Feral for Love

I

Feral for Love

A Fated Mates Shifter Romance

Ruthless Alliances Collection

VJ Silver

Feral for Love

A Fated Mates Shifter Romance

Ruthless Alliances Collection

by VJ Silvey

Published by Bibliotherapy Publications LLC

VioletJeanWrites@gmail.com
www.violetjeanwrites.com

ISBN: 978-1-960653-17-8

Dedication

For the girlies who go
just a little feral
for the right man...
...especially
when he matches energy.

Ruthless Alliances Collection

Between Ruin and Salvation

Cursed by Fate

Unravelled by Darkness

Avenged by Fire

Destroyed by Redemption

Between Fear and Obsession

Wild in Spirit

Wild at Heart

Wild for Love

Standalones

Wrecked by Chance

Feral for Love

Content Warnings

It is important to note that this book contains themes, actions, and dialogue revolving around several heavy topics.

Including:

Language
Violence/Death
Sexual Assault
Sex/Nudity

Chapter 15 and Chapter 16 contain on-page sexual assault

Table of Contents

Prologue

October 1994

"Ajax, I'm sending you to Houston. Don't fuck it up."

Ajax's jaw clenched, his head snapping up to stare at his father's stoney expression. "Alone?"

"I just need one of you to go, and I don't trust anyone else."

What he meant was he only needed one son safe. One son was enough to take over the pack one day, but the other was expendable. The silence between Ajax and his twin brother stretched wide as Axel's eyes met his. Axel was the older one, the most important, the one most like their father, and that knowledge hung in the air as their father continued making plans like his words held no weight. But they did. Especially when one son was always the one taking the risks.

"This war is far from over, and something bigger is being planned. It's been too quiet. The vamps have been lying low, and there has been no sign of witches, or even another pack encroaching in months."

"I think we sent a strong enough message in the first three years of this Goddess-forsaken war. They know not to fuck with us, and they've moved north. That's all." The muscles in Ajax's neck tensed, knowing even the smallest challenge to his father was a risk to his temper.

"No. Nothing is that easy. And the second we let down our guard, or make any type of exception, then we compromise the pack's safety."

The harshness in their father's gruff voice called for no quarter. So, they stayed silent, waiting for him to continue debriefing and give his final orders.

Tuhuy, the Tuisa Alpha for almost twenty-five years now, rose from his desk, the heaviness of leading this pack weighing on him. He paced, and like a caged lion, it put them all on edge. But his pacing had been an integral part of his lectures for all their lives, and he didn't even look at them as he spoke anymore. "It's been almost a year since there's been any activity within the state lines, and suddenly, I'm hearing rumors of a Supernatural Council that's formed. That information is flooding in, like a calculated campaign, from anyone I've spoken to. Supposedly some sort of alliance for peace being made with representatives from witches, wolves, fae, and even vampires. Vampires!" A low growl of disbelief escaped his throat, and Ajax couldn't help but agree with that point. Witches, wolf shifters, fae…he'd seen good and bad of both. But vampires? No such thing. There was no compromise with the undead demons. They only cared for themselves and would stop at nothing. "Sounds suspicious, and I don't trust it or them. They want us to get comfortable, let our guard down, while they work some angle, making bullshit connections that will restrict our businesses, choke the life from our resources, then watch for our weaknesses. I can smell it."

Axel nodded, adding his two cents when their father paused. "I agree. It only makes sense for them to be organizing against us. We have to go back on the offensive. We've been passive for too many months now." His brother never questioned their father. He'd always been the twin who most took after him, who'd had the temper, the deep-seated anger and suspicion, but Ajax couldn't help but challenge everything they'd known, everything they'd learned in the one hundred and fifty years since their people had settled on this land. Stay close, stay private, build success from within, and keep everyone else out. It was what they lived by. Despite that, over time, his father had loosened up, especially with the influence of the free-spirited witches as their ally next door. It had been the glimmer of hope he'd had his whole life.

But now, Ajax clenched his jaw, trying to keep his own frustration from bubbling over at their old-fashioned ways as his father and brother bounced the same conspiracy around the room.

"The Supernatural Council has to be fake, a front for something more. A rumor, a tactic to get people to relax." His father spoke louder now, his hands clenched as he worked through whatever fears had taken over his instincts and his logic.

Axel stood, rolling open the large map of the United States and flattening it on the large desk. "Think about why they would make something like this. Why would any of the supernaturals work together after trying to kill each other for years?"

"I can guarantee it's not everyone willingly forming this alliance—just the ones who still have power…and resources. They've already absorbed smaller packs and covens. Look at the locations of all the big players. Everyone who is left, all the big packs…they're up north, far west, and only a few in the deep south."

"And covens? They're hiding out everywhere, but I know their numbers are decimated all over. We saw that when we did our runs to Alabama last year. Even if the shifters and witches teamed up, what use do they have for vampires and fae if they truly wanted peace? There's more to it."

"Protection. A coalition…promises to consolidate money and power. Greedy, murderous bastards."

Ajax sighed at the suggestions, at the way his father and brother riled each other up. Maybe it was all true, especially since his father was almost never wrong, but he knew them, especially when it came to fighting an enemy. If they weren't reigned in, they'd assume the worst, and they'd react to the fullest consequence. It could be nothing.

Leaning forward to stare at the map they were poring over, he shook his head, trying to downplay their fears. "Come on. We've said it for a long time. The way to strength is to have strong allies, and it's not a new concept. That's why we allied ourselves with Rathlin Coven in the beginning. They are the reason we were able to survive amongst humans at all—the reason we were able to build our whole ranching business to be the biggest in the country. Hell, it's almost the biggest in the world. It was with their help, their magic. You know this. We all do. Maybe this Supernatural Council is finally seeing the precedence we've set. Alliances bring peace. It did for us."

"Don't be obtuse. This new alliance doesn't want peace. Our connection with Rathlin is bigger than that, and you know it. They are family." Axel frowned down at him, annoyed at the comparison.

"You don't understand, son. It's not that easy. Look at the bigger picture. None of them, not one, has the strength or wealth that we have accumulated on our own. Especially in the past fifty years. We've made ourselves indispensable to humans. If there were a true alliance between supernaturals in this country, they would need us to be a part of it. But there has been no word. Only silence. Too much silence."

"You seriously wonder why they haven't included us? We've killed any person that's come within our reach. Rathlin alone, with the concentration of the Daughters of Danu, has more power and magic than any of the covens on this continent. But no one knew that before they went out. Nobody knew where the Daughters of Danu had settled until Cahaira and Rhiannon were sent out scouting. For over a century, they've been hidden here, and no one looked their way. But look how that recon mission turned on them when they walked into the midst of fighting with no backup. They were forced to destroy covens, attack wolves, even confront the fae. They had to show their hand, to show how much power the two of them held individually and together. That's not what they wanted to do. But it's what they had to do. I guarantee it sent a message to the world. Why would this new alliance come to Rathlin or Tuisa for a peace treaty? Not when we hold so much power. They learned not to fuck with us. End of story."

"For fuck's sake, did you forget Cahaira was almost killed several times? If Rhiannon hadn't been there…" Axel shook his head, his brow furrowed at the memory. "She was being reckless, trying to save people. That brought on all the attention she didn't want. You act like everyone ran away from the girls. Shifters may have backed off, because their power is easy to see when it's unleashed, but Cahaira's or Rhiannon's presence didn't deter the rest of them. It only showed them they needed to be stronger before their next attack on us. We shouldn't have let the girls go. It showed our cards, and it showed the world all the power we have concentrated down here. The only good that came out of her attempt to bring peace in the beginning was her finding Linc."

He closed his eyes at that. At the reminder that their best friend, the eldest daughter of the current Rathlin Head Priestess, and the strongest in the line of Daughters of Danu, had almost died. She and her mirror, Rhiannon, were only supposed to go on a recon mission around the country—to see what was happening and bring back news. She had only been twenty at the time, not even fully in connection with all her power yet, and everything had gone wrong.

It was a big part of why Tuisa had gone on the offensive, why they had left the confines of their almost one million acres in South Texas, to show the other supernaturals not to fuck with them. His father had said it was for all of their protection, but the silent agreement between the three had been to avenge the attack on the two Daughters. The witches had always been their weakness, more than just allies. Almost losing them had made it personal.

Within days of Cahaira and Rhiannon arriving home broken and bleeding, thousands of Tuisa's fiercest fighters had overrun the battle zones across the south, and their bloody victories were still fresh in his mind. Cahaira's mother, Kathleen, had kept the girls home after that, refusing to let them go out on their own again. She had decided their coven would only go on the offensive if they were under attack and would stay in their area of the world. Their line of descendants, the source and root of all witch magic, were a direct link to the goddess Danu, and it was dangerous for all witches if they were to be put at risk anymore.

"All I know is that whatever goal this Supernatural Council has, it isn't for good. Together, they will run through our country like a vacuum, sucking and taking resources and life from the desperate without actually bringing peace. They are there to consolidate power, resources, and money. I won't allow them anywhere near here."

For almost four years, this war had been waged, no real sides drawn, no one truly understanding what started it. Only constant grabs for power, land, and money, with rumors, fear, and distrust running rampant. Other packs had been crippled, covens eliminated or scattered in the wind, vampires holing up and hoarding resources and money from the cities, but not Tuisa.

In South Texas, the Tuisa pack, the largest and fiercest pack in the country, had held strong. They'd always had their reputation, their connections, and businesses in the human world, and combined with the Rathlin Coven, and even the Aisling Pack presence nearby, they'd drawn their line in the sand. Or in this case, they'd drawn their line in the broken and bloody bodies left by the Tuisa warriors.

It had only taken three years of Tuisa's counterattacks, a gruesome and merciless campaign against any supernatural within three hundred miles, before the fighting stayed permanently north of them. His father had used their army to protect their own, their people, their allies, their land, their legacy. And he'd done it by any means necessary. No mercy. That was the Tuisa way. It was how they had survived the last two centuries, hidden, yet thriving, within the human world.

He'd done it with Axel and Ajax leading the armies, the first in every attack, their brutality an example to all. The blood stained his hands, but it was who he was, what he was meant to do, and that had been drilled into him since the day he was born. Which meant that even with the supernatural war still raging throughout the rest of the country, others had learned to avoid Texas. Or at least, they had avoided direct attacks anywhere south of Houston within the past two years.

Inwardly, he sighed with resignation. They were right. They made sense. And if they weren't right, it wouldn't hurt for him to do the recon on his own. It was better than sending anyone else that he cared about. "What's my mission in Houston?"

"Blend in with the humans. Watch the vampire activity. I know they're there, and they think we aren't. Find out everything you can. It will be a long game. I can feel it."

"Rathlin is on board with this?" Ajax's thoughts flitted to Cahaira, then Deidre, her younger, gentler sister, and what they would think of him leaving for Houston by himself. Rhiannon, Cahaira's magical mirror and Dark Daughter of Danu would urge him on. Her cynical realism and tendencies towards violence as the protector of the magical line of witches often fit in with the violent Tuisa ways. On the other hand, Cahaira would have a fit if she knew the details.

"Yes. They also said they would not be pledging any type of allegiance to whatever this Council is pretending to be, even if they are asked."

Ajax nodded, his brows furrowed. There wasn't a doubt about that. Rathlin and their witches were not just Tuisa allies, they had always been their closest friends growing up, along with Nubia, Axel's mate. "Last I spoke with her, Cahaira said she had a bad feeling about all of them."

"And the runes? Did Kathleen say anything?" Axel stared at the wall blankly, his mind clearly running through all the possibilities.

"No. Not since…not since his death, she won't check the runes. She has gone into mourning. Says the runes are unreliable, and she refuses to consult them anymore. Cahaira has practically already taken over in her stead." Ajax's voice almost cracked, remembering the way his best friend had sobbed in his arms, how the loss of her father, and the inconsolable grief of her mother, had crippled them.

"We will keep Rathlin safe until they recover. They are ours." It was the one thing all of them agreed on.

There was an awkward silence, and between the three of them, they all knew what had to be asked. "And Aisling?"

The Aisling pack had a short but painful history, one that walked the line between both Rathlin and Tuisa. Originally formed by Kathleen's mother and her fated mate, who was a rogue Alpha wolf, they had used land between Rathlin and Tuisa to create a hybrid pack, one that invited both wolf shifters and witch outsiders in. They had formed a smaller, more open-minded cattle ranch, modeled after Tuisa. Its boundaries had been walled and warded, protecting all within by the powerful Daughter of Danu magic. Until one of their own turned on them. And now, they had Alpha Rick, the shifter who'd challenged and killed its founders.

The takeover by Rick, the man who had challenged and killed Kathleen's youngest brother after her parents died, leaving him as the current Alpha, had devastated all three communities and made the relations between all of them shaky. A change that none of them had recovered from, especially when all the witches in Aisling went back to

Rathlin. But it had been twenty years now, and neither Axel nor Ajax remembered it, as they were just toddlers when it happened, but the ramifications had been clear. While Aisling was begrudgingly included in their territory, none of them wanted anything to do with the community who had stayed in Aisling. They just didn't have much of a choice. Their lands intertwined with both Rathlin and Tuisa, boundaries on all their sides touching. Originally, it had been that way for a reason. Aisling used to be family too. Yet now…now there were bigger issues at play.

"I reached out to the Aisling Alpha. Rick was not interested in combining forces, but he also does not trust the Council. He had other reasons, but at least he is on the same page as us."

"Bastard benefits from just our fucking presence." Ajax couldn't help the bitterness that crept into his voice. It was where both Kathleen and Cahaira had been born. It should have been their home. And spending his whole life hearing the lore, feeling the pain of losing Kathleen's mother, he knew exactly how it had crippled Rathlin.

"He benefits from the Rathlin wards that are still in place. That is all the benefit he needs. He's cocky." His brother's voice broke through his thoughts. At least they agreed on that.

"Then it is decided. Ajax goes to Houston."

He cleared his throat, already focused on what he would do to infiltrate a vampire nest. He would need magic to shield his identity. "How long?"

"As long as we need. Settle in. It might take a while to figure out what they're up to."

"And if I get noticed? No one else is coming to give backup?"

"Don't get noticed. I trust you can handle yourself. Be careful, son.

Chapter 1

Ajax

December 1995

Fuck him. And fuck his old-fashioned ways. He thought following the old traditions and closing the pack off to the world was the solution? That this new and unknown Supernatural Council would just leave them alone? Fool.

His brother's last words rang in his ear, and he grit his teeth at the betrayal. "If you leave again, don't come back. You've turned your back on your pack and your responsibilities. You're making a choice, and I will not make an exception for you."

Ajax tightened the grip on his handlebars and pushed the engine harder. He couldn't get away from here fast enough.

A year. A year of secrets, undercover work, living alone amongst humans, all while fighting to stay alive by himself. Then two months leading the Tuisa army in a bloody decimation of the Houston vampire nest. He'd hunted every last one of them, tracing their connections throughout the rest of the country, and leaving a wake of dead vampire dust and empty businesses. The Supernatural Council had gotten the message from Tuisa loud and clear. Neither they, nor the vampires who encroached, were welcome.

He'd been angry at first, separated from the pack for so long, away from everyone and everything he knew. The subterfuge and pretenses that went with spying and blending in had been hard to get used to at first. A merciless brutality, a reality filled with violence, was all he'd known his whole life. He'd been taught since he could walk that he would use his fists, his claws, his wolf, to fight for the pack. The pack was the only thing that mattered. Until he found something else to fight for.

Freedom.

Freedom from the constant plans for war, freedom from the suffocating and secretive pack life, freedom from being watched, freedom from the expectations of being the Alpha's son. His second son. Freedom from the pressure to run the largest pack in the country with his twin.

In the past year, as he'd gone back and forth from the pack to Houston, he'd found a calling. Had tasted this new freedom and independence and never wanted to let it go. The freedom had allowed him an escape from the constant flashes of violence, death, and suspicions that filled his thoughts. There could be more to life.

The irony of that freedom had come with the one thing he was naturally good at. Violence.

His first stop in the city had been a gym, a place to take his mind off the loneliness, a place to work the tension from his muscles, and work through his anger. From there, it was easy to take up a personal trainer role. These humans took one look at his physique and begged him to take jobs in their gym. Eventually, coaches and sponsors convinced him to fight in tournaments, turning his skills into entertainment. He didn't need money, but it had felt good.

Without telling his father or even his brother, he'd joined the amateur boxing world. And he'd been undefeated so far.

He was only supposed to be gathering intel for his family, getting information on the businesses and movements of the Houston vampire nests, and he had. It wasn't hard. They hadn't expected a lone wolf to slip in and out of their midst, listening to rumors between the men in the gyms, honing in on the business deals, getting in good with the vain vampires who led with pride and ego. They'd been easy to spot, especially since he had magic lent to him by Rathlin. With his scent and aura hidden by one of Cahaira's spells, his work had been successful. That was all his father cared about, and he'd done it.

The day he'd come home, the minute he'd stood next to his father, listening to him report the deaths and victories to their pack, he knew he'd wanted more. To be more than the vicious enforcer. More than his assigned role in this pack. He had so many ideas.

With the successful year spent in Houston, and an end to the war under his belt, he thought his father would relax, that he would hear him out. After all, he had to trust him to lead the pack in the next few years.

But he hadn't.

Now, with the roar of his motorcycle reverberating through him, he shook his head at that, at the dreams he'd had only a few short months ago. The visions he'd had of opening Tuisa up like a normal pack. A pack that let their shifters come and go, live in and out of the pack like never before. He saw Tuisa as a model for a new wave of relations between supernaturals. It didn't have to be like this.

He didn't know why he thought he could convince his father to find a compromise. Didn't know why he'd been so optimistic after five years of brutality. But he was convinced it could be good for all of them. The pack needed something more.

"I want to start a private gym. One for shifters from all over. It doesn't have to be inside our boundaries—I can set it up in the city. Teach our fighting, our ways. Have shifter-only tournaments, a sort of entertainment for the supernatural world. A way to release aggression without killing. It would be a peace offering of sorts."

"Peace? What is this peace you speak of? There is no peace for us. There never has been. We fight for our lives, our freedom, our way of life. Not for some silly vanity."

"Not anymore. The war is over." He'd been frustrated with his father, knowing it would be a fight, but had hoped he could chip away at the typical stubbornness that ran in their family line. "You've heard the goals of the Supernatural Council. We should be uniting and working as one. Supernaturals shouldn't be fighting amongst ourselves. We should be fighting to rise in the human world. And we've done that. We could help others do the same."

"You have much to learn, especially when it comes to people like the Council. They lie. Whatever goals they are selling, we are not buying. We do not rely on others, only ourselves."

"That's bullshit. We have Rathlin. And we used to have Aisling. Packs are communities, and you used to know that. Hell, you made sure we understood our history. Shifters band together to survive."

"No. Tuisa will stand alone. We do not need another pack. That is final." His father had slammed his hands down on the desk, the muscles in his neck pulsing in anger. "Do not question me."

For a second, he'd felt defeated, had felt like the child from long ago, but he didn't give up. "I'm not saying we need anyone. It is clear we do not. I am saying that we can expand our businesses. We've conquered the ranching business, why not more? This is just another business. Another opportunity to make a name for ourselves."

"A name?" His father's nostrils flared, and the emerald green of his eyes darkened and his jaw clenched. "I do not care about our name. I care about our survival and our safety. Being the biggest has only put a target on our back. I will not risk infiltration, weakness, or letting down our guard for a little hobby. Put this idea behind you."

His father had always been a hard man. He had to be, and Ajax understood that. The burden of caring for this pack was obvious, but he had been more open to expansion in the past couple of decades. At least, he'd been more modern than his father before him. His people could ask for leave, had been able to take vacations, go off to school, and even shop in the big cities if they took escorts with them.

Until lately. Until the war changed him, had hardened him even more than anyone had thought possible, and had closed him off to anything. Ajax had walked away from that conversation bitter, but not beaten. Maybe his father was right. Now wasn't the time. Things were too volatile even if the war was officially declared over after five years. He could try later.

He wouldn't give up. Hadn't given up.

But his brother was no better now.

Especially after their parents' death.

It had only been three months since the day his life changed. Three months since the thud of their bodies hitting the ground had begun to haunt his dreams. It was a sound that had permanently changed his perspective and his mind forever.

The unexpected attack, a tragic exception made for a supposed new family mate, and a betrayal at the hands of a trusted man, had allowed a deadly infiltration of fae into a family gathering.

Fae.

They'd never even met a fae before, other than Linc, Cahaira's mate, and he'd been so logical, so friendly. Fae participation in the war had never been confirmed, never been seen by them. Fae were mysterious, moved in silence, sneakily with magic that stemmed from the illogical, from the mind. They were known to play tricks, to go for the long game. But Fae had never made it this far south. They'd never expected an attack, especially this long post-war.

When his father fell, the sudden break in all of their links to the powerful Alpha had shocked them all. All except his mother. Larana Blackwolf hadn't hesitated. And she paid a heavy price as she fell beside Tuhuy in the dirt. Rage flew through them at the bright red blood splattering at their feet, and it hadn't taken long before the traitorous and disguised fae had fallen to their death. Between him and his brother, they'd torn their leader to bits, but not before Axel had taken a severe slashing across his face that never fully healed. Fae magic would do that. It left a mark on shifters, and it had certainly changed everything for them.

In the aftermath of that day, things had only gotten worse as Axel decided to shut down the pack completely. No one in or out. No one.

Weeks of chaos followed, and as they grieved, he had stepped back, allowing Axel to take on the Alpha magic alone. He couldn't do it. Couldn't imagine his world without them.

Where Axel had sought revenge, searching tirelessly for the links back to the fae who'd sent the traitor, Ajax had only thought of the future. Of how things needed to change to get better. But as hard as he tried to function, he'd only been left with an empty void, a need for meaning in his life, and he thought his own twin would support him.

He was wrong.

"We need to consider taking this pack in a different direction. What we're doing isn't working. Shutting everyone out puts a bigger target on our back. We should be building our allies, reaching out and training friends. I can go back out and strengthen those connections. Send me."

"You are needed here. With your people. Not running around the country on some bullshit quest. You are to act as my co-Alpha. We will rebuild, we will honor our father and grandfather, and all their fathers before them. It is our way."

"Maybe it is time for our way to change. Maybe you should go out there yourself. See what it's like in the human world. It might change your perspective."

"You're a dreamer and a fool. That is not how any of that works. Your life is here and only here, as is mine. The faster you accept this shut down, the better."

"I don't want that. Any of it. I want my own life."

"That is not how it works here—"

"Who fucking cares? Then change it. Look where all this has gotten us? Mom and Dad are dead. Our pack is—"

"That is wolf life. We die. We move on. We keep our people and our legacy safe. There is nothing else."

"There has to be. I refuse to believe that this is all there is."

"You don't have that choice. We cannot risk another infiltration. I will not put my family or our pack at risk. Nubia is barely functioning as it is without her sister. If we lost our son…"

"But that's wolf life, right?" He'd thrown his brother's words back in his face, and he'd watched him shut down, especially when he brought up his first-born son. Makaii wasn't even a year old, but his nephew's birth had changed Axel just as much as their parents' death had.

While Axel's expression remained stony and unreadable, his voice softened with a dangerous reminder. "I want to share this role with you, Ajax. I want you by my side, running this pack with me. But you don't have to. I can do it myself. And I will. It is my duty, with or without you. By now, you've had plenty of time to decide. If you won't accept this destiny, then that is your choice."

"You're right. It is my choice. And I refuse. I can't live like this. If you won't listen to my ideas on how to bring our pack into modern times, then…I need something more, something else. I need to go see the world."

"We are no longer an open pack. You know that. If you leave, it will mean that you renounce Tuisa, and you will regret it. You will go rogue and lose your mind. I will not accept you back."

He'd stared hard into his brother's face, one identical to his own, contemplating all the things he had inherited, and all the things he hadn't. The physical traits couldn't be denied. The Blackwolf Alpha legacy had run strong through their line, passed down from their father and their great- grandfathers before him, far back, six generations, to the original Alpha male and Alpha female who'd helped settle Tuisa. The faded and tattered paint portrait of them both held a special place in his mind, their story an instrumental part of their lore. Despite the age of the portrait, it was always clear the two of them, both Alphas in their own right, were meant to lead a legendary pack. His great-grandfather's strong indigenous facial features, pin-straight, long, black hair and thick, muscular physique blended with her softer, deeper brown skin, haunting beauty, and glittering green eyes, cementing the inherited features of the Tuisa Alpha line, setting the leaders of the Tuisa pack apart generation after generation.

But Ajax kept his hair short, the slightest wave in his own jet-black strands just long enough to run his hands through, where Axel left his hair long and braided down his back, like the tradition of every Alpha before him. This was his silent rebellion against the role he had inherited. It used to be their only difference. But now, the still fresh, pink, jagged scar on his brother's face marked them forever different from each other. It practically throbbed with remnants of the fae's foreign magic, one that symbolized the type of power that could still jeopardize their lives. The only one they truly feared, as no one understood it. Not even the witches. But they couldn't live in fear forever.

His brother was no better than his father. No, he took that back. His brother had become worse. His father may have been controlling, but he wouldn't have turned his back on him.

"Then that is a decision you will have to make when the time comes. But don't worry. I won't be back."

With his motorcycle pointed west, Ajax left home, left his pack, and left Texas.

He didn't need any of it anymore.

Chapter 2

Marti

Monday, September 16, 1996
San Diego, California

Marti hadn't been in the office for ten minutes when she heard the door bang open. Sighing, she kept typing, hoping it was one of the regulars who decided to show up early. A fool's thought. Not at six in the morning. She knew who it was, and there was nothing she could do about it.

It was her responsibility to open the gym early, and she usually enjoyed it. It gave her time to do her job as bookkeeper without the hustle and bustle of the night fighters. But not lately.

Glancing at the office door, she wished she could just lock it and close the blinds, but he would absolutely just bang on it till she answered. It was better to just deal with him.

Ben's body took up the whole door when he appeared, bag still slung over his shoulder, dressed in a gym stringer tank and tiny spandex shorts. As usual, he wore them extra tight so that his penis was on display. She shuddered inwardly, and her stomach rolled. It's not that he was bad-looking. He was a bodybuilder who pretended he could fight, and muscles ripped through him, but she didn't think he actually knew how to use them.

Pure vanity. That was his personality, though.

Overly slick and perpetually making inappropriate jokes, he looked at her like he would lock her in a basement dungeon in a heartbeat, but she'd brushed that off in the many years she'd known him. Any time alone with him was a dance in how she would avoid his overly touchy advances. While any other time, she'd probably put an end to his creepiness, he spent a lot of money here, and she only had to deal with him for a few minutes every morning. But really, he was harmless.

Keeping her eyes on the books in front of her, she murmured, "Good morning, Ben." Her only hope was to seem distracted and busy. That was always her game plan, even if it never worked.

"Mornin', sweet cheeks. You are looking extra delicious today."

He rounded the desk, picked up the tax documents she was working on, and moved them over, so he could lean onto the faded wood, crotch in her eye line, before swiveling her chair and forcing her to face him. "You should come help me with my workout today. No one else is here to spot me."

She mentally took a deep breath, forcing patience into her voice, then looked up into his dull, brown eyes. "You know I couldn't spot you, even if I wanted to. If you waited another hour, there are plenty of people here who could spot you."

"Yeah, but I don't want to take any of them home and make them scream my name."

She pushed away from him and stood up. Walking out into the main gym, away from the privacy of her office, was always the best course of action. "We've talked about this, Ben. I'm not interested. Have a good workout."

She stood at the door, waiting for him to leave, so she could make a show of locking it and going to make her rounds cleaning the bathrooms.

He leered, his eyes sweeping her up and down as he walked through the doorway before blocking her in, leaning close, too close. She clenched her jaw, pressing herself as far away from him as possible as he paused to squeeze her waist roughly. "One day soon. Our babies will be beautiful."

His voice had dropped the slightly teasing tone, and she was taken aback by the serious tone. She'd been dealing with him for years now, ever since she'd come back from college, and never once had she heard the hard threat in his voice. Was she imagining it?

"Ben. That's not funny. You need to move aside."

His eyes locked on hers, and any trace of humor was gone. The only thing left was a promise that scared her slightly. "I'm almost ready for you. Everything's falling into place."

Then he winked. His mocking smile appeared so easily, she thought she imagined his change in demeanor. When he finally moved away, ambling over to his first machine, she forced herself to relax, her mind reliving his words as she let out a slow, even breath. She needed to get away from him and this new level of creepiness. Making her way to the back, she disappeared into the laundry room to pick up extra towels to place in stacks around the gym. One thing was for sure, if they weren't readily available, no one wiped their machines down around here. This gym catered to either men who trained to fight in some way, or bodybuilders. It wasn't exactly welcoming to women, so it wasn't surprising that they didn't have a single female member.

Other than her, she didn't think there'd ever been any women in here. But that didn't bother her. She'd grown up here, and their home was behind the gym. Everything about this place was hers, even if she didn't use a single machine.

By the time she finished laying out towels, two more regulars had shown up. Only a friendly wave from the first before he started his routine, but the second guy, Felix, came to say hi first. He was another large man, but with a more natural muscle build, which was good because he barely worked out. He was also her best friend from college, and he never missed a morning with her, not since his family had let him move to the city after graduation. Said it was his freedom run before taking over his family business.

"Hey Martiiiiii, beautiful morning, isn't it?" He grabbed a fresh towel from the stack she had just laid out and threw it over his shoulder. "Get any work done today before your admirer showed up?"

She chuckled. Ben didn't hide his perverted ways, and most of the other regulars didn't like him, but he was especially wary of Felix, and

Felix always tried to get there as soon as possible just to help her out. "Not really. I swear he gets here earlier and earlier every day."

Felix snorted. "And his spandex gets tighter and tighter."

She giggled, cutting her eyes to Ben, and the way he postured in front of the machine. Despite being in his early 20s, Felix was not a fan of the new apparel trends.

"I'm gonna get started. You head back in there. I bet he won't bother you now." He winked before picking his bag back up.

"Thanks, Felix. You're my hero."

Back in the office, she settled in to finish up the monthly books, then began working on the upcoming tournament. It was only three weeks away, and she had a lot to do. They held them twice a year now, and her dad insisted this one needed to be bigger than before. There was a lot of chatter in the amateur fighting world about big money fights, and he was insistent on recruiting more of the top fighters. She'd rolled her eyes at that. They were a smaller gym, and those big names didn't give them much attention, so she didn't know how he expected her to work miracles.

To her, these tournaments were nothing more than human cock-fighting, and some of these men didn't have enough experience to be fighting at all—which meant it was basically a bloodbath. She had watched enough men train over the years, and most of these amateurs thought they could just muscle their way through fights and win. Too much muscle and not enough actual sparring practice was the exact problem.

Nevertheless, it was the newest thing. At least once a month around here, often every weekend in the larger cities, some local gym in the area ran underground tournaments for anyone off the streets to step in and challenge one of the bigger names. Their hot-shot gym members loved to fight the amateurs, and her father had started participating a few years ago, so now they were up to twice a year in their little place.

Really, it was just an excuse for the bad behavior that ran rampant in their world. There was lots of gambling, drinking, and fighting—in and out of the ring. Unless her dad needed her to help with one of their own gym members, she didn't go. The fighters won money the further into each tournament they went, but they also got bloodier. There were no real rules, and it made her sick to watch. Too many fights had ended with a trip to the hospital.

But, from these tournaments, sometimes real fighters emerged. They were talked about and passed around as the next biggest things from gym to gym. Gyms would battle to represent them in the bigger tournaments. The sponsored tournaments. In the business world, it made sense to build a reputation around good fighters. It drew more members and money. But, to the gym owners, it was about ego, reputation, and prestige.

This was her world. Outside of her job as the accountant and general catch-all for anything her dad didn't know how to do, she organized the promotional tournaments they did twice a year. She recruited around the area, kept her ear to the ground for the newest trends, and marketed the hell out of it. Those events drew big names and big money. These tournaments and the profits were what would keep their gym afloat for months.

After sitting on the phone with one of the major law firms for almost an hour, she was able to hang up. Writing 'CONFIRMED' next to their name on the sponsors list, she stretched her body and cracked her neck.

"Hey, Sunshine. Everything going smoothly?" Her father strode through the door, dropped a kiss on her forehead, and pulled up a chair across from the desk.

"Like butter." Her dad was a gruff man, all about business on the outside, but had a soft spot. Even if they didn't see eye-to-eye on everything, he'd do just about anything for her. Telling him about Ben's behavior was out of the question though. She didn't even want to consider what he'd do to him, and they needed Ben's business way too much, as he'd periodically brought in tons of other customers over the years. She put up with him for the sake of the gym.

"Good. Got a call late last night. We got him. Finally." Settling into his chair, he uncrumpled a slip of paper from his pocket, smoothed it out, then lifted it up to read after adjusting his glasses, and she waited patiently for whatever news riled him up this early in the morning. "Finally figured out Ice's real name. Ajax Tuhuy."

"Ice?" She sighed. She'd heard of him. Everyone had. The buzz around the mysterious fighter had everyone scrambling. Brutal, vicious, cold. He talked to no one and cared about nothing. He was undefeated and the rumors about his skills were out of control. "You realize he's probably been undeclared this long for a reason? I doubt—"

His bushy black and grey eyebrows furrowed, the deep wrinkles in his dark, weathered skin more pronounced, and he pulled his glasses off. "Marti. You have to convince him. I want him for the fight, as our headliner. We already have his opponent set up through one of our big sponsors, but they want Ice. You just needed to get in touch with him, and I know you can convince him. This—he—will be our big break. Maybe he would even let us rep him permanently. Big rumors that he's headed to the UFC soon. Right now, he has no official gym, just shows up wherever there's money to be made. And I have a feeling about him. He's supposed to be here. I just know it."

"I'll do what I can." She rewrote the name in her notebook under her list of other contenders. "Did you decide what vendors you want? I have to replace the food guy you fired last time. Any preferences?"

"Yeah, anyone who can do their job. But nothing fancy. I want to be able to use my hands and catch a beer with the guy after."

"Gotcha. Pretzels and hot dogs it is. I was thinking of adding some promo items, like beer coozies, t-shirts, or coasters. We can get some smaller businesses to pay for them and add their name to the bottom. We can make money off that, and even more if we charge for bigger items." She knew this was a stretch. He hated spending money, especially if he didn't think it would change anything.

He sat back in his seat, arms crossed, one hand rubbing the stubble on his chin as he thought. "Actually. Let's do it. Something free, something cheap, and something more expensive. Maybe mock up that logo you've been talking about and add that. Make sure the businesses pay out the ass for their names on them."

"Great. I'll get that done this week." She leaned forward and began writing in her notepad, trying not to show how excited she was that he not only took her advice, but was going to let her design a logo. She had been asking about that for months. This Ajax guy must have really put him in a good mood.

It took her over two hours of calling businesses, and finally, she was given a number to someone who claimed to be his manager.

"Yo."

"Looking for the manager for Ice? Ajax Tuhuy?"

"You got him."

"I'm a promoter for a gym in San Jose, and we have a big tournament coming up in three weeks. I wanted to invite Mr. Tuhuy to be our headliner. We will—"

"I'll get back to you."

"Sir—"

The call went dead, and she rolled her eyes. These arrogant managers were a pain in her ass. He wasn't the only one. They liked to be coddled, praised, thanked, and killed with kindness. She would try again tomorrow and the next day, and the next day. He would get tired of her eventually.

For a week, she booked contender after contender, crossing off her to-do list quickly. Each line she marked as complete left her with a feeling of satisfaction. But the one thing she couldn't mark off was that headliner. Her father asked her every day, and it took everything in her not to tell him to give up.

Each call she'd made had resulted in either being sent to an answering machine or him telling her that he would let her know. He was playing hard to get, so today, she'd decided to drive up to the gym where she'd found the manager and make him talk to her. There had been another big tournament the night before, and she'd heard Ice had swept the house.

That meant he was still there, probably sleeping it off, so he couldn't avoid her.

Los Angeles was two hours away, but the weather was gorgeous, and the drive flew by. Any day spent outside those musty gym walls was always a win. She'd brought a book, knowing that the fighters weren't exactly morning people, and she may have to wait until night to get him out of the bed, but she wasn't worried. She would get her way, she always did. Persistence was key.

The LA gym wasn't hard to find, and not exactly in the best part of town. It was newer, but not corporate, and the guy working the front desk had his feet propped up and barely gave her a glance. "No solicitors."

"My name is Martina Andrade, and I was hoping you could help me find someone." She flashed a winning smile and pushed her thick black glasses up her nose. She wasn't the kind of girl who dressed fancy often, or even did her makeup, but today she'd thrown on a boring pantsuit trying to look professional. The kicker was, she knew she looked young with her oversized glasses and single braid falling over her shoulder, and often men were almost always willing to help out some young girl who made them feel strong and manly. Didn't matter that she was actually twenty-six and not the eighteen years old she looked.

"Looking for Ice, yeah? We've gotten your calls."

"Exactly. Are you his manager?" She was surprised his manager was working the front desk, and even more surprised he would be up before noon. She glanced around the mostly empty gym. The floor was still littered from last night's event, and it was a huge mess.

"He doesn't have a real manager. Does what he wants. And I don't have good news for ya. He likes to run off. Disappears for days at a time. Can't corral Ice."

"That's okay. I can wait around and see if he shows up. I'm not in a hurry."

She took a seat by the window and pulled out her book. He was lying, but that's okay. They all did. Out of the corner of her eye, she watched him contemplate her, then disappear for a minute and come back.

"His bike is here, so he must be in his room. Tell ya what. You head up to his room—it's upstairs, and to the right. Whole suite of rooms up there rented out, so be careful which one you bang on at ten in the morning. Room 206. You can talk to him yourself. Be easier. He has a soft spot for pretty girls."

Chapter 3

Ajax

Sunday, September 22
Los Angeles, California

Distinct banging jerked him awake, and he squinted at the sound. The fuck was happening? The trails of another nightmare hung tightly for a second, the visions of his beast bloody, snarling, tearing through vampires with his pack members just out of reach, finally melting away. His heart was still racing as the dregs of the nightmare stayed with him, and he shook off the fear that engulfed him every time he closed his eyes lately.

His wolf was getting more and more desperate every day. Desperate to be home, to be a part of the pack again.

He groaned inwardly, shaking off his instincts, and thought he had imagined the noise. But the banging didn't stop. He rolled to the side of the bed, his feet hitting the floor, and the naked woman laying on him tumbled away with a murmur.

Who the hell was banging on his door?

Without dressing, he stomped over and swung it open angrily. In front of him stood a petite woman, her big doe brown eyes rimmed with glasses, and he froze when her eyes widened and dropped to stare at his complete nakedness. When those plush, pink lips parted in a gasp and she reddened, his eyes dropped to take her all in. Dark, wild hair, barely tamed into a long braid, draped over her shoulder, trailed down her chest and down to her waist. Curvy and soft, baby-faced and beautiful, she couldn't hide beneath the loose pantsuit she wore. But she clutched a notebook in her hands, pressing it to her chest as she stepped back, stuttering at his appearance. He took all that in moments before her scent hit him.

Honeysuckle and strawberries.

Mate.

His beast roared, and he couldn't breathe. The woman he'd waited his entire life to meet stood at his door, thousands of miles from his home. A gift from the Goddess. Nothing else mattered, and his need for her swept away every logical thought he could have mustered.

She was here for him. She was meant for him.

Unable to stop himself, instincts took over, and he wrapped his arms around her, one arm under her generous ass, the other circling her body, his hand snaking up as he lifted her into the air. In the narrow hallway, it didn't take much before he had her back against the wall, crushing her to his naked chest, her tiny squeal ignored.

This woman was his, the other half to his soul, and his wolf said to claim her here and now. He nuzzled his face into her neck, seeking out her calming scent, inhaling as his hand tangled through the braid at the back of her head. She was so soft, so pliable in his arms, her sounds of surprise egging him on. More. He needed more. Pulling her head to the side roughly before tilting it back and trailing his mouth up her neck, he found her mouth, and the stiffness in her body melted away. Her soft whimper was muffled by his lips as he kissed her, taking in every sensation before pulling back to suck on her bottom lip.

He barely acknowledged how her hands crept between their bodies lightly, her nails digging into his chest, until his wolf went wild at her touch.

"Mate." He pulled back to memorize every detail of her face. "I found you."

Confusion filled her eyes, and over the roar of his wolf, it hit him that she wasn't a shifter. Her scent was distinctly human. And the sleepy voice of the woman in the bed behind him rose between them.

"Ice?"

His mate stiffened, and in slow motion, he could see reality sink back into her mind, and she pushed him away, sliding down his body hastily. The shock of it all slackened his grasp, and he let her go.

Human. She was human. Not a shifter. She wouldn't know.

His mate stuttered incomprehensibly, picking up the dropped notebook and bag, and as she stumbled away, there was a slight panic in her eyes as she hurried down the hall away from him. He could only watch, stunned, until her final glance back shook him from his stupor, just before she disappeared. What the hell did he do about a human mate?

Too late, he realized he needed to go after her. What he would say when he found her, he had no clue. But right now, he didn't even know her name. Turning back to his room, he quickly pulled on a pair of loose shorts, tossed a terse command for the other woman to get out, and he hustled after his mate. He hit the bottom of the stairs, then pushed out the front door of the gym just in time to see her pulling out into LA traffic.

Stepping back inside, he looked over at the idiot who he let pretend to be his manager. He had tired of dealing with the phone calls, so he let the front desk clerk tell everyone no for him.

"Who was that?"

"Promoter who's been looking for you all week. Drove all the way here to convince you, so I sent her up to ask you yourself."

He paused to glare at him. "You thought it was funny to send her up to my room?"

"Got rid of her, didn't it?"

"That's what I hired you for. Get me her number, gym address, everything."

Back in his empty room, he stared at the number and the name on the scrap of paper.

Martina. His mate.

His wolf howled in his head, and he rocked on the bed, head in his hands. He didn't know what to do. His mind flashed through every detail of her, every curve he felt under his hands and against his body, and he yearned for her, ached to have her in his arms. But how did he mate with a human? She had already run from him without a word. And humans didn't know about the supernatural world. How would she handle it?

Picking up the phone in his room, he dialed the number on the paper. It had only been an hour, and he wasn't sure how far away her gym was, but he left a message and hung up.

Then, slowly, he picked up the phone again and dialed the only place he considered home anymore.

"Hello?"

"It's me."

After a long squeal session and waiting while Cahaira gathered her sister, husband, and mother around the speakerphone, he was finally able to speak.

"Tell us everything. What have you been up to!? Where are you right now?"

"I have a bigger issue, and I need your advice, as always."

They sat in shock when he recounted his morning, painfully detailing how he let his mate run away from him.

"You're going to fuck this up."

"Absolutely, he is."

"You have no faith in the man. Women fall over him. He's got this." Lincoln, Cahaira's husband and the only hybrid fae witch any of them knew, was the only one who seemed to have faith in him. But Ajax stayed silent, listening to his childhood friends predict his downfall.

"Wolf women. To a human, he's a little much. The intimidating, arrogant asshole look scares off good women." Deidre, as always, was the calming voice of reason, and he needed that.

"Then what do I do?"

Kathleen, practically his second mother, spoke above their arguing. "You do what feels right. It was meant to be. The Goddess wouldn't put you together if it couldn't be done." She paused as the room at the other end of the line went silent. "But you could probably try not to be too bossy and overbearing at first. Less like...well, you know. The rest of the Alphas in your family. That couldn't hurt. Just be yourself—but maybe, a little less in the beginning. Let her fall in love with you before you tell her."

"I don't know how easy I am to love. Not without a bond telling her to."

"Easy enough, Ajax. We love you."

"You have to. Can't get rid of me."

When he hung up, he felt a little better, like he had a plan. But just speaking with his friends and hearing Kathleen lecture him, sent the pangs of sorrow through him. Kathleen and his mother, Larana, had been close, and he knew every word she shared was something his own mother would say. Her soft and gentle ways had always been a balance for his father. She had been a hopeless romantic, had loved telling him about the old lore of their ancestors, sharing the moments her parents had met, and even the day she'd found his father. Finding your mate was a magical moment in their culture, and it hurt that she wasn't there to share in his happiness. One thing was sure, she would absolutely agree with everything Kathleen had said.

He needed to date her, take his time, get to know her—act like a human would when they were in love. How hard could it be?

Chapter 4

Marti

Sunday, September 22
San Diego, California

Marti drove like a bat out of hell, breathless, heart pounding, and mad at herself. Maybe if she hadn't been so sure of her abilities to convince him, she would have been prepared. She would have known she was being set up for something wild. In her head, she had taken all the warnings about his scariness as a challenge, one that she'd been sure was exaggerated. But up close, in the seconds before he'd lifted her into the air, his devastatingly handsome scowl and the dangerous flash in his eyes had her heart pounding, and she'd been speechless.

It hadn't helped that he had been naked, not shirt off naked or gym naked, no—in all his splendid glory naked, and she had felt his massive naked dick against her stomach. Naked. Jesus.

When he had pulled her into the hottest kiss of her life, so hot she'd sworn she was actually melting, and all reality had disappeared for those few short seconds, her world spun like she was in a dream. She felt like she belonged to him, like she was his forever, and she was the only one for him.

And then she wasn't.

When the woman's voice in the bed behind him called out, and he had pulled back, she had felt like an idiot. Why was she letting an intimidating and arrogant stranger touch her, kiss her, and make a fool of her? Even if it was for just one short moment, she had fallen for another man's game. A stranger's game. How embarrassing.

And with that, she refused. Not again.

But even as she pulled into the parking lot of her gym, she couldn't get him out of her mind. Couldn't help imagining the black, silky hair with a slight wave that curled around his ears just so, falling into his eyes…and what gorgeous eyes they were. Deep, emerald-green, they sparkled with a danger that she had been too ignorant to stay away from. And his face? Chiseled and angular, he had bronzed light brown skin that stretched across killer cheekbones. She could still feel the burn of his stubble on her neck and mouth where he had dragged it across her neck, even as he growled into her throat. She'd never heard a man do that before, to be so engrossed in pleasure that his body reverberated in satisfaction. It was heady.

She was foolish to even relive the moment.

Back in her office, she promptly crossed his name off her list, and focused on other business, desperately trying to free her mind from the mortification she had just experienced with a stranger. What she had allowed. What she had encouraged. That last fact hadn't escaped her, but she chose to ignore it.

"Successful then, huh? What kind of money did he want?"

Her father's voice was upbeat, excited as he dropped a scrap of paper on the desk in front of her. Ice's name and number were scrawled on it, and a short message.

Call me back.

She almost snorted. Like hell, she would. He probably felt entitled to do whatever he wanted now that she had basically thrown herself at his naked body like a cheap date.

"Actually, we couldn't come to agreeable terms, so we decided to go different directions." She kept it light, anticipating her father's disappointment.

He frowned. "That's strange. He seemed like he was good to go on the phone, just needed to iron out the details."

"I don't think so, but I'll call him back just to make sure." She rose from her seat, kissing her father on the cheek lightly. "Probably to ask for me to promote one of his other fights. He's headed to a big, televised fight for the UFC soon, and not interested in these smaller ones." She gave her father a big smile, trying to keep it light and chipper, to change the topic. "I've finished up here. I'm going to head over to the house and start dinner. Don't forget to take a break and come eat."

Her father ran all the nightly trainings, but he never failed to come home and snag the food she made. It was a promise that had always been important to her, especially since it had just been them most of her life. It was their time, no matter what was going on. That meant he deliberately staggered the nightly training schedule so that he had a thirty-minute gap at 6 pm. He was the one man she could always count on. That was something she needed to remind herself. She could only count on her Dad. No need for any of these men.

She slept like crap that night, dreaming of a green-eyed monster smirking down at her, laughing at the thought that someone like her would interest him. Repeatedly, visions of his heavy hand closing around her neck and pushing her against the wall shook her from her sleep, and his deep, husky voice still seemed to whisper in her ear.

"I found you."

What did that even mean? It should be fucking terrifying to have felt so helpless in his arms. Should have been. Yet, when she woke, a healthy fear heavy on her mind, she brushed it away, especially because she wasn't quite sure it was all fear. She *should* be afraid. Everyone else was wary of the fighter. Yet, when she thought about it, she couldn't shake the thrill and feeling of rightness that had filled her in those moments. None of it made sense, so it was better she forgot about it.

She had a million other things to focus on, especially the biggest positive. This whole week, Ben would be out of town on business, and he had made sure to tell her over and over, thinking she would miss him, giving her a little countdown each day. Gross.

But even more, his creepiness hadn't subsided. His short little bursts of anger, of dark promises, had lasted longer each day. She was almost to the point of telling Felix, but she'd told herself she just needed a break from him. That this week would be a respite that would reset his crazy.

So, she settled into the office, opened the graphics files she'd saved, and started working on a fresh logo. She had so many ideas, and as she clicked through the program, concentrating, she didn't notice the man standing in front of her until she heard the soft click of the lock from her office door.

"Ms. Andrade, correct?"

Startled, she looked up to see a blonde, handsome man in a business suit. He was smiling, but somehow also not smiling at the same time, and it was disconcerting. But she shook off the wary feeling and smiled broadly, reaching out her hand to shake his.

"Yes, call me Marti! Can I help you with something?"

"Is your father here?"

"He doesn't come in this early, but I can handle anything you need."

He took a seat, unbuttoning his suit jacket and looking around the room derisively. "Kevin Pennington. I'm here on behalf of Goulden Enterprises, making sure our shared interest in your company is clear as we get closer to the date of the tournament."

"Shared interest?" She frowned. The name sounded familiar, but she wasn't sure how, and a sliver of fear sliced through her at the slimy tone in his voice. "I know we have a small loan out, but I am certain we will be able to pay it off by the final due date. The tournament will give us the boost we need to pay it in full."

He barely broke a tiny smile when he asked if her father had shared the details of the loan. He hadn't. Not exactly, but she knew enough. Five years ago, her father had brokered a deal for new equipment and a whole gym remodel without her. It was against her advice, and she was still in college at the time, living across the state. Since then, he had only told her about due dates and amounts.

"Not especially, but I'm in charge of the books now, so I would love to find a way to take care of everything and get your company paid off." She forced a friendly smile. He hadn't done anything wrong or threatening yet, but something about him put her on edge.

"It's admirable that you want to pay your debt, but I'm afraid that's not possible. We have a much more invested contract than just the loan you speak of. We have a partnership of sorts when it comes to these tournaments. Just make sure it's bringing in lots of people, and we will handle the rest."

"I don't understand."

"Goulden's investment in your company is the same interest it has in many small businesses like yours. We want to be an integral part of the community, to give back. Which means we have our hand in each event. This one is important to us, for various reasons, but especially because it will pave the way to something bigger, not to mention a lot of revenue for us." He paused at the word 'revenue,' like he really meant something else. "We won't be ending that contract anytime soon, so get comfortable. I'm just here to make sure the tournament is a success, for our sake and yours."

"It will be."

"Good." He stood to go, buttoning his suit slowly. "A piece of advice. Make it easier on yourself and play nice with Mr. Benjamin Barnett. He's the only one with any say on your contract…and your future."

She swallowed hard. "Ben?"

"An important part of Goulden, a partner and founder. He asked me to keep an eye on you while he was out of town. Seems like he has a…special interest." The insinuation in his tone sent a shiver down her spine. What did Ben have to do with anything? He was just a regular.

"Maybe you can enlighten me on the other part of the contract that I don't know about, and any role that Ben is playing in all this. I don't appreciate being left in the dark."

Ignoring her, he stepped through the door, but before turning back, he looked her up and down, and clearly finding her lacking, his lip curled slightly in distaste.

"I'm not sure I understand Mr. Barnett's obsession with you either. Tell your father I was here and remember what I said. This tournament needs to be bigger than ever before. I trust you to make that happen. Good day, Ms. Andrade."

As he walked out of the gym, she pulled the stray strands of hair behind her ears and smoothed the single braid over her shoulder. She felt dirty suddenly, and more confused than ever.

What the hell was that man talking about? Her father had some explaining to do. Glancing at the clock, she realized he still had a couple hours before he would be here, so she settled herself and went back to finalizing the logo, attempting to banish the weird encounter from her mind.

But it didn't work. For an hour, she barely held herself back from stomping over to the house and demanding an explanation from her father. Instead, she picked up her book and got lost in a world of fantasy. Reading, especially if it was science fiction or fantasy, had been her distraction as long as she could remember, and it always served to calm her nerves.

When his smiling face appeared in the door, her heart melted a little. He wasn't a huge man, not even six feet, even if that's what he put on his license, but he was built like a bulldog, with bushy, graying eyebrows, and despite his loving, teddy bear personality, he was fiercely protective of her. Everything he did, he always found a way to make it right.

But she couldn't keep the sharpness from her tone. "Tell me about Goulden, Dad. I need to know everything, not just the bare minimum."

He was startled. "Goulden? I—uh, they are the loan company I used for the equipment."

"Try again. Kevin Pennington visited me in the office this morning, said he had a vested interest in the tournament?"

Anger filled his face. "They promised they wouldn't do that. I've made every payment on time, and I have cooperated with all their demands. He shouldn't be in here threatening you."

"Tell me, Dad. I have a right to know."

He'd stiffened, staring at her with a slight panic in his expression before he spoke robotically. "Ben approached me years ago, talking about going bigger, going legit with better equipment, an updated look, and making more money by taking bets, charging people, bringing sponsors, the works. Said he knew some people that could get me started. That it's a money-making venture for them. They get a cut no matter what."

"Forever? Dad?"

He sighed heavily, unable to even meet her eye as he sank into the chair opposite her. "I'm stupid. Signed a deal for the tournaments, and a different one for the loan. They convinced me it would put the gym on the map and get us out of debt forever. But, at the end of the day, the tournaments are only bringing in money for Goulden. Day to day…there's not much extra with our smaller tournaments. Nothing much left for us compared to what we give them. The area is too saturated with bigger corporate gyms. I figured that's why they came to me, to all of us. We are easy to target with promises of something bigger. The corporate gyms…they won't touch tournaments. Too many illegal things go on outside the fighting. Which means, I take all the risk."

"So, why now? Why are they applying pressure now?"

"Their own operations are getting bigger. I've heard they have similar deals with lots of the neighborhood businesses. They're taking over. Everyone owes them something, and now they want more of the reward."

"How do we get out of this?"

"I don't know." Defeat clouded his expression, then something more. Fear. But her father wasn't afraid of anything. "I thought I could just do a couple of tournaments, and then not organize anymore. Just keep making my monthly payments. Then, when you came back, you did so well with them, they were even happier. It made them lots of money. I approached them about my cut, about me taking all the risks, and said I would just stop the tournaments. They threatened to burn the whole place down…with you inside." He shook his head slowly, like he was working through his memories. "I never thought they'd do anything. Seemed like a scare tactic, like something out of a movie, and we're not in the fifties anymore. They seemed harmless, but I didn't want to risk a lawsuit."

She took a long, steadying breath. "So, what does Ben have to do with this?"

He frowned, unsure. "I didn't think much. I thought he just introduced me to them. I didn't think he was a part of it, and I never see him anymore. He started coming in the morning years ago, and I kinda forgot all about him."

She held her tongue. She didn't want him to feel more guilty than he already did. Ben had started coming in the mornings when she came back from college. And if he was in charge, like Pennington had implied, then he had been keeping watch on them the whole time.

Even now, she felt like she was being watched, and a feeling of disgust ran along her skin.

"He is a lot more involved than either of us knew, and he has definitely been keeping an eye on us in the morning. I will be more careful now."

Silence filled the air, and while she was still annoyed he hadn't told her, his resignation only had her bristling at the way this 'business' took advantage of her father. But they weren't people to be bullied.

She was considering all the ways she could get them out of this when the phone rang on the desk, its shrill interruption a reminder that business had to go on. They both stared at it, worried for a second it would be someone from Goulden, but that didn't make sense, especially with an out-of-state area code on the caller ID. Her dad picked it up and cleared his throat before answering.

"El Luchador. Who? Oh, yes." His face lit up, his grin unmistakable as his eyes fell on her. "I'm glad to hear you're still interested. Didn't think we'd get you. As a matter of fact, she said you couldn't come to an agreement. I do think she needs to get some details from you. She's right—"

Realizing who it was, she quickly shook her head no and mimed, "Take a message!"

"She's not here. Just went out the door. I can take a message, and she'll get back to you." He grabbed a pen and scribbled down the number again, staring up at her quizzically.

When he hung up, he was confused. "What's going on? We need him. Pennington's the one who got this information for me, and he insisted Ice needed to be our headliner. He was clear that everything hinged on it."

She swallowed hard. This was a problem. "I just am not in the right headspace to negotiate with him right now. I don't think we can come to an agreement anyway, but I'll try again."

How the hell did she explain this to her dad? And why did that man keep calling? What did he want?

Chapter 5

Ajax

Wednesday, September 25
Los Angeles, California

Three days later, he realized just how hard it was to get hold of her. Hard.

She wouldn't answer the phone. She wouldn't call him back. Human women had never been a problem for him before. But she wasn't just any woman. She was his mate.

Doubts began to plague him. Had he already scared her off forever? Had he ruined it? But he kept coming back to the look in her eyes, the hunger before the shock set in. He hadn't sensed anger, but whatever she'd felt had scared her. So, he held on to that thought—that meant he had a chance; she had felt their bond too.

He had to go see her. His wolf demanded it.

For three days, he had paced. He had worked out harder than ever before. He even drove out into the mountains to shift and let his wolf run free one more time. Usually, it helped work out the memories, the flashes of screams and blood that still clung to him from the war, and the loneliness of his life without a pack connection, but now, he needed to work through the fear that his mate might not want him.

Before leaving his pack, he was able to push those thoughts to the side, to pull on the strength of pack connections, but since leaving, since tasting the human world, and since becoming a rogue, it hit him harder each day. He'd shifted and run several times over the last few weeks, each time it giving him a little relief, but never enough. He thought as an alpha-born wolf, he could stay rogue longer without needing a pack, that he could be gone at least a couple years, but the call to go home had been getting worse over the last two months, and he was stubborn. He wasn't going to let his brother win. He wouldn't grovel, and he wouldn't give in. There was nothing left for him there.

For weeks, he had tried to brainstorm ways to make his wolf relax without a pack link, without a connection with another wolf. He knew eventually he would go feral as a rogue, forcing him to shift into his beast more often, until he lost control and became fully animal. For now, though, he could still fight. His wolf was a problem for another day.

What mattered now was that his mate wouldn't answer the phone, and that was driving his wolf mad more than anything. His instinct was to go to her business, to show up and…do what exactly? Demand she go on a date? What did humans even do romance-wise? He didn't usually have to practice pickup lines. Women had always thrown themselves at him in Tuisa as the son of the Alpha, so he'd never had to try hard, whether in the pack, or now on the road with humans. And knowing he would have a mate one day meant he had never made an attempt to get to know any women outside his friend group. How did he make a human love him naturally?

Every thought flew through his brain, making him more and more nervous, but he hadn't given up. He picked up the phone one more time.

"Cahaira? What…what do I say to her? How do I get her to agree to be around me even? She won't answer the phone."

"For someone so smart, you sure do act dumb. Go in person. It's easy to ignore a phone call. But you're hard to ignore in person. You're like a bull in a china closet though, so be easy. Try to be relaxed and just find ways to be near her. Don't force it. It will happen naturally."

He frowned. She had wanted him to fight for her gym. He wanted to just accept. That was the easiest, but the owner kept sending him back to her. So, in person? Was that too desperate? What if he lost control over his wolf when he was around her? Shit. All he could think about was how she felt in his arms, how he could have just picked her up and fucked her against the door right then and there.

"Hello. Earth to Ajax. Focus. Are you listening?"

"Yeah, I'm here."

"Once she is open to knowing about your wolfy personality, she should already be so hooked, she won't leave. Until then…ask yourself, what would Linc do?"

He laughed at that. Cahaira's mate was the perfect match for her. Relaxed, doting, completely in love, but still didn't take shit from his fiery wife. Just smiled at her and did whatever he thought was right. And he was a strong witch and fae hybrid. Together, with Cahaira's magic, they were a formidable force, and they always had his back over the years, even against his own brother. Cahaira and Axel argued almost all their childhood, his twin brother's extreme obstinacy even more overbearing than his own, and Axel had always butted up against Cahaira's sense of right and wrong. She had never hesitated to let him know.

This time, the only one left standing by his brother's side was Axel's own mate, Nubia, and even she disapproved of the way he pushed Ajax away. But what was done, was done. When he hung up, he had decided to think less like his brother and more like Linc. He could do this.

As a courtesy, he let the man pretending to be his manager know he was leaving, and that if he needed him, he would be at her gym, *El Luchador*.

"Dumb idea. Little gym, no money there. Ain't worth it."

"I don't care about the money. I told you that."

He'd walk away from everything, and his manager knew it, so the man walked a fine line around him. The manager wanted him in the UFC more than Ajax did. But he just wanted to show his brother he could be successful. He wanted to show him he was right. He wanted to do what he loved, not what he was obligated to do. If that was the UFC, fine. If it was something else. Double fine. Either way, he wasn't walking away from his mate.

A crudely written set of directions in his leather jacket, he mounted his bike, hopped on I-5, and just drove.

By the time he'd passed into the San Diego city limits, his stomach was in knots. If she was a shifter, this would be a no-brainer. Nobody rejected their fated mate—they were sacred and made for each other by their Moon Goddess. But a human didn't understand that and didn't feel the same pull that wolves did. Hell, the idea that wolf shifters were a real thing would run her off by itself.

His wolf was another problem. He had to rein him in. The beast in him wanted to mate and mark her immediately, her feelings be damned. But he knew better. Any other day, he would be in complete control, the domination of his wolf something they all learned early on. But now…without a pack, without the anchor that made shifters whole…his beast had been more and more in charge, and that scared him.

Instead of focusing on that, he focused on her chocolate brown eyes, her soft pillowy lips after she pulled back from the kiss—how they were pink and puffy, parted in shock. How she folded so easily in his arms. Shit.

El Luchador wasn't hard to find, but it fit right into the older neighborhood. It's worn down exterior on par with most other small gyms, it was a classic hole-in-the-wall that locals probably loved. So, when he stepped inside, he certainly didn't expect to see fancy equipment or a completely renovated look. It didn't match the neighborhood or the exterior. Despite that, it was basically empty of people, so the greeting from behind the desk surprised him.

"Welcome to El Luchador. Can I help you?" The older, burly Hispanic man sat up from where he'd probably been napping as he stretched and eyed him curiously.

"I'm Ajax. Looking for a place to train for a minute. I…uh…" Ajax looked around, nervously hoping to see her, but at the same time, he hoped he didn't just yet. "I spoke with Martina the other day. She wanted me to compete in a tournament you have coming up. Is she here?" He tried to sound casual and relaxed.

"Ice, right?" The man smiled widely, excitement energizing his demeanor almost immediately. "Absolutely. I'm the owner, and we would love to have you headline. Marti said you turned her down though. Did you change your mind? She said she called you back, and there was nothing you could work out."

Marti. Not Martina. He let her nickname roll around in his head before he realized the old man expected him to answer.

"Just a little miscommunication on my part. That's why I came in person. Didn't want to give the wrong impression again."

The old man grinned, reaching out to shake his hand vigorously, his strong grip pulling him closer like he was an old friend. "Name's Domingo. I'm excited to have you on board. I'm not great at all the details, but we can offer you the headliner position. And your choice of fair pay. We have prize money, along with a guaranteed pay rate or a possible cut of the door. What's your price?"

The bell on the door jingled, but he didn't have to turn around to know it was her. Her scent of honeysuckle and strawberries hit him, and he faced her as she walked towards them both.

"What are you doing here?" She frowned at him uncertainly, and her beautiful golden skin flushed as she locked eyes with him, then quickly looked away.

"Marti, Ice here is interested in the event now. Says there was some miscommunication that he wanted to clear up."

She didn't look at him again until she was behind the desk, like the counter could keep her safe from him. And maybe it would, because he couldn't think to speak with her that close to him.

He drank her in, immediately taking in details he hadn't noticed. He had felt her curves before, but she had been in a loose pantsuit, dressed for a meeting. Now, she was softer, even younger-looking, and adorable in baggy overall shorts with little sunflower appliques ironed on. One strap was hanging loose, and underneath the overalls, she had a striped, tight sweater that was cropped to see glimpses of her curves under the bib. The single braid that fell loosely over her breast begged for his touch. He couldn't stop picturing how he would wrap the length of it around his wrist and pull her to him. Which meant he hadn't noticed that she was speaking to him until his gaze landed on her lips. They were pursed and annoyed right now. A far cry from the pouty, swollen lips that he remembered. When she pushed her round, black-rimmed glasses up her nose and spoke again, he snapped out of it.

"I'm not sure we can work out a deal. He is training for a UFC bout, and I'm sure he doesn't want the possibility of injury—"

"I'm not worried about injury. I've reconsidered. I want in. When is it?"

When she didn't answer, merely glared at him, he smiled in amusement. Her anger was cute, like a little kitten whose toy was taken away.

"October 5th. Next Saturday. What are your conditions? Do you have special restrictions you want to be put in your contract, or is a standard agreement okay with you? Marti can whip it up real quick, so you can get back to your day."

He didn't glance away from Marti's face as he answered the old man. "Whatever you believe is fair. Something about this place speaks to me. Something beautiful here." Domingo's presence was practically forgotten, and at that moment, all he wanted was to see her smile, to turn the glare on her face into laughter. He wanted to hear about her likes and dislikes just as much as he wanted to hear her whimper and moan in his ear.

"I know the machines are sexy to some guys, but calling them beautiful is a first." Her voice was gentle, lilting, but firm as she eyed him, her instincts pushing her to step back when he moved towards her.

"I have to say, I agree, but I think he means you." The jovial look on Domingo's face had dropped away instantly, the older man's body suddenly angling itself between Ajax and Marti, like she needed protection, even as his voice took on a reproachful tone. He cleared his throat, then emphasized the next two words. "*My daughter* is in charge of all the paperwork, and she can get that going for you. We have a deal, then?"

His daughter. Hell. He didn't know why he hadn't realized that. And here he was, lusting over her in front of him like a teenager.

"Sounds good." He shook his head, trying to relax and smile, turning on the charm for Domingo now. "I do still feel bad about the miscommunication between us, all the back and forth, and wanted to make sure I apologized. Whatever cut you think is standard and an apology for the lady?"

Her father frowned at him, like he was considering his words, weighing them against whatever instincts he had, then looked over at Marti, trying to figure out what was going on. "Unless she objects. Marti?"

"Apology accepted for the misunderstanding. I can get the contract drawn up in just a few minutes and get you on your way."

Her father's look was still suspicious, like he was inclined to turn him away now, so he rushed forward with the deal.

"Then it's settled. If you have a recommendation for a nearby hotel, I will get a room. Since I'm staying for the tournament, I will train here until then. I have no ties in LA."

"Even better than a hotel, we have a couple of private dressing rooms for out-of-town contenders. There's a pull-out couch, a bathroom, and a TV. You can stay here in the gym. I'd hate to see you waste money on a hotel."

"Perfect. I'll sign whatever contract you want, and I would love it if Marti could give me a tour and maybe explain how the tournament runs here."

A smile slipped back on Domingo's face, and the slight confusion eased between them all. "This is gonna be great. You'll love it here. If you want to join any of my classes, or hell, teach one of your own, you're welcome to it. My gym is your gym."

The bell of the door tingled again, and a few clients walked in, their chatting a necessary distraction, and it was clear they were there for a training session with Domingo. So, the man shook his hand and headed over to a sparring mat, leaving him alone with his mate.

Marti looked at him warily, and he couldn't help himself. "I don't bite. Is there a place we can speak privately?" He leaned onto the counter, flashing his biggest smile at her. "Just want to apologize properly. For everything else."

She looked at him in surprise, then tucked a stray hair behind her ears and adjusted her glasses before nodding and walking off. He followed her to an office, and before he had even stepped into the room, she'd lifted the blinds on the big window facing the sparring ring, making sure everyone in the gym could see into the office.

So, she was nervous around him. Or she didn't trust herself, and he considered that information thoughtfully.

"Close the door, please. But don't lock it."

When he turned back to her, she had pulled out some paperwork and was clicking away on the computer. "No need to apologize. It was just an unfortunate case of mistaken identity. I woke you up from your sleep, and clearly, you thought I was someone else."

"No, not at all."

She looked at him sharply, but didn't say anything as she typed away at the computer.

"If you're implying I didn't mean to kiss you or that I regret it, then I don't. The only thing I regret is letting you go and wasting three days without you."

"That's a little much, Mr. Tuhuy. You don't even know me." Her tone was firm, but she was breathless, and he could feel her slight panic in the air.

"Why do you think that? You don't believe me." It wasn't phrased as a question, more a statement. Like either she didn't think highly of him or herself.

"We aren't exactly in the same bracket. I don't plan on falling into your bed just because you flex your muscles. Been around guys like you my whole life. I understand the game, and I'm not interested. I don't date gym guys."

"That's an awful lot of insinuations you just made about me and even yourself."

"I'll say it again. I'm not your type, Mr. Tuhuy. So, what's your angle? I'm not a virgin, and I'm probably older than you, despite how I look. What makes you think: Yes, let me chase the weird, older, frumpy girl. She looks desperate. No, thank you. There are plenty of women, including the one you had laying in your bed that morning, who would love to chase you. I'm sure you're not hurting in that department, so why me?"

"Ajax. Call me Ajax. Not Ice. Not Mr. Tuhuy. I want to hear you say my name. Even in anger."

She blinked at him rapidly, her face getting red. "Out of everything I said, that's all you heard?"

"It's the only thing you said that mattered to me. Everything else was ridiculous, so I'm not entertaining it." He leaned forward on the desk, and she stiffened. "Please. For you, just Ajax."

She didn't answer, but his wolf's senses told him everything he needed to know. Her heartbeat pounded in his ear, and she stared at him, frozen. He lowered his voice, letting his gaze fall to her full chest, then back up to her lips. The only allowance he made himself. The only time he let his control slip. The words he really wanted to say were still under wraps for the moment.

"There is no apology for kissing you. I don't regret that." He leaned in more, closing the gap between them to only inches. "But I won't touch you again without your permission. For that, and for making you angry and however else…you felt, I am sorry."

Chapter 6

Marti

Thursday, September 26
El Luchador Gym

"This is so fucking silly, Marti. Get yourself together."

She walked around the gym, setting out fresh towels, restocking the vending machine, and muttering to herself. With Ben still out for the week, she had the early morning to herself, so she should have been relaxed. Instead, she was jumpy and nervous. Every few seconds, she looked over her shoulder, expecting him to be there. What pissed her off was that she was disappointed when he wasn't.

Seeing him yesterday had ignited feelings that she couldn't control, and she was frustrated that her body had betrayed her at every turn. Growing up in a gym full of men meant she was practiced in the art of kind rejections, smiling even as she brushed off lewd comments or half-assed proposals. That was part of it. But this felt so different. So...encompassing.

Even now, she couldn't help but wonder what he looked like as he slept. If he was still fully naked, or if he kept his socks on. Maybe a side sleeper? Was he curled up, or did he spread out? He probably snored. He looked like he snored. She grit her teeth at that. Why did she care? Why did she want to so badly walk the thirty yards to his door, just around the corner from where she stood, and see?

He was a fighter, and not any fighter. One who had a reputation for brutal fights, ones that ended in blood and violence. That's how he had gotten his nickname and his reputation. He was cold, dangerous, and brutish. That's what everyone said. But it's not what she felt, not what she'd experienced.

She scrubbed one of the dirty machines with a vengeance, the ridiculous back-and-forth conversation she was having with herself only frustrating her more. Instead, she refused to glance at that door again, because despite her brain telling her she didn't want him, her body had other ideas. Yesterday, every part of her had lit on fire when he spoke, his eyes undressing her, pinning her in place. No one had ever made her feel this way, not any of the men here, not her ex, not the randoms she had dated in college.

And he hadn't even touched her. So, when Felix showed up, his smiling face was a welcome reprieve from her own traitorous body.

"Hey, Martiiiii, you enjoying your week off from the spandex dick?"

Felix dropped his bag on the bench and made his way over to her, laughter in his face.

"I should be, but here I am, scrubbing ball sweat off of machines, living the dream." She forced a laugh, refusing to let that man intrude on her thoughts anymore. She hadn't told Felix about Ajax because she knew he would get all protective, then ask a million questions. While her dad had always been purposefully ignorant of her dating life, Felix had taken it upon himself to screen anyone she'd ever had an interest in from the beginning. Especially after her ex ran off with all her money. So now, she didn't want to make him into more of a thing than he was.

But she had called Felix and talked to him about Goulden. He had become serious real fast, telling her that she needed to find a way out of the contract with them. They were bad people, and he didn't like any of it.

"One day, I'm going to get one of those tiny spandex body suits, follow him around and make him uncomfortable, show him what a real dick looks like in spandex." She giggled and looked up at her friend as he approached nonchalantly, and then he stopped mid-stride. "Is there someone else here?"

"What's wrong?" And why did he look like he was sniffing the air around them, turning in circles and tensing like he was an animal expecting an attack?

"I...there's someone else here. Marti, answer me. Who else is here?" He had stepped closer to her, and when a door opened and shut, the sound echoing through the empty gym, Felix took up a protective stance. She stood from her scrubbing position and frowned. How the hell did he know that?

"Yeah, our headliner for the tournament has decided to stay in the private dressing rooms. But he sleeps late and shouldn't be up this early. How did you—"

Just then, Ajax came stomping around the corner of the hallway, hair disheveled, wearing thin grey shorts and pulling on a tight black t-shirt as he walked. Her breath caught seeing him again. Might as well not have put on a shirt at all. The sleeves clung to his biceps like a second skin, and the shorts were slung so low, she could see the distinctive outline of his dick as it swung, yes, literally swung between his legs. Jesus, Mary and Joseph. She needed to get it together.

She was pulled from her trance by a growl coming from Felix as he stepped in front of her, shielding her from Ajax. A growl? Did her friend just growl like an animal? What was going on?

She had barely blinked, and Ajax was in Felix's face. She had been so caught up in Ajax's body, she hadn't noticed his murderous expression as he went straight for Felix.

What the fuck was happening?

Neither of them moved, but they both were filled with an intimidating energy that snapped her from her shock. Only a few inches shorter than Ajax, but nowhere as thick, they weren't evenly matched in any way, so she grabbed Felix's arm and tried to step between them as they stared each other down.

"Felix? What has gotten into you?" Putting her hand on his chest, she pushed him back, and he allowed her, relaxing a bit as he stepped away from Ajax. "This is Ajax Tuhuy, the fighter they call Ice. He is headlining our tournament next week." Taking a few steps back, Felix relaxed a little more, then ran his fingers through his light brown hair in aggravation, never looking away from Ajax.

She whirled to face Ajax. His face was tense and stiff, dangerous looking, almost unrecognizable for some reason, like his features were slightly distorted, and his hands were clenched into fists at his side. He didn't look at her, only beyond her at Felix. Here was the man they called Ice. Here's who everyone was afraid of. Who she should be afraid of. But she wasn't. She was pissed.

"And you! Felix is a member here and my best friend. You need to get yourself together. I don't know what kind of gyms you are used to, but we don't treat people like this here. Have a little common decency."

"Are you fucking him?" The question was almost inaudible, it was so icy, low, and furious.

She gasped at his audacity, her mouth open in shock for several seconds before she said something. She could hear Felix's bark of laughter behind her.

"What?"

"Are you fucking this beta?" He moved again, closer to Felix, who had fully relaxed and was smirking now.

Beta? What does that mean? Was that some sort of insult from Ajax's hometown? It didn't matter. She was furious. How dare he talk to her like that?

"Fuck you. Who I fuck is none of your business. You are crossing a line, and I don't care who you are, you can get out of my gym. I won't stand by and watch your machismo bullshit. Get it together or get out."

Stomping away towards the office, she was so angry she couldn't breathe. She slammed the door as hard as she could, hoping the sound knocked some sense into him, but really wishing his thick head was in the door, so she could smash it in.

Through the window, she could see Ajax hadn't moved, but Felix had casually wandered over to a machine and was doing reps. Pushing the power button on her computer tower, she turned her back to the window while it booted up. She didn't care if he had a little crush on her. He had no right to talk to her or her friends like that. She forced the confrontation from her mind and began working on her to-do list. She had several things to do now that they had him as a headliner, including running some newspaper ads, changing up graphics, printing the bet lineup, and so much more. So, she got to work, refusing to look up, refusing to give him the satisfaction, for a long time. Until she couldn't bear it anymore. Had he left?

A quick glance out the window, and she could see they were sparring in the ring, but this time they were both smiling and laughing casually. Seriously? Men were insane. But she watched a while longer. Felix never sparred with anyone, said he got enough of that at home with his brothers. That he only came here for the machines and the company.

He was surprisingly good at it, even with Ajax being bigger than him.

Able to relax now, she let her mind wander. What was it about Ajax that made her feel so crazy? She didn't like to be rude to anyone, but so far, he'd been really good at getting under her skin. She'd never lost control and screamed at anyone before, even when her ex screwed her.

Back then, she thought she was in control, that she knew him. But he had used her all along. Had convinced her of his loyalty and love, that they would be married. And the whole time, he had set her up as the fall guy for one of his scams. He'd disappeared with all the money in her savings, leaving her name on documents that the police found when he stole from so many others. She had been charged with fraud, lost her scholarship, and was left broke. And broken.

Thankfully, she was able to avoid jail when she proved she was innocent, but it didn't get her scholarship or savings back. So, she worked her ass off, taking classes part time to afford school, and finishing her degree later than planned.

Now, she was a 28-year-old accountant who ran a failing gym business with her father. And couldn't trust anyone.

Especially not this giant of a man she just met.

She refused to be scammed again, and there was no way he was for real. She just hadn't figured out his angle yet. Glancing out the window again, she watched as he sparred effortlessly, sweat shimmering across his toned back, and her gaze strayed down to his nice, bubbly ass. Damn. Did he have any flaws on his body?

She pulled her thoughts back in annoyance at herself. She never dated the jocks who came to the gym, their attitudes tended to focus on themselves, and after a lifetime of it, she sought out men who leaned more towards books or numbers, like her. It made sense. It was safe. Or, it had been.

Hell, despite all her father's pushing as a kid, she never even learned self-defense. It just wasn't in her. She'd faked sicknesses, hurt ankles, and at one point, when she was like eight, she'd just laid on the gym floor and read a book during a jujitsu class. Anything to get her out of it. Eventually, her father stopped pushing her to be any kind of athlete and let her be the book nerd she wanted to be.

Finishing up in the office, she watched as Felix and Ajax wandered the gym together, picking machines to work on, then headed over to the free weights. They were laughing and getting along like old friends, and that annoyed her for some reason.

Gathering her bag and all her paperwork, she packed up to head out for her errands. Her dad would be down any minute, and the gym had begun to fill with other people. Closing the office door behind her, she couldn't shake her annoyance at their sudden friendship.

"I see you worked it out without any bloodshed." She'd gone over only to tell Felix bye, or at least that's what she told herself.

"Just a small misunderstanding. Thought I knew him from somewhere, but he just has one of those faces." Felix casually lifted a free weight and flashed her a smile.

She looked up at said face, and Ajax was staring, his eyes burning into her as he paused his own lifting to study her. "Just one of those faces? Huh. I've never seen a face like his." He smirked at her, and she flushed. She didn't know why she said it like that. "As in, seems like he has a face only a mother could love. Most fighters do. No brains, just muscle."

He smiled at her despite the insult and dropped the weight to the ground, his attitude from earlier completely gone. "You headed out somewhere, beautiful?"

She frowned at him. "That's none of your business. I'm not sure how you got this notion in your head that anything I do should matter to you. Shouldn't you be lifting something?"

Her tone didn't faze him, and he casually leaned on the pole nearby, sweeping his eyes up and down her body again. Today, she just had on neon purple bike shorts and an oversized sweatshirt with a Hitchhiker's Guide to the Galaxy print. It wasn't gym attire, nor was it accountant attire either, but it was what she liked, and she couldn't for the life of her figure out why she was so defensive and hyperaware of her wardrobe every time he looked at her.

"I was thinking I need a tour of San Diego. Hadn't been here before and it's legendary, right? Who better to show me than you? You did promise me a tour last night."

"Of the gym, not the city." She glared at him. She knew she was being rude, and it wasn't like her, but she couldn't help it.

"I think it's a good idea. You should keep him around when you run errands, especially after what we talked about yesterday. Just to be safe until the tournament's over." Felix's voice of reason had her gritting her teeth, and she shot daggers at him. She wasn't going to broadcast her father's business to this man.

"What did you talk about yesterday? Is someone bothering you?" Ajax had stepped close to her, and his heat had her flushing before she could push it away.

"You're the only one bothering me. But go get dressed if you're coming with me. I'll wait, but not long." He smiled big, the soft look melting away the intimidating lines of his face, along with her resolve, before nodding to Felix and striding away.

Once he was out of earshot, she turned to Felix and pointed at him. "You're a pest."

He shrugged and gave her a knowing look. "You know I'm right. That Goulden guy said he'd be watching. I was going to stick around myself and keep you company, but a guy like that on your payroll? He can do double duty."

"Clearly, I don't want to be around him, and you're my friend. You're supposed to have my back."

"Not when you're wrong. And since when do you talk to people like that? You don't even treat Ben that way. What's gotten into you? Other than the misunderstanding earlier, has he been rude to you?"

She groaned in frustration. "Not really. There's just something about him that gets under my skin, and I don't like it."

Felix put down the weight and stood to face her. "Maybe just give him a chance. Seems like a nice guy."

"When did you decide that? When he was trying to rip your head off or when you were feeling each other up in the ring?"

"Definitely the ring. We had a connection." Felix's eyes twinkled when he laughed, and she resisted the urge to throw something at him, considering everything around her was dangerous.

"I'm so glad you find this funny."

"That was a silly misunderstanding. He apologized, and we worked it out. I like him. And I think you will too, if you drop the armor for a second."

"Fine. You're right. I've been a little prickly with him. I can be nice, after all, he is doing us a favor."

"That's my girl." He headed back over to finish his free weight reps, and she sighed. "See you tomorrow."

Making her way back to the desk, she waited for both Ajax and her father to show up. She couldn't leave anyway until he came to watch the gym. They hadn't hired anyone else in an effort to save money.

She drummed her fingers on the counter and thought about what Felix said. She could feel her own disposition changing with him around, and that annoyed her doubly. She liked being the brightest, most cheerful person in the room, and she had only been a sourpuss since meeting him.

She sighed. She could make more of an effort to be nice, even if she was going to turn him down. Maybe he would get the hint then. But she had to admit, despite being angry at how he acted and talked to her, his flash of jealousy over her felt a little exhilarating. It felt like he actually had feelings for her, not the carefully professed love of her ex.

She really needed to get her head checked.

"Good morning, Sunshine. How's my little girl this morning?"

"I'm good, Daddy. Just going to head out and run some errands." She kissed her dad's cheek as he settled in at the front desk. This was his fortress, and he loved manning the desk just as much as he loved teaching the classes. He was a talker, and he knew everyone's business. More of a chismoso than anyone she knew.

"Ah, good, good. Grab me some seltzers while you're out, please."

"Of course." She felt Ajax's presence almost instantly when he came from down the hall, and she took a calming breath. "Mr. Tuhuy is going with me. He wants a tour of the city, and I figured I could do that at the same time."

Her father barely glanced up from the newspaper he was reading to acknowledge Ajax when he walked up, just nodded. "Good idea. Take your time and have fun."

She grabbed her bag and pushed through the door without checking to see if he was following, but she didn't have to. She could feel him behind her, and when she stopped to unlock her car, he was right there, almost touching her, but not. He leaned against her door, preventing her from opening it, but she didn't look up at him, not with him so close, merely waited for him to move.

He bent to her ear, the heat of his now minty breath wafting over her cheek, sending goosebumps across her skin.

"Ajax. Not Mr. Tuhuy. We discussed this already. Don't forget."

She faced her door still, unmoving as he loomed over her from behind. "Can I open my door now?"

"Say it."

She took a breath. Why was this so hard? It's not like it was a special name or anything. She was just honoring his request like she wanted him to honor hers. So, she turned her head, angling her body just enough to look up into his green eyes, smoldering as they studied her profile.

"Ajax."

God, that was a mistake. This close, all she could think about was his lips on hers again, and she resisted the urge to lean into his jaw and feel the dark shadow of stubble against her skin. The memory of it dragging across her throat flooded her, and she could barely pull away.

"Was that so hard?"

"No." Breathily, she ignored the double entendre that popped into her head and gestured toward her door. "Do you mind, *Ajax*?"

He smiled slowly, pulling away from her enough so that she could breathe, but not going anywhere. She could no longer feel his heat on her neck, and immediately, she missed it.

In that moment, the urge, no…the need for him to kiss her washed over her. She wanted him to touch her, to press his body against hers again in every possible way, and when molten heat spread from her core, the flush leaving her heady, she faced him as she took a shaky breath. Her eyes dropped to his lips, and she lost all train of thought.

"Tell me what you want, beautiful. Use your words." The deep rumble of his voice carried through his chest, and he leaned forward, reaching around her.

She hadn't realized just how angled she was towards him, with her hand lifted to his chest, steadying herself, until she closed her eyes, waiting, heart racing, wanting more despite everything her brain screamed.

Chapter 7

Ajax

Thursday, September 26
San Diego, California

He knew what she wanted, what his closeness was doing to her little human body, how the mate bond was playing havoc on her emotions. He could feel it, could see it in her eyes, hear it in the racing of her heart, but it wasn't enough. Not yet. He wanted more than her body. He needed her to want him. All of him.

Which meant, he would get to know her, every part of her first.

"This? This is what you want?" So, despite wanting more than anything to pull her into his arms and explore every inch of her with his mouth, he reached around her for the door handle. Pulling the door open and gently moving her to the side, he watched as her eyes flew open in confusion, then embarrassment. "To open your door, yes?"

"Oh. I—"

She was flustered, and when she sat down in the driver's seat, he resisted the urge to finish what he started. Instead, he closed the door, then headed to the other side to settle into the passenger seat. She started the car without a word, and they had been driving for several minutes before she spoke nervously.

"Now I'm the one who needs to say I'm sorry."

He cocked an eyebrow at her, not expecting that. He thought she'd be angry, maybe tell him off from earlier, be annoyed with him for not kissing her like she expected. But she didn't look at him, merely stared at the road as she spoke.

"I am not normally so…aggressive…and mean. No matter what you choose to do, I shouldn't let it affect me. We have to work together as business partners, and there's no reason to be at each other's throats." She cleared her throat before speaking again. "Or anything else. So, I wanted to apologize for crossing lines and being rude to you. I shouldn't have been banging on your door unannounced on Sunday, and from there, it kind of went downhill. Felix had to remind me that I wasn't acting like myself, and that changes now. I have a few errands to run today, and things to get done on a deadline, and then I can run you to whatever tourist sites you want to see. You are our guest and are doing us a huge favor."

This woman was a surprise, to say the least. Here he was, hoping he could get her to forgive him, and she did it without a second thought. No rules, no expectations. She just forgave him. Something inside him softened, releasing a bit of the tension he always held. Usually forgiveness held a price.

"I'm the one who is sorry. I've been acting like an animal with no manners. There's no excuse for it…but business partners sounds so cold—I hope we can at least be friends. What do you say?"

He gave her his best smile, reminding himself to not do anything to scare her away or make her hate him. This morning had been a disaster in that department, and he thought he had ruined it the second she walked away and reality sank in.

Only hours ago, the barely contained rage from his beast had almost forced a shift on him when he scented another wolf with his mate. Ajax knew he had lost his mind, along with his chances with her, after talking to her that way. He had never spoken to a woman like that, let alone his mate, but he couldn't stop that boulder from rolling down the hill. He had challenged the beta wolf, unable to see past the other man touching her, claiming her before he had a chance. She was his, and his beast had been ready to kill for her. It had taken several minutes of focus to realize Felix had walked over to a machine casually, and when the rage had subsided, the shifter had glanced up and asked, "She's your mate?"

When he had only been able to nod, the beta had launched into a random story about his sister. "Man, the first time I met my sister's mate, the Alpha of a pack up north, I thought he was going to kill me when I gave her a hug. He asked me the same thing, and I was so confused." He chuckled, loosening the tension between them. "I was so dumb, all I could think to ask was 'Why would I fuck my sister?' That didn't go over well, but we got it sorted out. New mates, especially alpha-borns, tend to have irrational wolves."

"She doesn't know." He managed to only croak out his misery.

"Yeah, I figured that. I've never seen an alpha and a human, especially a human who lives nowhere near a shifter pack. She doesn't know about shifters, and my pack is at least an hour away. You're in quite a situation, aren't you?"

"No shit." He had wandered over to a neighboring machine, distractedly running through a few reps while Felix talked. "And I keep messing it up."

"You'll be fine. I've spent years mixing with humans, especially when we were in college, and they're all a toss-up of personalities, but Marti? Marti is the kindest person I know. She just needs time to get to know you, and she'll be hooked. If you're fated, then she's your complement. Just maybe try not to make her mad or rush things."

"That was the goal, but I didn't expect to wake up and scent another wolf near her. My beast didn't like that."

"Yeah, so what's your plan?"

"Spend as much time around her?"

"Sure, makes sense, but how?"

"No clue. Thought I'd figure it out in the moment."

"Well, unless you have a reason to sit in the office with her, I'm not sure how that will work. She is only out on the gym floor until her dad gets here, then she works in the office or goes home."

"She doesn't train or work out or run any classes?"

"Nope. She likes to say she's allergic to sweating. Give her a book all day."

He thought about that for a minute. He used to love reading when he was younger. Mainly comic books and adventures saving the princess, but that was a long time ago. His father hadn't given them time to waste on frivolous leisure like reading. Too much to learn about running the pack.

"And there's something else I think you should know. I only found this out last night, and normally, I wouldn't tell her business, but I think there's a reason fate brought you together right now. Have you ever heard of Goulden Enterprises?"

He frowned. "I don't think so."

"They are a company run mainly by our local vampire nest. Real pieces of shit. One of their people—the head vampire elder—came and visited her yesterday. Her father made some kind of deal with them a while back, and they are putting pressure on them for the tournament. He said he would be watching her, then mentioned one of the regulars here at the gym as someone in charge. That part I didn't know. But I did some digging. Ben is his name, and he's a big player in their world. Their main human partner. And that guy…he's a whole other piece of shit. So, if they are in it together, she needs to be careful. I actually had planned on taking some time off and making sure she didn't go anywhere alone for a few days. Already had it cleared with my Alpha."

His head spun with all this info at once. After questioning him for several more minutes, and hearing all about this Ben asshole, he had grown angry again. Vampires thought they could push in on Marti and her business? And this cocksucker creep who didn't leave his mate alone had crossed the line. Wait till he showed his face here.

"Let's spar. You seem like you should work out some tension before she comes back out here."

An hour of sparring later and he finally felt like he had an even fight for the first time since he left Tuisa. He knew it wasn't fair fighting humans, it's why he'd wanted to open a gym and hold tournaments just for shifters, but here he was, doing what he loved, just with humans.

Sparring with Felix reminded him he definitely missed the fighting style of fellow wolves, and the release of the worry that his opponent could be hurt or die at his hands. That would be a whole different kind of fallout to deal with. Wolves moved rapidly and healed quickly. Humans did not.

Afterwards, they took a break, especially since there was a crowd of gym-goers watching now. He had a couple people stop to talk to him, recognizing him as Ice, and then a few people chatted with Felix.

By the time they had taken a break, they headed over to the free weights, comparing technique. When they were alone again, Felix looked at him weirdly, like he was struggling. "I will say...no I can't say, because it's her story to tell. Just know there's a reason she's not in a relationship and hasn't been in a long time. She will need to trust you, and it might not be easy. You won't be able to rush her."

And that last piece of advice rang in his head right now.

His whole morning with Felix had been more enlightening than all his conversations with Cahaira and anything he could have dreamed up about her himself. He felt more confident, and he made himself a promise not to rush her, to wait until she was begging for him before he touched her again. If that meant they began as friends, then that's where he would start. He couldn't scare her away.

He just needed to convince his wolf to go slow.

So, now that he was in her car, staring at her delicate features, the messy wisps of hair escaping her braid, and her glasses perpetually slipping down her nose, he desperately wanted to make sure he didn't fuck this up. She didn't take but a moment to contemplate his question, and she turned to him with the first smile he had seen from her, and it took his breath away.

"I think I can handle friends. Never hurts to have an extra friend."

Ajax stood by her side as she ran in and out of several businesses, staying to talk to every person like they were old friends. He watched her ask about people's parents, children, siblings. She made jokes and laughed at silly stories. And she always introduced him, telling people about his accomplishments like she was a proud mama hen. He had to admit that part took his breath away. His life had been full of expectations, not accomplishments, and certainly not praise, especially not after choosing this new path.

"Hey, Tom! How's Maggie and the kids?"

"Still tiny terrorists driving her crazy. She needs a poker night with the gals soon."

"Ohh, you know I'm in. I'll give her a call as soon as this tournament is over. Planning is taking up all my free time."

"She'd love that. Is that why you're here? You ready to run that advertisement?"

"You know it. And I have the headliner himself here. Tom, this is Ice. He's been killing it up and down the coast for like a year. Undefeated, right, Ice?"

Ajax didn't like the attention, didn't want to be known, but that's what comes with it, so he usually just stayed away from questions, media, managers, promoters, the whole lot. But for Marti, anything she wanted.

"Yeah. No big deal. I enjoy it enough."

"That's always a reason to do something. It's why I still run this little community paper. Barely break even, but it's something I love. And I bet people would love to hear about you. Hell, a picture would be even better."

"Ohhh. You have any headshots? We can add it to our advertisement, and we'd have every single woman in the county knocking down our doors." Marti teased him but raised her eyebrow in question.

"No, I actually don't do pictures or media, really. I like to keep a low profile."

Marti frowned in concentration. "That's why it was so hard to get hold of you. Took weeks to get your real name and number, and even then, it was our partners who got it. I can respect that. If it makes you uncomfortable, we don't have to put your name." Her warm eyes looked up at him in concern, the little scrunch between her eyebrows making him melt. Hell's bells.

"It's fine. I am okay doing it for you. It will be good for your gym, so I'll do whatever you need, but I don't have any pictures to submit."

"That's okay. I've got my camera in my office. I'll be right back." Tom disappeared, and Marti frowned at him.

"Seriously, you don't have to do this. People will come for a million other reasons. I don't want you doing things you wouldn't normally do. Not for me or the gym."

Ajax shook his head at her worry. "I promise, it's fine. It's going to happen if I go to the UFC, so might as well do it for a small business first. I'd be honored."

She smiled softly. "Thank you."

Tom wasn't gone long, and when he walked in, he was swinging a fancy Nikon. "How about this? Everyone in the city knows Marti—she's the face of El Luchador. If you pose for a pic together, then I will give you the front page, and a nice little blurb, whatever you want."

"Tom, that would be awesome. How much?"

"No charge. I already know Maggie will take all your money in Hold 'Em, so it wouldn't be fair. Besides, with Ice on the cover, the copies will be flying."

"Sounds great! Where do you want us?"

"Let's do it on the side of the building against the brick. Good lighting, even background."

They headed outside, but Tom stopped suddenly. "You got any gym shirts with you, ones with El Luchador on them? Would be better in the pic if you were wearing them. Or you could run to the gym and grab some."

"Absolutely. I give them out all the time, so I'm sure I have some in the trunk. Let me check."

He watched her hustle over to the car and rummage around in her trunk, then walk back with two tops. "This was the biggest one I could find. They're not exactly top quality, but I think it will work if we stretch it a little."

"No problem."

She handed him a black shirt with the gym name scrawled on it in gold, and before she could turn away, he pulled his t-shirt off and started stretching the smaller shirt in his hands.

"So, we're just…gonna change…right here. Cool." He looked up at her, and she was turning red, trying not to look at him. She turned away, pulled off her cute little movie shirt, and was standing there in her sports bra and purple bike shorts for about six seconds before she whipped on the neon pink cropped sweatshirt over her bra. It also had El Luchador in big block letters across her chest, and she pulled an oversized sweatshirt around her hips and tied it off, but not before he took in every curve of her plump ass.

She refused to even meet his eye, only fussing over the shirt he'd squeezed on. "Yeah, that is a little tight on you. Hey, Tom, hold on, I gotta make some adjustments so Ice can breathe."

She pulled him back to her trunk, and she pushed him down on the edge, then started digging through some more bags. When she held out a pair of scissors and grinned maniacally, he couldn't help but flinch.

"This trunk is like Mary Poppin's magical bag of infinite goodies."

"Just hold still. You look like a busted can of biscuits right now."

The cool metal of the scissors slid along his armpits and back, and he felt the material tearing and releasing around his biceps. He held his breath as she moved from one side of him to the other, and with him seated, he was eye-level with her chest as she concentrated on cutting his shirt. Her soft hands slid along his ribs and around his arm as she worked. Then the tight shirt released from around his waist as she sliced the shirt along the seams, leaving only the last inch of hem attached all the way around.

"There. Now you look like every other gym guy." She slapped him on the shoulder and squeezed just as he met her eye. She hesitated, and he could hear her heart beat faster for a second before she looked away. "Picture perfect. Let's go!" Her voice was chipper, a little too bright before she turned, walking briskly towards where Tom was waiting.

"Okay, let's try a couple of different poses, so I have something to choose from. Can I get the typical muscle pose from you, Ice? Both arms up. And same with you, Marti. Let's see those noodle arms, but you go down with them…So funny, Marti."

The tone of Tom's voice changed at the last part, and Ajax looked down. Marti was straining comically with overdramatic clenched teeth and closed eyes before she stopped and smiled at Tom.

"But did you get the picture?"

"I'm not using that one. Let's do another one. Ice, superman pose. Marti, stand in front of him and mirror his pose. You gotta have the same facial expression though. Look fierce. Fiercer. Yeah, nobody is going to believe that." Tom sighed, dropped his camera, and stared at Marti in disapproval. She only laughed and shrugged her shoulders.

"I can only be as good as my photographer, Tom. Come on, put that photojournalism degree to work. Make me front page worthy."

He scowled at her. "You're like a five-year-old. Okay, one more. This time, Ice, put one arm around her shoulders, and Marti put one hand on his stomach, like you just slapped him. Big smile. See, that's perfect. Finally found a picture you looked natural in."

His arm slid around her shoulder easily, and he realized almost immediately he had broken his no touching rule. He felt his wolf practically purring as he tucked her into his side, safe and protected in his arms. There was over a solid foot difference in their height, and every part of her was soft, perfectly connected as she wrapped her back arm around his waist and rested her front hand on his abs, leaning into his body. Shit, shit, shit. Down, boy.

He willed his body to cooperate, hoping he didn't have a full-on tent in this newspaper picture. And when she finally released him, she gave him a little squeeze, then walked away laughing with Tom. He stood there for a minute, giving his dick a little pep talk.

"Calm down. She's not ours yet." He muttered to himself, taking his time as he followed them back into the building, where they were already poring over a tag line.

"Just Ice for San Diego's fav gym. Ultimate luchador here to put us back on the map."

"I like it. There's a play on the words with justice and your gym name. All kinds of hooks going on. You should be working here with me at the paper."

"Too restricting for me. I got to have my hand in all the pots." Marti looked up at him, and he swore he saw a twinkle of humor in her eye when her gaze flicked down to his crotch and away again.

"Do you want to give any of his stats, hometown, home gym, personal life? Things to make people interested?"

His stomach clenched at those questions, but before he could decide how to answer them, Marti spoke up.

"Nope. We are sticking to: 'Tall, dark, and mysterious hottie hits the circuit in a whirlwind of undefeated wins. Picked up by the UFC, be prepared to see more of this luchador on TV in the future, but come see him in person right now.'" She looked over at him, almost like she knew. "Sound good?"

"I don't know about hottie. That seems a little much, but everything else is good."

"Don't be modest. Anything else you need, Tom?"

By the time they were back in the car, she was in a great mood. "People love the San Diego Snapper. It's a small community paper, but it's pretty popular for unique news that won't be in the Tribune. But I put a small ad in the Tribune too."

"Where to next?"

"We are done with my errands. Now, you get to decide. What do you want to do?"

"I want to buy you lunch. I'm starving. What do you suggest?" Just a few moments together, alone with all her focus on him. That sounded perfect.

"What about tacos? Nobody does tacos better than San Diego."

"That's a big claim, especially when I grew up on South Texas tacos. You'll have to have a strong contender."

"I have the perfect spot. Hope you don't mind a wait."

"I've got all the time in the world."

Chapter 8

Marti

Thursday, September 26
San Diego, California

"So, what's the verdict?"

Smugness had crept into her voice, and she knew immediately that he was considering lying to her. Marti couldn't hold back the triumphant she felt as he finished chewing and swallowed his first taco. "It's really good. Like, fuck yeah, kind of good."

She chuckled, then took a bite of her own taco. She didn't even wait to finish chewing before she waved her taco in the air at him. "Told you."

"Didn't anyone teach you not to talk with your mouth full?"

She chewed slowly, savoring each bite, even scooping some of the juices running over her chin with her finger and licking it dramatically before answering. "Nope. Dad said not to use my manners. Would scare all the boys away, and he liked that idea. Does it work?"

"Not in the slightest. I enjoy watching juice drip from your lips and flecks of food fly across the table. Hottest thing I've ever seen."

"Hardy-har-har. I knew you liked it. So, South Texas? You dropped that little tidbit, so now I'm interested. You grew up there? Is that where you spent your whole life cultivating these muscles in some home-grown gym?"

"Not a gym exactly. I grew up on a cattle ranch near the coast." He threw that information out nonchalantly, like it was no big deal, but she knew better. No one knew a thing about him, except her. Something about knowing that he trusted her with that information made her feel protective of him.

"A ranch? So, you're a cowboy? I thought cowboys were lean and wiry. What horse could carry you around all day without dying of exhaustion at night?"

"Only the best. I was more in charge of other things, not just the cattle. We have security and business issues that I was a part of."

"So, a hired gun to protect all the cattle? That makes sense. I bet cattle thieves take one look at you and piss themselves." She giggled at her jokes, and he looked at her wryly.

"Okay, funny girl. I told you about me. How about you? You run the business, but did you have to train growing up with your dad? He make you participate?"

"He tried a couple times, but I was such a complete failure, he gave up. He let me man the phones and read my books."

"You seem like someone who could do anything she chose to do though."

"You're absolutely right. I chose not to sweat. I figured out how to get out of things I did not enjoy. Be the worst, and people exempt you from it."

"You got it figured out."

"Absolutely, and I got to read my books, write my little fan-fics and watch other people sweat their ass off. Not for me. I'm absolutely against all strenuous activities. You won't find me sweating."

"Never?"

"Nope. There is no activity in the world that will be great enough for me to get sweaty and gross. I'll let that fall to you."

"No activities at all? Maybe you're not doing them right." He smirked at her, and she caught on to his insinuation a little late. She felt the heat in her cheeks, and she pointed her fork at him.

"I stand by my statement. I don't even care what you're implying. Sweating is the worst. I'd rather sit on an air-conditioned cushion in sweats with a book in my hand."

"Whatever you wish is my command, but give me one chance, and I'll show you an activity worth sweating over."

"Uh-uh. You said friends. Don't ruin a good thing."

"I didn't say what kind. Just because you assumed platonic, and I did not, is not my fault. You should always check the fine print. Besides, friends don't let friends live a boring life. I think you need a little spice here and there."

God bless. Every word he uttered bounced between sweet and hot, a move that had all her emotions tangled. All day, she had to force herself to keep her thoughts straight, and she had created a chant in her head when her mind had strayed to the gutter.

Trash cans, Dad's beer, porta-potties, throw-up bucket.

But all her thoughts today had leaned anywhere and everywhere but platonic, and hearing him say it out loud sent a searing heat through her body, and she flushed.

"Anyways."

"Tell me what books you like to read."

Now that was a topic she could talk endlessly about. Most people didn't want to hear about her fantasy books, or her obsession with Hitchhiker's Guide to the Galaxy, but he looked genuinely interested, and she went on for several minutes before she paused.

"Sorry, I get excited. I know it's boring. I used to get told—I mean, no one wants to hear about my book obsession. My dad would listen, but others would ban it."

"Who are the others?"

"No one. I just mean that I appreciate you not mocking me over it. Just wanted to say thank you. I've had a lot of fun today."

"Tell me who, Martina. Please."

His voice had lowered slightly, and maybe she imagined it, but it felt menacing, and she blinked at the request. "It's no big deal. My ex just had a rule about how much I could tell him in one day. But that's my fault. I don't realize how much I've talked until people keel over with boredom."

His face had changed dramatically, shutting down all emotion for a second, then it softened, and he reached his hand out, turned it over on the table, and she slid her hand in his without hesitation.

"No one gets to downplay the things you care about. Talk as much as you want because I enjoy hearing you go on and on about something you love."

She swallowed hard, and he squeezed her hand before releasing it reluctantly. "You're right. But that's enough about me. I fed you the best tacos in the world. Now, what do you want to do?"

"You're the local. Where can we go this late in the afternoon?"

Her mind raced over all the typical tourist things, trying to think of what would surprise him the most. "Hmmm. You grew up in the Gulf of Mexico? How much time have you spent in the water of the Pacific Coast?"

"None."

"We have to fix that. Let's go, or he might be gone already."

She grabbed his hand, tossing their trash and hurrying out the door. She knew exactly what she wanted to do, but she didn't know if it was too late in the day. It was almost off season, so maybe she had a chance since they were already within walking distance. She raced over to the San Diego Harbor and down to the pier.

"What are we doing?"

"No questions. Especially because I can't guarantee it will happen. Oh, look! There he is! Donnie!"

One of her high school friends sat in the sun, slumped in his captain's chair, baseball cap over his head, snoozing away. "Donnie Montez. Sleeping on the job, I see."

Donnie's wiry frame jumped up in his seat, and his hat tumbled to the ground. She hopped over the side of the bobbing boat easily, picked it up and slapped it in his hand as he spoke. "Marti, always a sight for sore eyes. Why are you disrupting my Thursday afternoon nap? You know those are the best siestas."

"Because I want a private tour. My friend here is in town, and he says nothing beats the boat tours in the Gulf. He's from Texas, so clearly, I need your help proving him wrong." She squeezed Ajax's hand as he joined her, ignoring how natural it felt to hold.

Donnie looked up at Ajax and frowned before putting his hands on his hips. "Well, we have to fix that, don't we? I know just the spot. Seen some blue whales still hanging around just yesterday. You ready to head out right now?"

"No time like the present."

Before they knew it, Ajax was seated at the bow of the boat, leaned back on the bench, arms draped over the side, and she was across from him, enjoying the spray of the salt water on her face.

"See how pretty! You can't tell me the water in the Gulf is this clear."

He just grinned at her and shook his head. He was still wearing the cut-up shirt from earlier, and the water sprayed him liberally, wetting the shirt and his lightly bronze skin in the late afternoon sun. They sat in silence, staring out at the water until they heard the yell from Donnie.

"Port side! Turning now and cutting the engine. Maybe they'll let us get close."

She squealed in delight. She hadn't taken the time to see the blue whales in years. Joining Ajax as they hung over the side where he was, the boat floated along quietly, and they waited. When the dark shadow of the enormous whale drifted toward the boat, the water rolled them away slowly, and the tail rose into the air, flopping down inelegantly, but oh so beautifully.

"So pretty. You can't tell me there are whales in Texas."

"No whales. But it is, indeed, one of the most beautiful things I've seen today."

She glanced up at him in satisfaction and realized he wasn't even looking at the whale. He concentrated on her, and she was suddenly conscious of his arm around her waist, keeping her from tumbling over the side.

She looked back at the whale quickly, and they watched it glide out of sight. Soon, Donnie powered up the motor, and they headed back to shore. When the sun started to set, he twisted on the bench, propping one knee up, pulled her between his legs, and tucked her body against his, both of their gaze settling on the receding sunset.

Something about the movement felt right, and she lost all desire to resist, sinking against his chest to watch the orange and yellow of the sky turn to pink and dark blue. She pulled her knees to her chest, and couldn't help but slide her hand in his, tracing the veins and meaty fingers with her nail before setting his hand on her leg. It felt right. Comfortable. And hot. So, when his thumb began rubbing slow circles against her thigh, the languid movement had her stomach clenching in anticipation.

"And the sunset? Can't see those on a Texas coast." *Trash cans, Dad's beer, porta-potties, throw-up bucket.* But it wasn't working. Even the deep rumble of his voice vibrated through her body, sending her naughty thoughts into overdrive. This trip out on the water was a bad idea. She was sure of it.

"Mmmmh. You got me. The sunrises, though, are spectacular. But, I think the company is what makes it better. To test it out, you'll have to come back with me to Texas and see. True experimentation requires controlled data."

"You don't want me in Texas. I'll just have to take your word for it."

"See, that's where you're wrong. I want nothing more than to take you back to Texas with me. One day, I will. That's a promise."

She chuckled softly, playing the game with him, but instinctively she knew he wasn't playing. Something about his tone had become serious, less wistful, and more resolute. And now, she was staring down at his hand where it rested on her thigh. Where it burned heat into her skin, her whole body aching for more of his touch. She squeezed her eyes shut, making one last attempt at keeping this professional. "As friends?"

He leaned down, dipping his head against her neck softly, only a whisper away from being cheek to cheek, and her eyes popped open as her heart raced. "You can call this whatever you want. Doesn't change it."

By now, growing need had taken over, and she squirmed against him, trying to relieve the increasing heat between her legs, and she shuddered at the closeness of his breath against her throat. She leaned back further,

her body wanting his lips on her neck, something, anything to sate the fire running through her veins right now. But he held back, tormenting her, until every few seconds, she felt the tickle of his lips and stubble skimming her shoulder teasingly. Like he was waiting for her.

"Please." Her strained voice sounded foreign, even to her.

"Please? Please, what? I told you I wouldn't touch you unless you asked. Tell me what you want."

She arched her neck, reaching one hand back behind his head, trying to force him to her neck. Somehow this was easier with him behind her, out of sight of those all-knowing eyes. "Kiss me. Please."

"Who? Who do you want to kiss you?"

"Ajax." Breathless, and almost indiscernible, the words hadn't fully left her mouth before his lips blazed a trail of heat up her neck. His arm slid from her knee up to wrap around her throat lightly for a second, a quick sign of heated possession, then skimmed up her chin and across her cheek where he turned her head, and she was forced to face him, her body quickly following. Still in his lap, her breath caught at their closeness, just as his mouth gently found hers. Slowly, mesmerizingly, their lips were in sync, soft and warm, his tongue moving against hers, and the world seemed to stop, yet go on forever. When she pulled back slightly, overwhelmed by the situation, and whimpered into his mouth, she felt his groan turn to a growl that ripped from his chest.

One arm wrapped around her waist, steadying her, the other slid up her ribs and under her sweatshirt, pushing her bra up, giving his hand free access. When his thumb brushed her nipple, flicking, teasing, she gasped into his neck. How did something so small give her so much pleasure? It felt right, hot yet desperate. She clung to him, head buried in the crook of his neck, one arm around his shoulder, the other trapped under his. No one had made her feel this way before, and her brain was on fire—it only wanted more, more, more with no rhyme or reason.

"Almost back to the pier, guys. Brace for some bigger waves. Gonna start to get dark out there when that sun sets, you want me to turn on some deck lights?" Donnie's voice crackled over the intercom from his captain's perch.

"No!" She pulled away from Ajax hastily, the moment broken just as a spray of water splashed across the deck, soaking her back as they slowed to trolling speed.

Jesus. That spray of cold water was just what she needed. She couldn't be falling for him, for his moves. It was too easy. She was giving in like she had zero spine. Red flags flew up in her brain, and she scrambled backwards. She reached under her sweatshirt and pulled her bra back down, straightened her glasses and smoothed her hair back, refusing to meet his eyes.

He reached for her, and she pulled back. "I think this was a bad idea."

"I think you're soaked, and with the wind, it's going to get cold. Let me keep you warm, at least." He moved to an inner bench, his back now to the captain's box, and away from the edge of the boat, safe from the worst of the salt spray.

She eyed him warily, not trusting herself or him, especially with that knowing gleam in his eye. But he was right, she was starting to shiver. The California wind had a distinctive bite, especially on the water. "Okay, but no more funny business, mister."

"I believe you were very specific with your instructions earlier. I only followed orders. Your orders."

She glared at his mocking little smirk. "You know what you did. You are practically oozing sex appeal. I need you to turn that crap off."

"Yes, ma'am." He mimed inserting a key into his belly button and turning it. "Officially off. Everything else is on you now."

He grinned hysterically at his own joke, and she couldn't help smiling back at him even as he grabbed her by the waist and pulled her back to his stomach, wrapping himself around her.

"I'll admit, you are like a heater, even your hands are warm."

"Probably be better if you took your wet sweatshirt off." He rested his chin on top of her head, his hands moving up and down her arms to warm her.

She snorted. "Fat chance. We are almost to shore anyway." She wiggled to get comfortable on the bench between his legs, and he lifted her to sit sideways in his lap. She was suddenly super aware of his muscular legs and…his large, very hard dick against her thigh.

"I thought you turned it off." Her own voice sounded hoarse in the air.

"He doesn't listen. Has a mind of his own. You want to try talking to him yourself? See what you can do?" His words were muffled as he spoke into her hair, and she swore he was sniffing her in long, heavy breaths.

She giggled. "Does he have a name? We could talk him down gently."

"Mjölnir." At that, she laughed out loud.

"Really? You named him after Thor's hammer? I mean, it fits, you being a perfect Thor and all, but I would have never pegged you for someone who knows about Norse Gods or even Marvel comics."

He scoffed. "You assume I'm some illiterate brute? Which do you want? The comics or the legend?" She shifted in his lap, not willing to look him in his face for this strange conversation, but he continued. "'Whosoever holds this hammer, if he be worthy, shall possess the power of Thor.'"

"Sounds like a cheesy pickup line you learned to get girls."

"I don't need cheesy pickup lines."

"I bet you don't, not with Thor's hammer over here."

"Mmmh. But you miss the most important part of that. Not only must you be worthy, but you would hold all power in your hands. You'd own me, body, mind and soul."

His words sounded so perfect, so earnest and romantic, she let them affect her for a moment, pretending he wasn't just trying to fuck her. She closed her eyes, enjoying the feeling that she could ever be good enough to be someone's forever, before closing off that part of her again. She didn't want that anyway. All love was just a long-running scam. Maybe what she needed was to just fuck him and get it over with. Get it out of her system, get through the tournament, and send him back out of her life. She could put her jade-colored glasses back on and continue her easy life here with her father.

But for now, it felt good to pretend.

"Well, let me know when you find the one who is worthy. It will be a sight to see."

He was silent for once, no charming comeback, only the solid warmth of his arms wrapped around her body, protecting her from the bite of the cold wind. But the hardness against her thigh didn't lessen, even in the silence as they approached the pier.

Chapter 9

Marti

Thursday, September 26
San Diego, California

"Thanks, Donnie. That was amazing. He won't say it, but it was definitely better than the Gulf. No whales there."

"Anything for you, Marti. I'll be at the tournament next week. Can't wait to see you fight, Ice."

They walked down the dock, and she resisted the urge to hold his hand. One day was all it took to change everything. She didn't know what it meant, or how it happened so fast, but she felt her resolve softening. They had only walked a couple hundred yards down through Harbor Island Park when she felt his attention move elsewhere.

He stiffened, staring off into the distance, and Marti looked up at him in confusion when he came to a full stop. Following his eyeline, there were several groups of people hanging out in the grass, the sun still up just enough to see them, but it was the single woman leaning against the tree that held his attention. Marti admitted she was beautiful. Even with the sun almost gone, her blonde hair shined, her dainty features highlighted by her blood-red lips. A leather jacket, low-heeled boots, and black jeans highlighted her slight figure, and she didn't hide that she was staring back at Ajax.

Immediately, a burst of jealousy filled her, then shame and anger with herself as her thoughts spiraled. She let Ajax's charm sway her again. He could have any woman he wanted, clearly. Once he was bored with her, he'd move on to someone he was more used to. Was she just an oddity he wanted to conquer because she turned him down? A challenge? He probably never had a woman run from him before, and that's all this was, a game. Marti didn't look like the girls he would be with. She didn't work out, nor was she naturally slender. No toned abs or lean arms for her. She liked her tacos, and her stomach was soft, thighs were thick, and her hips wide. Suddenly self-conscious when faced with this woman who held Ajax's attention, she stepped around him, keeping her tone light, like she didn't care.

"You should go say hi to her. She's pretty. More your type."

Distractedly, he frowned, but didn't look at Marti, his gaze never leaving the captivating woman. "Do you know her? Recognize her from anywhere?"

"No, but she's clearly interested in you. I'll stay here. You go talk to her."

Finally, he looked at her, realizing her demeanor had changed as she tried walking away again. "What are you talking about? I'm not interested in her like that, she—"

"Seriously, go. We're just friends. I want to see you relax before the tournament. You probably have time to take her to dinner. I can head home."

"Don't be crazy. She's here for you. She's a part of Goulden. We should get out of here."

She froze at the name. She hadn't told him about that. And how the hell would he know who is a part of Goulden? She hissed at him as he pulled her in the opposite direction.

"How do you know about Goulden? Ajax? Answer me!"

"Not here. Unless you want to see me kill her, then we should get going."

She snapped her mouth shut, glancing back to see the woman moving towards them at a surprisingly fast pace. They moved quickly though,

Ajax practically dragging her until they reached the car. Pulling out of the parking lot in silence, they were almost back to the gym before she said anything. She had to get her anger under control.

"First. How do you know about Goulden? I haven't mentioned them."

He waited for a minute before answering. "Felix warned me. He was going to stick with you until the tournament and keep an eye on you, but we decided it made more sense for me to do it."

"Keep an eye on me. Like I'm five."

He didn't say anything, only stared out the window, his mind elsewhere.

She felt her eyes tearing up, and she tried to stop the flow of tears. She was an ugly crier, but at least it was silent. He had only wanted to hang out with her today because of some sense of duty? A favor for Felix? So, he was just bored, and everything was fake. A lie.

Once again, she felt like her world was crushed and crumbling beneath her. Like with her ex, all over again. Yet, she had been with her ex for over a year, and it didn't hurt nearly as bad as this. She had only been around Ajax for one day. What was wrong with her? Too trusting, yet again.

When she found her voice, it cracked, but the longer she spoke, the stronger it became, and anger took over. "So, you volunteered to hang out with me as a job or a favor? Or maybe some sense of duty. Gotcha. You aren't responsible for me, nor my gym. I will release you from your contract, and you can go."

"Marti, that's not—"

"Did he pay you? Felix? He didn't want to be around me, so he paid you to take his place? Or are you actually a part of Goulden? Is that how you know who she is? Because that makes sense. They're the ones who found your information. They're the ones who insisted on me getting you and only you. Is this some elaborate scheme? Did Ben put you up to this because I turned him down?"

She pulled into the parking lot of the gym, stopping in her reserved spot. "Get out."

Instead, he turned to her, and in the dim lights of the streetlamps, she thought she saw pain in his eyes, or even fear. She didn't know, and she didn't care. He was just a good actor. It was all fake.

"I volunteered because I already wanted to be around you. He told me because I was already planning on asking you to hang out, and he wanted me to be aware in case something happened. There was no elaborate plan to trick you. I just want to be around you, and it was a bonus that I can make sure you stayed safe from those scumbags."

He reached up, wiping the path of tears that had dried on her cheeks, then cupped her chin in his hands gently.

She had softened as she stared into his mesmerizingly green eyes, easily believing his words, like a fool, before the other hammer dropped.

"You can trust me. I'm not like the other men you've been around. I won't hurt you."

Those words snapped her back to reality. Other men? So, Felix was just spreading all her business around to people he didn't know. Clearly, he told Ajax about her ex, as well. Fuck these men. All of them. All of their pretty little lies and their mind games.

"So, Felix is just a fountain of information, and you got to be the lucky one who passed his test." She jerked her head from his hands, then leaned over him to open his door. "Get out."

He stilled, staring at her, like he was fighting a battle in his head, then turned to step out of the car. But he didn't close the door, only stood there staring.

"I'm sorry. It's not what you think, but I am sorry. I will make this right. See you in the morning."

"Like I said, I will terminate your contract, and you can go. I don't want to see you, or Felix for that matter, ever again. Close my door. I have somewhere else to be."

"Where are you going?"

"None of your business."

Without waiting for him to close the door, she backed up, ripping the door from his hands, and letting it close on its own as she drove away. She wouldn't be a victim anymore, nor would she be pitied. Whatever truth there was in either story. For all she knew, he was a member of Goulden himself and playing a part.

She laughed through her tears at that. This wasn't some action film. No one was out to get her like that. Just a few manipulative men who liked to fuck with her head. It hurt that Felix had been a part of it too. One of the only men she'd ever trusted.

When she finally pulled into the spot in front of the house on La Jolla Farms and Blackgold Roads, she locked her car and grabbed an extra sweatshirt from her trunk, throwing the wet one away and layering on another shirt underneath. She even pulled on sweatpants from the same bag.

He was right, this was like a Mary Poppins trunk.

Angrily, she pushed thoughts of him out of her head, reminding herself that she knew nothing about him. Just that he was from somewhere in south Texas. He could be a serial killer, set on his next victim, for all she knew. All the serial killers were handsome men, luring in their prey, right?

Closing the trunk, she grabbed her book and set off down the concrete path to Black Beach, ducking under the security gate. It was rarely used, especially at night and this time of year. Too many other beautiful beaches with easier access. But she loved to come here and think, to be near the ocean, read her book and be alone.

Dropping a small blanket onto the sand, she settled her back against the cliff and stared out at the water for a long time. She'd been coming here for as long as she could remember. Her dad used to come with her, telling her story after story of her mother, and how much she loved the ocean, the waves and her books, too, just like her. She was only four when her mother died, and her memory had faded to just mere seconds in time, moments she desperately tried to associate with the only photographs she had left of her.

Pulling out the laminated bookmark with her and her mother's face, she traced her finger along the outline. Here, on the beach, it was easier. Her best memory was her mother lying on her stomach in the surf, right beside her. They would giggle every time the tide came in and swelled around their bodies, squealing at the temperature. But it was only a blip in time, and then that moment was gone. Other memories weren't as vivid, or not as long. Just flashes of giggles as they read together on the beach, and her dad joking with them about missing out on the ocean.

All these memories became stronger when she was here, with the sound of the water soothing her thoughts. When the good memories were strong enough to drown out the newer, suckier ones, she could breathe again.

But she couldn't get rid of the sinking fear that it would come for her too. That the cancer that took her mother would probably doom her as well. It didn't take a rocket scientist to see it in her mother and grandmother's family history. It was genetic. It was already pre-determined in her head. She just wanted to outlive her dad, that's all. He barely survived her mom's death, and she didn't want him to suffer through hers.

For her, there was no longer a driving need to find someone and settle down, to plan out some fancy life. As she'd gotten older, after being exhausted by the dating world, she'd accepted it, like it was already a reality. Even if it was one she hadn't spoken about.

Every time her father mentioned her starting her own life and not worrying about him, she just laughed him off. There was no point. Men were untrustworthy; her life was unpromised. For now, she had her books, her dad, and the simple things. Everything else, she could live without.

She wasn't wearing her watch, so she wasn't sure how long she sat there, reading with her little battery-powered book light anchored around her head. But when she closed the last page of the book and stretched, dropping the headlamp into her bag, her butt was so numb from sitting, she got a cramp when she tried to stand.

"Oof, girl. You're getting old. I need to start bringing my beach chair. Can't hit thirty with a bad back." She muttered to herself, stretching as she packed her stuff back in her bag, and headed back towards her car. Long shadows under the moonlight stretched across the paved trail, and when she paused to readjust her bag, she swore she heard a rustling noise behind her, and a shadow skitter away.

Looking around furtively in the dark, she picked up her pace, trying not to panic. Her mind immediately jumped back to Kevin Pennington and his warnings that they were watching her. She hadn't really taken it seriously. These guys were just bullies, all talk. Why would they follow her onto a beach? Her movements had nothing to do with their business dealings, and he shouldn't have any personal interest in her. Even Ben didn't follow her around town, did he?

Either way, she cursed the long uphill trail slowing her down. Like hell would she let those pieces of shit Goulden people make her sweat over some empty threats. Deliberately, she slowed her pace and reached into her bag, digging around the bottom as she walked. Her hand closed over the cylindrical can of mace, and she let it fall to her side casually, like she was holding nothing.

All the way to her car, she tried to remain calm, and even once she was inside, fumbling the keys into the ignition, she didn't let go of the mace, not after checking her backseat, not after staring up and down the street for anyone walking around, not after driving back to the gym and parking her car in her spot.

Locking up, she stepped through the garden gate, opening it just far enough it wouldn't creak, then made her way around the side of the gym towards their little home in the back. She was almost to her door when she heard the roar of a motorcycle pull into the gym parking lot. Motorcycle? The girl in the leather jacket probably drove one. It would make sense. Well, she wasn't scared of those pricks, pretty or not.

Dropping her bags inside the front door, she quietly took up a hiding spot on the path right behind the gym. She could see her front door from that curve, and they couldn't see her. When the gate creaked from being opened too wide, she got her mace ready, clenching it in her hand and holding her breath in the darkness of the night.

It wasn't a woman who walked around that corner, but it didn't matter. No one should be back here, and she reacted. Without waiting, and without a word, she flicked up the safety latch and pressed the button, aiming directly for the man's eyes.

Chapter 10

Ajax

Thursday, September 27
San Diego, California

If he hadn't been so far in his own head, worried that she was taking unnecessary risks, stressed that she hated him again, and mad at himself for fucking it all up, he would have realized how strong her scent was when he turned that corner. His father would have been disappointed in him for letting someone get the drop on him, especially a human.

But it was truly what he deserved.

When the first blast of pepper spray hit his eyes, pain seared through him, and he dropped to his knees, covering his head from the never-ending spray.

"Fuck. Marti! Stop, it's me. Fuck, that shit hurts." He groaned as he leaned his head into the ground, squeezing his eyes shut, willing the pain to stop. But it didn't. It had gotten into his lungs, and it burned as he coughed. There was a cloud of pepper around him, and he kept inhaling it, couldn't get away from it.

Crawling forward on his hands and knees, he bumped into her shins, and she didn't move. He went around, letting his wolf lead him to a less contaminated area with his heightened senses. He ripped the gym shirt off his body, pulling it up to wipe at his eyes.

Fuck. It was covered in the mace spray too, and it only made it worse.

He was barely able to think when the cold spray of water hit him directly in the face. He felt her foot up against his ribs, and she pushed hard enough to get him on his back. Immediately, the water hit hard against his face, and when he opened his eyes to yell, the jet increased and shot right down his throat.

Damnit, this was not how he would die, waterboarded by his own mate. Sputtering and coughing, burying his face in the ground to escape her maniacal torture, he covered his face with his hands. "Marti, please. Fuck, let up for a second." He pleaded with her, rolling around until he realized the burning had stopped, and he could breathe again.

Sitting up on his haunches, then squinting up at the blurry figure in front of him, he blinked a few times, hoping his wolf would heal him fast. But she'd disappeared while he worked through the pain, appearing a few minutes later with a gallon of milk, which she also proceeded to dump over his face silently. For several minutes, he panted on the ground, letting his wolf heal him while she stared. When he finally could speak, he didn't even look up at her.

"This shit hurts."

"Honestly, yeah. I'm glad it hurts. Why are you following me?"

"I told you. I just wanted to make sure you're safe." He wheezed, pulling to his knees, then crouching as he tried to focus on her face.

"I've been safe my whole life without you. Try again."

"Because I fucking care about you, and even if I'm the reason you're upset, I wanted to make sure you were okay. I swear."

"You've known me for like three days. You can't care about me. What's your game?"

"No game, I swear on my parent's graves. I just want—" His eyes had finally cleared, and he blinked rapidly just as she lifted her arm to spray him again with the pepper spray. His instincts finally kicked in, and he leaped forward, pressing her up against the wall, grabbing her hand and ripping the pepper spray away from her, leaving only the water hose in her other.

She gasped as he pinned her arms above her head, his body pressing into hers. Then, it was the fear in her eyes that had him pulling back slightly, but not letting go.

"I'm sorry. I'm bad at this. I've never cared about someone like I do you. This is new to me too. Normally, I don't go around stalking people. Hell, I've never even been on a real date with someone, and I'm not doing it right. All I know how to do is fight, and whether your safety concerns are real or not, protecting someone is the only thing I know how to do well."

Her chest heaved against his, and she glared at him. "I would say that you aren't doing that well either if I knew you were there and got the drop on you. If I had a gun instead of mace, you'd be dead right now."

"Fair enough." But she didn't soften her glare. "If I let you go, are you going to try to drown me again?"

The hose was still in her other hand, even if it was pinned under his grip, and she smirked. "Maybe. How do I know you're not a serial killer, full of lies and bullshit?"

"You don't. You have to trust me on that."

"I don't trust anyone except my father, and even then, his judgment is iffy. He seemed to like you, and that's sign enough that he's losing his touch."

"For fuck's sake, Marti. I could have killed you several times by now. Why would I let you introduce me to half the town if I was trying to kill you?"

She paused, furrowing her brow while she considered that. "True. Let me go. I won't spray you. I was just trying to help relieve the pepper spray pain."

"I feel like you enjoyed my pain a little too much."

"Oh, there's no question about that. I would do it again."

He released her and stepped back, holding up the mace. "Then I'm keeping this far away from you."

She walked over to roll the water hose back up against the building, before giving him one last comment. "It's cute you think that's my only one."

Then she simply walked back into her house and closed the door without a backwards glance.

Fuck. This woman was wild. She was stubborn, she was impulsive, and she was fearless. And she was his.

He just had to figure out how to convince her he belonged to her, just like she belonged to him. He ran his hand over his face wearily and let himself inside the gym to shower and sleep. But even once he laid his head down, his mind raced with all the possibilities. How the hell was he going to change her mind?

He didn't know when he finally fell asleep, but the banging on the gym doors definitely woke him up. Pulling on some pants, he stepped out into the office area, attention immediately drawn to the front doors where Felix stood pounding on the glass.

"Marti! Seriously, let me explain. Open the door. Marti!"

Even through the door, Felix could be heard hollering at Marti, and he froze. Looking out into the gym, he saw Marti casually placing towels, cleaning machines, and tidying up. She was ignoring Felix, and when he cleared his throat, she glared at Ajax.

"I haven't changed my mind. Get out of my gym."

He sighed, then shuffled over to the door where Felix looked at him furiously. "Hey man, what the hell happened? Let me in."

One of the upgrades this gym had that he had never seen anywhere was an electronic entrance. Members had cards that opened the door during slow hours or when no one was manning it. It protected Marti in the morning from people wandering in while she was alone. Something he had instantly appreciated when he was given his card to get in and out. Strange that they had such state-of-the-art technology in a place like this.

Opening the door for Felix, he lifted his eyebrow at him. "You locked out?"

He ripped the sign off the door and held it up for Ajax to see. "She deactivated my card. What did you do to her?"

He paused to read the sign, and if both Felix and Marti weren't so angry, he would have laughed at her spunk.

Feral for Love

No traitorous, secret-telling friends allowed. Membership cancelled. Friendship cancelled. Family Fitness down the street is open.

"Both of you can go fuck yourselves for treating me like a child. Talking about me behind my back. Telling my personal information like you have any right. I've gone through my life safe and sound without either of you, and I can continue that just fine." Marti had closed the gap across the gym angrily, and she pointed a toilet brush at both of them, then walked away to her office.

If looks could kill, the one Felix shot him would have taken him out on the spot. "What the hell is she talking about?"

"I told her I knew about Goulden. We ran into a vamp, and she was confused. I got her away from them, but I had to tell her you told me, so I could keep her safe."

Felix set his bags down on a bench and began pulling on his gloves slowly. "That's it? I mean, yeah, we could have told her that it was a secondary reason for being around her, but this is a little much."

"I may have tried to calm her down by telling her she could trust me…"

"And?"

"By saying I wasn't like her ex, and that I wouldn't hurt her."

Felix groaned. "Goddess, you are an idiot. I didn't even tell you anything."

"Well, now we are both lumped in with all men who are untrustworthy. She's told me she's terminating my contract several times, and pepper sprayed me last night." He took a deep breath, then rubbed his face wearily. Saying it out loud made everything hit just a little harder.

Felix's jaw dropped, and he whistled low and slow. "You're fucking shit up left and right. I never thought it would be so hard to get your mate to like you."

He growled at him. "I was doing fine up until then. Now, I don't know how to fix it."

"Well, let me fix my fuck-up first. I don't want to be associated with any of your fall-out." Rubbing his hands together, like he was preparing for a fight, Felix took off towards the office where Marti was working.

Ajax stayed behind him, just out of sight, but close enough to hear as Felix opened the door.

"Marti-tarty, life of the party. You know you can't stay mad at me."

"Try me, Felix."

"Come on. I was just worried about you. You're my friend. That's my job."

"So, now our friendship is a job? A duty to you?"

He heard Felix take a deep breath. "That's not what I meant. I value our friendship, just like I value your life. I know the Goulden people on a personal basis. If they came to see you, then you're in more danger than you think. I had already taken off work to hang out. That wasn't a secret. Ajax wanted to do it instead, since he was already planning on hanging out with you. It made sense. Besides, you can't blame me for not wanting to be a third wheel."

"We don't even know him, Felix. He could be the next Ted Bundy. And you decide to not only assign him to follow me around pretending to like me, but then you tell him my personal business with my ex? Tell me. Is that a part of the job? A chapter in the friendship handbook?"

"Okay. You got me there. But I have great instincts. He is interested in you. Since the moment he saw you, that's real. He's not pretending."

"Don't speak for him. You're not around, and you're not some magical matchmaker. I have zero desire for any type of relationship with a man, real or fake, serious or casual."

"Marti, damnit, you're being stubborn."

"I'm allowed to be stubborn regarding my boundaries and my life."

"Yes, you are." Felix sounded defeated, and he shook his head. Marti's logic was sound, and now, Felix saw what he'd been working with. "I'm sorry though. I had nothing but the best of intentions."

"The road to hell is paved with good intentions. Why should I trust you not to override my own boundaries?"

"Because you love me?"

"Jesus. All men are the same. You think you can bat your eyes and declare your love, and we are supposed to fall at your feet. I can't wait till you meet the woman of your dreams. I'm going to sabotage the shit out of you. Go work out before I tell my dad to cancel your membership for real."

"You're a fucking peach, Marti-bear."

"Yeah, yeah. Get out."

Felix practically flew out of there smiling. As he passed by, he mouthed, "You're up, good luck."

He leaned against the door frame, knowing damn well she knew he was there. "So, I'm the man of your dreams?"

She paused her typing and scowled at him. "Of course, that's what you got from that."

There was a long pause as she went back to work.

"That doesn't answer my question."

"Yeah, because I dream of using all of these cans on you again. Daily, for a hundred years." Yanking open her top drawer, she pulled out seven more pepper spray bottles, lining them up on her desk. "That's one a day until the tournament. And I have several more boxes of these around here somewhere."

"Only one a day? I think that's a win. I'll take one a day if that means you'll let me hang out with you. So, what's the plan today?"

"My plan is to do my job, then fall asleep early, reading my new book. I don't know what you're doing. Maybe you should train some more. Your reflexes are a little slow, and now I'm worried you've been winning by pure luck."

"The zoo it is."

She looked up sharply. "Why the zoo? That's all day."

"Zoos in Texas aren't world renowned, and I figured I've been acting so uncivilized that it was appropriate to put me with the animals."

"God, that's cheesy. But true."

"So?"

She sighed heavily, shuffling around some paperwork and glaring at the dark monitor of her computer screen. "I have things to do, and my dad doesn't get here until ten. But please, feel free to beat up on Felix. I'd love to see both of you bloody."

He smiled softly at her gruff words, knowing she was agreeing in her own way. They were going to the zoo today.

"For someone who refuses to sweat, you're awfully violent."

"I'm just working smarter, not harder. If I can get other people to do it for me, why not?"

Chapter II

Marti

Friday, September 27
San Diego Zoo

"I can't believe I forgot about the new pandas! They're finally here. It's so exciting!"

"They aren't on display yet, but after their quarantine period, you'll be able to see them. We have to make sure they adapt before being exposed to the public." Even the light and informative voice of their tour guide couldn't ruin her excitement. Only a few more weeks, and she'd be the first in line.

She leaned back in the seat of their rental cart, the private tour she'd insisted on being the best decision she made all day. The zoo was her soft spot, and she had suspicions that Felix told him that too, but she didn't care right now. She had never done a private tour, always opting for the new Kangaroo stops, or the big, open-air bus. Watching the animals never got old, and there was always something new to see.

"Okay, but we have to see the flamingo exhibit next. They're so pretty. I wish I could take one home with me."

Ajax's arm was wrapped around the seat behind her, and she made it a point not to lean back. She didn't want to give him a chance to touch her more than he already did.

"Are they edible?"

She whipped her head over to him and frowned. "Stop playing."

"Flamingo meat is illegal to eat here in the United States." The guide's tone switched quickly to sharp and disapproving, but the older woman didn't turn around, just pulled up to the exhibit, then ignored his comments, as she should be doing too. She wasn't going to let him bait her into liking him. He could use all the charm he wanted today.

"That doesn't answer my question. I bet they taste fishy. Or maybe like duck. Also, how can you be punished for an illegal activity if there's no proof left when you're done?"

She only looked at him as they sped off to the next exhibit, but he continued. "I see why you wanted a private tour. Look at all these poor souls walking up and down these hills. I bet they're breaking a sweat."

She snickered at that. "I told you. Work smarter, not harder. You won't get me to sweat if I can help it in any way possible. Besides, you're paying."

They zoomed around a particularly tired group of parents with kids, and Ajax leaned out to get one of the kid's attention when they slowed for a second. "Pssst. Ask your parents for one of these. Or at least make them carry you around."

Almost immediately, the kids started screaming for a golf cart, and Ajax chuckled even as Marti grinned. "That was mean. You know they're going to drive their parents crazy now."

"You're the only person I'm nice to, little one. I'm a bad dude, haven't you heard?"

She frowned at that. No matter what she said about him, hearing anyone say that, even him, annoyed her. It weighed on her because she thought back to all the rumors she had heard about Ice before meeting him. Even his manager had acted like he would bite her head off.

So many people had said he was vicious, rude, and cold. Now that she thought about it, he hadn't been any of those things with her. Even as she'd watched him interact in the gym, she hadn't seen it either. Her father had certainly been talking her head off about him. Somehow, this stranger had already weaseled his way into her life like he'd been there forever.

They grabbed lunch at the food court area, sitting down for a mediocre cheeseburger before they finished their tour, and she considered him carefully. She'd tried to be aloof all morning, just going through the motions of taking him to the zoo but refusing to be "friends" again. That was a slippery slope. Business partners was all she was willing to be for the next week. Then he could move on, and she could go back to her normal life.

"So, have you seen any boogey men or women here to trying to do unnamed scummy things to me?"

He looked at her casually, ignoring the tone in her voice. "Nope. All clear."

"Was that your strategy for your job today? Keep me busy, so I'm safe from these imaginary monster business men in suits? They might stapler me to death if we're not careful."

"If I wanted to do that, I'd insist you stay at home, away from the public. That would be smarter. I wanted to see the zoo, especially since you're running me out of San Diego the second I win the tournament."

She scoffed. "You wanted to see animals, seriously? I just don't see it being your thing."

"You also seemed to think I was illiterate, if I recall."

"I didn't say illiterate. Just not well-read."

"So judgy for someone who doesn't want to be judged."

She felt herself redden. He was right. She had assumed a lot of things about him. "To be fair, you encourage people to think the worst. You don't share anything about yourself. I barely know your real name and the state you're from."

"You still don't know my real name." He chewed slowly, staring at her, waiting for her reaction. "And Texas is a big state with lots of ranches. You'd never figure it out if I didn't want you to."

"You don't want me to, clearly. You know entirely too much about me, and you want me to trust you, but now I find out Ajax isn't your real name?"

"Ajax is my name. Just not Tuhuy. It was my father's."

She grit her teeth, not wanting to push that button, to hear more about his father, especially since the past tense had been clear when he said it. The psychological implications alone were off limits. "So, you have a different last name? How do you even get paid?"

He shrugged. "Who said I wanted to? I have everything I need."

"You might be the most frustrating man I've ever met."

"Man of your dreams, don't forget."

She huffed and stood to throw her food away. "You're impossible."

"And yet you don't deny it."

She picked up his trash and threw it away for him without a word, then stomped off to the waiting tour guide. She hadn't noticed his arrogance yesterday, but today it was infuriating. She didn't know if she could do a whole afternoon of this, yet as soon as they were back on the tour, the animals took all of her attention. They spent a while at the new Polar Bear Plunge, where the tour guide stopped to let them wander around. The area was kept slightly chilled, and again, she felt the cold in the air, but this time she'd come prepared.

"Cold?" He cocked an eyebrow, but she pulled another sweatshirt out of her bag and tugged it over her head.

"See. I don't need you. I got a Mary Poppins bag with me today."

He mockingly put both his hands in the air in surrender. "You're right. Another Hitchhiker's Guide to the Galaxy sweatshirt?"

"Actually, yes. I have like a dozen. I don't like being cold, and it's my favorite series. My shirts are all Marvel comics though. Can't leave my superheroes out, especially Thor."

"I guess I just thought you only read books, not comics. You don't really look the type." His voice was mocking as he repeated what she'd said to him.

"Okay, I deserve that. I love fantasy and sci-fi, any type, and that includes comics. But I fly through those, and they are easily ruined, so I don't bring them out of the house."

"That's what I loved as a kid. Comics. Any and all. But I haven't kept up much lately. My dad didn't think I should be wasting time on reading. Didn't serve a purpose for my future."

"Your dad sounds like a dick."

"He was, but he's dead now, so I should pick it back up again."

God. What was wrong with her? She'd clearly heard it in his voice earlier. Why would she call his father names? "Oh, I'm sorry. I didn't mean to—"

"Don't worry about it. My mom's gone too, in case you want to avoid that subject too."

"Oh. Um." Panic ran through her, then softened when she glanced up at him. His face was inscrutable, yet somehow softer.

"She wasn't a dick though. Kinda the opposite."

She glanced away, pausing to watch the polar bears play in the water. "My mom died when I was four, but I'm really lucky that my dad has always been my number one supporter. How long ago did they die? Like, were you a kid? Do you remember them?"

For a long time, he didn't say anything, and she stayed silent, certain she had crossed the line. "I'm sorry. You don't have to answer. I get not wanting to share. I won't ask anymore."

"No, it's okay. I don't have anything to hide from you. I'm just not naturally a sharer. Last week was one year since their death. It's why I was gone when you called my manager. I spent time hiking through the mountains, trying to forget. I'll tell you about it one day. It's just better you don't know for now." His voice was gruff, strained, lacking the arrogance she had been hearing all day.

She didn't say anything, but her instincts kicked in, and she grabbed his hand to squeeze. When he didn't move, just continued staring off into space, she scooted closer to him and wrapped him in a silent hug, burying her face in his chest. Finally, the stiffness left his body, and he rested his chin on the top of her head, squeezing her back. Silently, they made their way back to the waiting tour guide and headed out. But something had changed between them, and in the silence between the polar bear exhibit and their next stop, her body naturally snuggled against his, providing a comfort that they both needed suddenly.

Something about the way his hand gripped hers, despite the fact that it was so large it swallowed hers whole, made her feel needed, so vital to him, that…she didn't know what. She only knew that she no longer wanted this to end. Didn't want to leave his side. That was their last stop, though, and their day together was almost over. Maybe zooming through the zoo on a golf cart had one con. It hadn't lasted long enough.

When the cart pulled up at the exit, he held on for just another second, then they walked to the car together in silence, not touching now. Even as she put her car in gear and slipped into San Diego traffic, she worried that she'd broken him somehow. With just a few sentences, she'd found another part of Ice that wasn't so cold, wasn't so hard.

She'd only just snuck a glance at him when he cleared his throat to speak. "She was opposite my father in a million different ways. Social, fun, always smiling. Everything my father wasn't. Always told me I should relax, to not take life so seriously, no matter what my dad said. She was the one who insisted I spend so much time with…um…with our neighbors. They were very different than us. Said they saved her, and they would save me one day too. After she married my father, before I was even born, she made friends with them, had to when she came to live with my father. Told me she was worried about living so far away from everything she knew, but our neighbor was so light-hearted, even in the face of my father's…insanity. They reminded her that life didn't always have to be taken so seriously. That nothing was so wrong that we couldn't make things work. More importantly, she always said I would need to let others in if I ever wanted to be whole."

"She was happy? I mean…she chose your dad. He must have made her happy."

"He did. In his own way. She very much loved him. And he loved her. Looking back, I know my grandfather was even harder on him than he was on me. That my mom paved the way for a long period of less rules and more relaxation. She made him better. Until…until she couldn't. She still made sure we all had other influences. Those neighbors became a second family. And now, my only family. They're a big part of the support I had for doing this. For the tournaments, for leaving."

"Your mom would be…excited for you? This is what she would want?"

"Yes. She was ready to go to bat for me. Wanted me to get out here on my own. Even if it pissed my father off, she wanted me to have a chance away from our family business."

"But not your dad." It wasn't a question. It was a realization that he beat himself up anytime he acted too much like his dad.

"No."

"Sounds like you became a great balance between the two of them. I bet she'd be proud of you."

"Maybe. Actually, no. She'd be pretty mad at me right now." She hadn't expected that answer from him. Thought that her words would make him feel a little better. But he only turned to her, staring at her profile as she drove. "I didn't exactly go about it in a smart way. Lost my temper a little. Not really any chance of me ever going back. She wouldn't have liked that."

"I don't believe that. I think there's always a chance. Unless you let your own pride get in the way."

At that, he smiled. "That's exactly what she would say. 'You boys and your damned pride.' That was how she ended every argument. Then she would stomp her foot and walk off. Told me all the time that we were too much like our dad."

"We?"

"My brother and I. Him more than me, though, if that makes you feel better. I can be soft once in a while."

Marti snorted at that, looking over at him, grateful for a red light so she could check to see how serious he was. "You? Soft? Where? Point to a soft spot."

He looked down to his lap, his grin and line of sight obvious. "You may be right. Nothing soft down there when I'm around you."

"You're ridiculous." Her face heated at that thought. The sweet moment had turned silly fast, especially when he winked and lifted his eyebrows suggestively.

"Right here." He grabbed her hand from the gear shift, lifting it to where his heart should be. "I'm a softie down deep inside."

"Feels more like ice to me."

"You want heat?" He moved her hand down over his chest and across his abs, but she yanked her hand back before he could go any further. The sound of his chuckle filled the air as she concentrated on the road in front of her.

"So funny. Ha ha. Would be a shame if we crashed because you can't keep your hands to yourself."

"It was more like your hands on myself. Either way, worth it."

"You sound insane. Or maybe you've had one too many hits to the head in these fights."

"So then, that means you've never actually seen me fight." He shifted cockily in the chair and sent her a winning smile. "I don't take any hits."

"Your ego is a real problem. You should get that checked out."

Pulling into her spot at the gym, she shifted into park, her mind already on her own father. It was just after four in the afternoon, so she was home just in time to start dinner with her dad. She had skipped it yesterday, but today, she needed some daddy/daughter time. Anything to get her mind off the giant stranger in her passenger seat because she desperately needed some space between them.

"I hope you enjoyed the zoo, and I'll see you around. I have to get home. Dad runs a couple great classes tonight before family dinner, but he takes off on the weekend, so you should catch them while you can. Have a good night."

She tried to be professional and even reached out to shake his hand. He frowned down at it, then looked back at her. "Really?"

"Business partners, tour guide extraordinaire, and temporary landlord; it's all you're getting. Nothing more." She swallowed hard at the look in his eye, unable to decipher it, only that she swore they flashed black for a second.

"I thought…we…"

"You're a nice guy, even if you pretend not to be, and there may have been some moments between us. But I'm just not interested. Now or ever." When he just stood there, refusing to take her hand, she pulled it back and nodded before turning to head around through the gate to their house.

It had to be done. She had to keep things cold between them, and she'd forgotten that for a minute, but she could do this. Even if he had looked devastated.

By 7:30, dinner had been on the table for over an hour, but no sign of her dad. She hadn't thought anything of it at first, knowing exactly how much her dad liked to talk. He probably just got caught up.

But Fridays were supposed to be different. Only the bare minimum classes, and he was done for the night. Straight home, and they always played cards together afterwards, while she told him about the books she was reading. It was one of her favorite parts of every week.

She had just started to pack up the chicken pot pie, along with a bowl of salad that she would insist he take, but he never ate, when he came through the door laughing it up.

"Dad? It's after seven. Where have you—"

"Marti-bear! I invited Ajax to join us tonight. He could use a home-cooked meal, and I told him what a good cook you were. Just like your mama." He pulled her in for a huge bear hug, lifting her off the ground and squeezing until she couldn't breathe, the smell of liquor filling the air. Several times she had to pat his back to get him to let go, and she looked at Ajax over her dad's shoulder. He stared at her, lifting a half drank whisky bottle to his mouth and taking several swigs before raising it to her in a salute. But there was no easy-going smile now, only a moody intensity in his eyes when he looked at her.

"Marti-bear, I ever tell you how much I worry for you? You need someone to take care of you when I'm gone. And you'd be such a good mama. I'd like to see a little mini-Marti running around here."

His breath fanned across her cheek, and it reeked of whisky. No wonder he was late. Ajax convinced him to drink instead of coming home. She glared at the infuriating man in front of her, even as he took another swig from the bottle. That meant she was going to have two big, drunk men to deal with tonight.

"Dad. I can take care of myself, and you're not going anywhere. How much have you had to drink already?"

"Just a few shots. I just haven't ate today. Ajax got some good stuff too. Wanna take a little shot with us? Loosen up? Maybe make me some little babies? He's a good guy. I've decided, Dad approved."

"DAD. You can't be serious. Go wash your hands and sit at the table." She rarely raised her voice to her father, but he was out of control, and he knew it. Him talking about her making him grand-babies wasn't new, but never once had he tried to hook her up with one of his gym guys before.

"Yes, Sunshine."

Her father shuffled out of the room, and she furiously gestured at Ajax. "Seriously? He doesn't drink. How did you accomplish that? And now, you've put ridiculous ideas in his head. Give me that." She reached for the bottle, but he held it above her head and smirked.

"I'm still drinking. I have a long way to go before I even feel a buzz." He stepped around her, checking out the kitchen table. "That smells delicious though."

"You can go wash up too. No sweaty hands at my table. Use my bathroom. Second door on the left."

Furious, she poured some water for both of them and sat down at the table to wait. Soon, they both lumbered back in and sat down, hopefully sufficiently chastised. She helped herself to the food, stabbing her salad and foregoing the pot pie. She was too annoyed for a cozy, heavy dish right now. This was supposed to be her recharge for the week, her family time with her dad. But now, she was in a sour mood.

"I haven't had food this good since my mom's. I appreciate you having me over at the last minute. You're a real treasure." Ajax had ignored the glass of water, continuing to drink straight from the bottle as he ate half the pie. His earnest demeanor put on a good show for her dad, but it didn't work on her.

"I told you. Great cook, and I don't even know how. God knows I didn't teach her anything. Self-taught. My girl can teach herself anything from a book. Luckiest dad alive." She flushed at her dad's praise, still refusing to look at Ajax.

"Dad, drink some water. I don't want you to have any excuses when I whoop you in cards tonight."

"You don't have to worry about that. Ajax here is going to join us. It's more fun with three than two any day. I only wish we had a fourth person, then he could teach us 42. I ain't played that in years. I need to be retaught."

"What's 42?" She looked over at Ajax quizzically. "Like from Hitchhiker's Guide?"

"No, it's a game, like spades, but with dominoes. Played it a lot growing up with my best friends. Real dependent on strategy. You probably wouldn't like it."

"You don't know what I would like right now." That got a chuckle out of him, but he deliberately picked the bottle up and took another swig.

"You know, Felix said he was free tonight. I bet he could come over, and we could all play." Ajax lifted his eyebrows, a mocking smile drifting across his criminally handsome face.

"I'm sure he's busy. He goes home on the weekends. Don't bother."

"That's a great idea! Tell him to bring some tequila. That whisky got me fucked up, but I can hang with some good Mexican tequila."

"Why don't you call him for us? He's your best friend, right?" Ajax's gaze narrowed on her, like a challenge.

She grit her teeth, frustrated with him. He was using her father against her. Slowly, she stood and picked up the house phone, dialing Felix's number and never breaking eye contact with Ajax.

"Hello?"

"Hey. It's Marti. Didn't think you'd be home. Ajax is here with me and my dad. On a Friday night. Dad wanted me to call you to see if you want to come over and play a game of dominoes. I understand how busy—"

"Of course, I love playing games with you and your dad. Been a long time since you invited me though. Any special occasion?" She could hear the laughter in his voice, even if her dad and Ajax couldn't, and she knew what he was doing. She glared at Ajax because, somehow, she felt like they planned this together.

"It's okay. I totally understand that you can't make it. Maybe next time."

"Awww, you don't want me to come over. You still mad at me?"

"Of course."

"I'll be there in five minutes."

"Bring some tequila!" Her dad's voice rang out gleefully from behind her.

"Is that your dad?"

"Yes. Ajax, so sweetly, got him drunk before dinner."

"Tequila it is."

"No! Don't—" Then the line went dead. She was going to murder him. And Ajax. Then bury them somewhere she could dance on their graves daily.

She hung up the phone and walked away without looking at either of them. They were deep in conversation about some other fighter who was in the class, and she didn't want to hear about it. In the bathroom, she splashed water on her face and stared into the mirror. What was she doing? She was letting this man get under her skin, mess up her life, all for a few days of fun.

A few days of fun.

He would be gone before she knew it, so why was she letting him dictate her emotions and mess up her week? She should be the one using him instead of torturing herself. If he was willing to fuck her, and she wanted it, why not? She was grown, hell, more than grown. She was almost thirty. She could do it. She would enjoy her time with him, then he would be gone.

Yeah. She could do that. Just don't get attached, don't get emotional. She could let go and have fun. She could.

They wanted to play games, then she could play games right back. Let's see how he likes it. Opening her closet, she reached up to the top shelf. She had a full bottle of vodka she won at a poker party a couple of months ago. Neither whisky nor tequila was for her, but she could do vodka all night. We will see who wins this round.

A door banged at the front of the house, and she could hear her dad hollering at Felix. Biting her lip, she glanced in the mirror nervously. She wasn't good at games like this. But she squared her shoulders, determined not to fold under pressure.

No more sweatshirt. Instead, she pulled on a tight black spaghetti strap undershirt and a pair of silky red pajama shorts. Not too short, but not too long either. Pulling the hair elastic from her braid, she shook out her hair, letting the slightly frizzy waves flow over her shoulders and across her breasts.

Nothing too crazy in front of her dad, but it would send a message. By the time she was done changing, she heard the distinct rattle of dominoes being dumped on the table, and her dad calling her name. Grabbing the bottle of vodka by the neck, she walked through the kitchen and straight to the fridge. Opening it and pulling out the lemonade jug, she grabbed an empty glass cup and took her seat at the table, slowly pouring a shit ton of vodka and a smidge of lemonade. She took three long gulps before she paused and looked at Ajax. He lifted his eyes to hers, and she wasn't sure if it was the liquor kicking in or she was going crazy, but she swore they swirled, the green and black churning like storm clouds.

"Are you going to teach us something or you gonna sit around bullshitting all night?"

Chapter 12

Ajax

Friday, September 27
San Diego, California

"That's when your ass got turned down. That girl looked at you like you had seven heads. I'm tellin' you, he thought he was such a playerrrr."

"I was. Just havin' an off night. Everyone gets those, Marti-tarty, life of the partyyyy." Felix held the last of the tequila bottle high up in the air, letting the dribble of liquid pour into his shot glass before throwing it back.

Marti's father sat slumped over in his chair, snoring slightly, and Felix and Marti were reliving their glory days of college. Even after his bottle of whisky was almost finished, Ajax was barely feeling anything, especially since Marti walked out with her own bottle looking like sex on a stick. He made sure he stuck to his limit because if he was too drunk, his wolf might take over and do something else he would regret. So, he had slowed down, letting her take shot after shot until she could barely sit straight, while he stewed in silence.

He didn't know what his goal was for tonight, but he couldn't handle the way they ended the day. It was like a kick in the gut, to hear her reject him, for her to tell him she didn't want anything to do with him and never would. Another person that wanted nothing to do with him. She'd closed the door on him, just like his brother had. But she'd done it with a smile.

And yet, he couldn't give up. He couldn't let the last thing she said to him before he went to sleep be that he would always be nothing to her. His heart hurt, and there was a darkness building in his mind.

He had already been feeling himself become more and more feral without a pack link, and now, his wolf yearned for the connection with his mate. It was maddening to need, especially when there was nothing he could do about it. He needed her, in any capacity he could get, so when she said it was family dinner night, he decided to push his way in, no matter what.

But now, he worried that he had pushed her too far. She had come back out different—reckless, flirty and deliberate. He couldn't count the number of times she had run her hand up his thigh and made crude jokes that her father didn't catch on to. It felt wrong.

He really hadn't anticipated her father being such a lightweight, but he was so out of it, he barely knew what was going on. And Felix didn't help like he thought he would. He only encouraged her new attitude.

They half-assed played a game of 42, but then had abandoned it for a drinking game at least two hours ago. Now, every time one of them came up with an embarrassing story about the other, they had to drink. It was definitely Felix's idea to piss off Marti, and it worked for him. He learned more about her in an hour than he had in two days. Apparently, after her ex messed her up, she became the life of every party.

"Oh my God, you know how much I hate that name. One day, I'm going to tattoo it across your stomach, so you'll have to explain it to every girl you fuck."

"You'd rather I call you Marti-bear?"

"I'm going to cut off all your toenails and shove them up your ass. Only my dad can call me that. Keep it up, Big Poppa!" She stood up when she made her threat, but as she began to sway, she plopped back down and giggled uncontrollably.

"This is a good one too. Get ready to drink up, Felix. We were at this one party, a real snooze fest. Nobody wanted to dance or do anything.

Someone kept putting on some dumbass smooth jazz mix because they thought it was funny. And just as the house got quiet during a saxophone solo, everyone could hear a girl screaming, 'Yes, Big Poppa! Yes, more, more, Big Poppa!' I walked right over to the closet in the hallway, opened the door, and this special boy fell through the opening, pants down, ass in the air. He got called Big Poppa everywhere he went for the rest of the year. Hands down, best ending to that night possible. Drink up, Big Poppa!" She poured him a shot of her own dwindling vodka, and Felix took it, winking at Ajax.

"I think we need to hear some fun stories from Ice over here. You're going to have to tell on yourself, and don't hold back."

"I don't have fun stories like that. I wasn't allowed to go to college, but I love hearing about Marti here."

"Nope. Nope. Nope. You don't get off that easily." Her words slurred, and she could barely hold her eyes open as she talked to him, but she scooted closer, pouring him a shot of her vodka. "You have to drink when you can't think of anything to tell us. You can't tell me you don't have any wild sex stories like Felix here. I'm betting you had women crawling at your feet."

He grabbed her shot, poured it down his throat, and almost choked. Hot vodka was not an easy swallow. He'd take a smooth chilled whisky any day.

They didn't want to hear his stories, not the violent and destructive ones he still carried from the war. "I have a story. One of my favorites, actually. I was on a boat once, just me and this girl, a real beauty— charming, funny, smart, popular. Everyone knew and loved her. You know, the kind of girl every guy wants. I'd been trying to get her to myself all day, she was…irresistible, yet she had no problem resisting me…but I didn't give up. It took a while, and despite playing hard to get, she'd finally found her way into my lap." He took his time, letting the details build, and Felix leaned forward, hanging on his every word. Purposefully, he kept his gaze trained on her face, watching as she poured herself another drink, her lashes fluttering as she stole looks at him, trying not to appear too interested as he continued.

"It had started real innocent-like, a brush of her hand, a reassuring squeeze, a *look*—you know the kind—then every moment that passed, she got closer. Asking questions, making conversation, keeping me guessing, really had me on the hook. Then, boom, right before we turned back to shore, she was clinging to me with every wave, whispering sweet words in my ear." Dramatically, he grunted his admiration, but this time, she stared back, unable to look away, her lips parted slightly as realization sank in. "By then, the sun was setting, and that soft light in her eyes had her looking like an angel. Water was soaking us both, and she was putty in my hands."

This time, he leaned forward slightly, like it was just the two of them in the room. "Every time I touched her, she begged for more, panted in my ear, pulled me so close, I couldn't stop. Every time she said please, every time my name fell from her lips, and every time she moaned in my ear, was a shot of heat to my cock. Another minute and her perfect lips would have been wrapped around my dick, and my hand would have been wrapped around her braid." Tension crackled between them, and he enjoyed watching her eyes widen at the picture he painted. But she broke the connection quickly, licking her lips and pouring herself another shot before he could even finish.

"And then what happened? Did you fall into the ocean or something?" Felix was clearly tipsy, having helped both Domingo and Marti finish the whole bottle of tequila and her vodka, along with several shots of Ajax's whisky.

"She disappeared, leaving me hanging. Said we couldn't even be friends. I was crushed. Still haven't figured out how that story ends. I've thought about her every minute of the day since then. My most embarrassing story will always be the girl who got away."

"Damn, bro." Felix looked at him in confusion, then it suddenly hit him as he looked over at Marti. She had lifted the whole bottle to her lips and was chugging, eyes closed. "Ohhhhhh. Sad story, for sure. Wonder how it ends."

But Ajax reacted quickly. "Hey, easy there. I think it's time you went to bed. Felix, you help Domingo to his room, and I'll get the party girl tucked in. We have a big day tomorrow."

"You got it." Felix pulled Domingo up, practically dragging him to his room, and he turned to Marti, ignoring her drunken flirty looks.

"Heyyyyy, big boy. What's tomorrow?" He pulled the nearly empty bottle from her hand and set it down just as she slid one hand around his neck, pushing her breasts into his chest and grabbing his dick.

"Fuck." He leaned into her hand as she stroked his cock. He wanted her, but not like this. This wasn't her. Reluctantly, he pulled her hand away, then picked her up, cradling her in his arms easily.

"Mmmh. Yes, take me to my bed. It's small though, not like you."

He pushed open her door, trying to ignore her lips on his neck, and quickly dropped her onto the pillows, her hair fanning out around her. She immediately arched her chest, rolling down the thin stretchy material of her top to reveal her breasts before moaning. "Ice…Ajax, please. I need you."

He froze in place, still leaning over her, taking in every inch of skin on display for him, her beautiful brown nipples puckering under the movement from her fingers, but he stood up straight and shook his head. "Not like this, little one. I want you to beg, but this isn't the way. When you're sober and can remember everything, I'll have you screaming my name."

"You are such a fucking tease. Fuck me, damnit." Eyes closed, she massaged her own breast, pinching and rolling her nipple while her other hand slid under the waistband of her shorts.

"Tomorrow, Martina Andrade. Tomorrow, I'm taking you on that date I promised you. Get some sleep, my little mate."

The hardest thing he had done all week was walking away from her as she called his name, but he didn't look back. Instead, he waited for Felix, and they both headed over to the dressing rooms. In no time at all, Felix was snoring away on the other couch, and he was stuck staring up at the ceiling, reliving everything he'd ever done wrong.

Saturday was her day to sleep in, but he wouldn't give her long. He had a full day planned for their date, and he had a feeling she wouldn't be easy to wake up this morning. His alarm went off at 8:30, and he dressed quickly, packing a bag of extra clothes, then popped into her kitchen to mix a hangover cure Kathleen used to make for all of them when they'd partied too hard at the coven. It was disgusting, and she was going to be so pissed, but maybe that's what she needed. She needed to work through all the repressed feelings she had with him, and he could give her a reason.

Pushing open her door, he flipped on the light. There was no movement from the big bundle of covers on the bed, so he grabbed something solid and shook until he heard her groan.

"Come on, sleepyhead. Time to wake up."

"Go awayyyy."

When she didn't move, he yanked the covers from her body and was pleasantly surprised to see she had ditched her whole top and was curled up in just her silky shorts. She squealed, burying her face and chest in the bed facedown.

"Why are you torturing me?"

"You're the one tormenting me." He eyed her behind, raised slightly in the air and barely covered by her shorts. "You have a spectacular ass."

She lifted her head to glare at him through her hair. "Are you here just to ogle me? What do you want?"

He set the hangover cure on her dresser and turned to rummage through her closet. "Our date. I asked you last night, and you agreed. I have a whole day planned."

"I don't remember agreeing to any of that. I need more sleep and some pain pills. Why do I feel so awful?" She had pulled the blanket back around herself like a cocoon as she squinted at him. "Where are my glasses?"

"Drink." He handed her the glass, and she sniffed it before cringing.

"I'm not drinking that. It smells disgusting."

"Drink up or I will throw you over my shoulder and carry you out the door like that."

She made a face, then drained the cup quickly, coughing pitifully before shoving the empty glass onto the dresser.

"Are these the only kinds of jeans you have? They all have embroidery. Or decals."

She wearily rolled her eyes. "They're fashionable. Why are you digging through my clothes?"

"I know you're hungover because you can't handle your liquor, but are you deaf too? I'm getting you ready for our date."

She groaned miserably. "It's your fault. I never drink anymore. I'm too old for that. What do I even need jeans for? Where are we going?"

"It's a surprise. Get some jeans on. You'll also need a bathing suit and whatever you want to wear after we swim."

"I can guarantee I didn't agree to this. You're taking advantage of me."

"No, ma'am. If I wanted to do that, I would have done it last night when you begged me."

Her head snapped up from her cocoon blanket. "What?"

"How do you think you got half-naked into bed?" He winked at her, and she blushed.

"Did we…did you…"

"First, I would never take advantage of a drunk woman. You'll be fully sober when you beg again. And, secondly, you would definitely know if I fucked you. You'd feel it for days, little one. Now shower and get dressed. We leave in twenty minutes. If you're not ready by then, I will strip you naked and scrub you myself. Let's go."

It took more like thirty minutes, and several more to convince to get her on his motorcycle, but he insisted, and she eventually gave in. His wolf practically purred when she wrapped herself around his back and held on for dear life.

When they made it to the horse ranch, he was feeling good, and she was looking much better. Or at least, she had color back in her face, even if she looked slightly frazzled. "I see a little wind woke you up. You're looking human again."

"Gee, thanks. That was only the most terrifying ride of my life. What are we doing?"

"You ever ridden a horse before?"

"Actually, no."

"Perfect. You've been showing me things that are better in California, but I'm going to show you how a cowboy rides the beaches in Texas. When I work security for my land, everyone rides horses along the border to keep out poachers, fishermen, any looky-loos. So, I may not have worked with the cattle much, but I still rode horses almost every day. Come on, you'll love it."

"So, a second terrifying ride. Oh goodie. I hope they have a big enough horse for you, or else you'll have to walk behind us. Maybe I can drag you by a rope."

"As much as you'd love that, I called ahead. They have our horses ready. I booked a private ride along the beach. Three hours, just me and you."

"No guide?"

"Just to get us to the beach and back. All the in-between, we get to be alone. And I can find out how many of the stories Felix told last night are true."

"I'm going to kill him."

Chapter 13

Marti

Saturday, September 28
San Diego, California

Secretly, she was having the best time, but that was the problem. She didn't want to get attached. A fling, that's all she had decided to allow herself. But now, they were either separated by horses, surrounded by other people on the beach, or just making jokes and enjoying each other's company.

That's the kind of stuff that makes you attached. She needed him to stop being so charming, so she could jump his bones and move on. Like that old saying, she needed to get under him, so she could get over him. It was the only way.

The problem was, he really enjoyed sharing his love of horses, and that surprised her. She knew he said he worked a ranch and grew up around horses and livestock, but it just seemed like something people from Texas said, but didn't actually do. His excitement was slightly contagious as he showed her how to maneuver and shared silly stories of his first time riding. It was like listening to her talk about her books.

And he was huge. What horse in their right mind would carry his big ass around all day? Even she was nervous about sitting on the beast. She was scared her weight was hurting the horse's back, and combine that with the saddle? She was sure someone was going to call the ASPCA at any moment. So, when she finally relaxed, it really made a difference. She was enjoying the methodical feel of trotting around and the rhythmic beat of the horses' hooves. She could get used to stuff like this.

"So, other than playing patrolman for loose moo cows, what did you do to get all those muscles? Just live in the gym?"

He smirked, glancing over at her with one eyebrow cocked. "You don't like my muscles?"

She flushed, then rolled her eyes. "I'm just wondering what made you so good at sparring. Your reputation is what it is for a reason. You train on the ranch? Or maybe with your brother? As an only child, I've always wondered what it was like to have a brother or sister."

He paused for a long time, like he wasn't going to answer. "Something like that. Brother or not, there were always plenty of others around to practice…fighting. Survival of the fittest in our part of the world."

"Oh, come on. It's not like you're out there fighting wars and killing people. It's an octagon with rope. Survival is a little dramatic, don't you think?"

He cleared his throat, his stare locking in on her, the suddenly serious expression on his face scaring her slightly. Did she say something wrong?

"None of that matters. It's behind me, and easier to look to my future now. It's much prettier than the past."

She scoffed at that, at his attempt to lighten his own mood. "I've always heard sibling fights were the worst. I had friends who would come to school with black eyes, chipped teeth, bloody knuckles…you name it. But their sibling always had matching bruises, and they were still the best of friends."

"Yeah. Sounds right. It's supposed to be easier when they share your blood."

"Like a built-in best friend. I'm jealous."

"Sometimes, the best of friends are the ones who choose you, not the ones you're forced to share a womb with."

"That's…that's sad."

"Yeah." He'd looked away, staring out at the water. "You're right, little one. The Pacific Coast…it's undeniably pretty. And very different from the Texas Gulf."

As the guide maneuvered them back to the ranch, she studied Ajax's features. He'd relaxed again, staring out at the water like he was in deep thought. "You miss your home? Your ranch?"

"Yes." That's not what she expected. Thought he would be all macho and say he didn't miss anything.

"Why don't you go back for a visit, at least?"

"I told you. I can't go back there, Marti. There's nothing left for me."

He dismounted the horse, handing the reins to the guide, then stepped over to lift her down. She slid down his front purposefully, this being the first time she was able to touch him all day besides the motorcycle ride. And it was worth it. Every muscle, every part of his body, was at her disposal like this. But it only lasted a few seconds, and then he set her out of the way while they undid all the buckles and ropes on the horses.

"That's not true. I watched you buy a little stuffed panda for your nephew. And you have your brother and sister-in-law. You may not have your parents anymore, but you have your brother. He's family. There's no way family would leave you to suffer."

"You don't know him. I'll send the stuffed panda to my sister-in-law in the mail. She would love to hear from me too. But, my brother, I'm dead to him. I can't go back there."

"I just don't get it. Were you not close growing up?"

"We were. Couldn't get any closer. Hell, we are identical twins. We were inseparable. Until now, anyway."

"Twins?" She felt her mouth open in shock. How can one twin abandon the other? "There are two of you? And you both look like…you?"

"That's what identical means."

That really shut her up. As someone who spent most of her life desperately wishing for a sibling, she couldn't fathom treating her family badly. No wonder he was seen as cold. No wonder they called him Ice. But that wasn't who he was. He wanted people to think he was a bad person, but he wasn't. So far, he had been thoughtful and sweet. Maybe moody, arrogant, and bossy, but he was right. He had good intentions.

Damnit.

She wasn't trying to fall for him.

"So, then, what will you do now? Just fight for the UFC until you're too old or too dead from concussions?"

He chuckled at that. "I'm hoping to settle down eventually. I dreamed of getting off the ranch, doing things I enjoyed instead of things expected of me. I guess it doesn't really matter what you do, it's the people you do it with." He hadn't been looking at her until right then, and she could feel the burn of his gaze. He couldn't mean her. This was temporary before he moved on.

"So, in a perfect world, with the perfect person for you, what would you do? What dreams did you have when you left home?"

He paused for a long time, shaking hands with the guide, then leading her back to his motorcycle. "I think I want to own a gym, kind of like your dad, just a little more specialized. I would want to spend my days making memories with my woman, going on adventures with my children, seeing things I had never done before. But only with the right person. For that person, I would do anything."

She laughed nervously because something in his tone had the butterflies churning in her stomach. Everything inside her said she wanted to be that right person, but her brain could not compute. That's what every man said, until the day something better comes along, or the person's usefulness runs out. Then there's pain. She wouldn't do that again. If it hurt that bad with her ex, then getting attached to Ajax and losing him would be even harder.

She couldn't let that happen, not even when it felt so easy.

She slid onto the back of the bike, snuggling in close to him, enjoying the rumble beneath her. With the helmet on, she had taken her glasses off, and he stored them inside the pocket of his leather jacket before they headed out. Such a simple gesture, but so natural feeling. Relaxing, she closed her eyes and enjoyed the feel of the wind and the roar of the engine. It was nice not planning things, not worrying and making decisions for once, so when he parked and she felt the wind and ocean, she was excited. Then he handed her glasses back to her, and she recognized her surroundings.

"La Jolla? We're going snorkeling?"

"I've heard it's a must-see. I rented kayaks for us. But first, we are going to eat at The Marine Room until the crowds die down a little bit. Let the tourists finish up, since I have my own personal guide."

She smiled big. "You're awfully confident that I know what I'm doing. What if I get us killed by a sea lion?"

Two hours later, they were kayaking through the water, snorkeling gear at their feet, surrounded by groups of tourists coming in from the caves. Glancing over at him gliding through the water surprisingly well, she grinned.

"Most people love high tide, so they can kayak into the caves, but my favorite is low tide. I like walking in them and exploring all the tide pools. So, I hope you're ready to do a little exploring!"

He laughed loudly. "I figured that would be too much sweating for you, but I'm ready if you are."

"Don't worry, the water is too chilly for me to sweat. Or I could always hop on your back, and you can carry me like the princess I am."

His deep chuckle carried across the water, and she smiled, a genuine happiness chipping away at all her resolve. He was insanely good at putting her at ease.

As they rounded the corner, she kept going, straight for her favorite cave, one that was most often overlooked, and at low tide, they could drop anchor and wade through. Trading out her glasses for the prescription goggles she didn't even realize he'd packed for her, she slipped into the water as deep as she could at low tide, excited to see all the beautiful Garibaldi fish and the occasional Leopard Shark. She'd done this dozens and dozens of times over her life, and it never got old. A quick anchor drop, and Ajax was splashing along right behind her.

Once inside the cave, she pushed forward, her water shoes helping her grip as the tide disappeared and she was able to walk along the rocks. Occasionally, she bent down in the tidepools, checking nonchalantly for Ajax's reaction as he stared around at the wonders in the cave. A soft orange reflection bounced along the walls in the moving light of the tide. She flicked on the flashlight attached to her life vest as they went deeper through the small tunnel, and she heard Ajax do the same. As the ceiling dropped and she kept going, she scooped to pick up a couple of the beautiful purple-blue shells she loved.

"Is this safe? How fast will the tide come back in?"

"Well, it's just now going out, so we have a couple of hours. Are you scared?" She turned and looked back at him, hands on her hips. He looked unsteady as he tried to walk across the rocks, and it was almost comical. The tiny life vest on his oversized body, goggles still on his head, and his bright orange water shoes reminded her that he was out of his element. For her.

She waited for him to catch up. "By the way, how did you know I go snorkeling? Is this another thing Felix told you about me? He sure does love running his mouth."

"Actually, it was an idea I got from one of the many stories you told last night. Something about how one of the guys you knew said some rude things to you, so you brought him out here and got him lost in the caves. Apparently, you barely got him out before he drowned."

"Ahh. Oops. I really need to watch what I tell people. It wasn't that close. Not really. Maybe a little. And he was always a little handsy with all the girls. He didn't mess with me or any of my friends after that."

"I'm just hoping you aren't going to do the same to me."

Her throat caught as he stopped only a few inches away and pulled off his goggles to look down at her. The glow of her flashlight created enthralling shadows across his angular face, and his eyes blazed light green, even in the darkness. "It would be a real shame to miss out on all this too soon."

It took a second for her to focus on his words, when all she could think about was his soft, plush lips, at how the light framed them just right, and how his grin showed off his perfectly white teeth. God, he was gorgeous. She forced a laugh and looked away.

"You're too big to lose. I'm not sure I should even take you the rest of the way. The tunnel gets pretty narrow before it opens up again."

"Then I vote we stop here for a minute. Wouldn't want you to get too sweaty."

"Sounds like you're a little scared, but this is a great place to pause. Nobody comes this far back."

He unclipped his life vest and dropped it next to him where he sat, even as he eyed the tide slowly moving out. She followed suit, undoing her life vest and finding a smooth rock to perch on as she admired his nicely toned legs. Unlike a lot of guys, he opted for a shorter swimsuit, and the white material against the deep bronze of his skin had her itching to run her hands along his thighs. This was what she'd decided, right? This was her chance. He hadn't made a move since the boat, and he made no indication he would again until she asked. But, for some reason, she couldn't bring herself to do it.

"I don't know if you can tell, but I've never been snorkeling. Just not a thing in Texas. It's beautiful in here, and yes, the water and marine animals are much more friendly than the coast I'm used to. Something so breathtaking about it all." He was staring around at the walls of the cave, but when his gaze stopped at her, her stomach did a little flip. "But I think it may be the company I'm with that makes it better."

"If you keep saying cheesy things like that, I'll have no choice but to believe you."

"I think we will have to do an experiment. One day, I'll take you to Texas, and we can see if it compares. For me, the thing I guarantee you can't beat is the stars. There's something about the big Texas skies that bring me peace, so I think you're right. I may have to go back home at some point, if you're willing."

She frowned at him. That's not the deal she made. Maybe it was only with herself, but there's no way he was serious. They had only known each other for five days. Five days. And she didn't want any of these romantic dreams filling her thoughts.

It had to be now. She needed to make her move, before he made more sweet promises that made her insides mush. Quickly, she tugged at her cover-up, the thin, soaked black material hiding the skimpy swimsuit she had bought long ago, but never worn.

When she dropped the material to the side, cognizant of every inch of her insecurities, she watched as his eyes lit up, glued to her body, and she was thankful for the dim light of the caves. She wanted him to touch her right now, to make her feel good, then move on. No connection. No promises.

She kept her hand light and teasing as she grazed his chest, then came to rest on his neck. He had leaned back on his elbows, and his nonchalance was confidence inducing, so she went in for a kiss. Soft and gentle, she took her time, and savoring the feel of him, she let her instincts lead.

When he repositioned, leaning to pull her forward by her waist, it felt natural to straddle him, not quite sitting, but facing him as she sat up on her knees. When his hand cupped her face hungrily, he pulled back to stare into her eyes, and they looked darker, broody almost. Shiver-inducingly dangerous.

"Ajax?" His head had dropped to her neck, sucking and nipping as he moved to her collarbone before dipping lower with his tongue. She slid her hands through his hair, yanking on the strands with a desperation that had built quickly. Sinking down onto his lap, she felt every inch of his hot, hard length, and she shuddered when his hands grabbed her ass, fingers digging into the bare skin under her bathing suit. His mouth moved down her chest as he gripped her cheeks, massaging and grinding her against him.

She leaned back, arching to give him access to her breasts, the straps of her swimsuit top giving way easily. Tingling, bursting sensations raced across her skin, and she moaned at the heat that took over her whole body. Every inch of her craved his touch, his mouth. Never before had she felt such a wanton need, and she rolled her hips, wanting…needing to feel him inside of her. The longer it took, the more panicked she felt, and she whimpered in desperation, not knowing how to get what she wanted. Not used to being in charge when it came to this.

She didn't need any promises or talk of the future, she just needed him.

When he bucked and pulsed upwards, matching the need she felt, then pulled her nipple into his mouth, she whispered, bracing her hands on his thighs behind her. "Please, more. I need more. I need you."

He groaned against her breasts, his teeth lightly grazing the nipple before he whispered hoarsely. "Marti. It's not time. You're not ready."

Her body was on fire, and he was telling her she wasn't ready? "How much more ready do I need to be? I want this. You want this. Fuck me, Ajax."

Using her weight, she shoved him backwards, lightly pushing his shoulders into the rocks. She kissed him, long and hard, letting his hands roam up and down her body, and lighting her on fire with his touch. When she finally released his lips, swiping lightly at his bottom lip, she had undone the string of her top from behind her neck.

With a groan, her top fell away, and she leaned forward, allowing his mouth to capture her breast again, sending little electrical tingles down her stomach. When he released her, his hands taking over, he growled, the echo filling the cave. "Fuck. Every part of you is perfect. Every single inch was made for me, Marti. You're mine. Mine."

Breathily, she moaned, his possessiveness sending her spiraling, so she pulled back slightly for leverage, rolling her hips, grinding against his dick, and whispering in his ear. "I rode a horse and a motorcycle for the first time today, and good things always come in threes. I need one more ride. Give me what I need."

Not slowing the motion of her hips, she pulled the strings from each side of her bikini, just as his finger reached between them and dipped inside her pussy.

"Ohhhhhhhhh, God. Yesss." Hands on his chest, she shifted, giving him room to stroke her clit softly. Eyes closed, head tossed back as she arched against him, his fingers slipped inside of her, curling with each thrust, and she almost lost it.

"Holy fuck. What are you doing to me?" She panted wildly, the sounds echoing and bouncing off the cave walls as waves of pleasure ambushed her. His fingers were magic, pure fucking magic. She had never felt such a deep, all-encompassing heat flood her body, and when he added his thumb to her clit, she thought she would pass out with each stroke.

"So much, too much, I can't…oh my God." Slowly, she lost strength in her arms, and she buried her face in his chest, her ass still in the air, his arm trapped between them, fingers pumping in and out of her.

"That's it. You're doing so good. Don't hold back. Let me feel you tighten around my fingers, give me everything, all of you."

When the gush of her wetness coated his hand, then her thighs, she dug her fingers into his shoulders, stifling a scream of pleasure as the climax moved through her whole body, the stiffening and convulsing hitting her harder and harder. She was boneless, exhausted and alive all at once, but he didn't stop. He used his knuckles to run along her hyper-sensitive clit, stirring tiny shocks of heat when she didn't think she had anything left.

"I'm not done with you, little one. I want to taste you, but I don't want you to cut your back on these rocks. Come, sit on my face."

"Mmmmmh. I…can't…move." Small gasps escaped her, as he slowly, lazily ran his thumb and knuckle over that sensitive bundle of nerves once more. But that pleasure built languidly inside of her again, and she couldn't think, couldn't focus on his words. Instead, her hands moved by instinct, and she sat up enough to tug on his bathing suit, trying to yank it down.

"Marti, baby. I don't think I can keep control if you touch me. I won't be able to stop."

"I don't want you to. Fuck me, Ajax. I don't want tender, soft or gentle. I don't want lovemaking. I want rough, hard, and fast." She finally got his pants down, and the biggest dick she'd ever seen sprang free. Grabbing hold of it with one hand, she sat back on his thighs. The pre-cum glistened in the dimness of the cave, and she ran her thumb over his tip, pulling the liquid down, and he groaned loudly, pushing the heels of his hands into his eyes and pulsing up towards her.

"You don't know what you're doing to me. I can't stop him. You have to understand the consequences, especially because I don't know if I can hold back."

"I don't want you to hold back, Ajax. Give him to me. All of you. I know what I want. And I want this…you…more than anything."

Almost immediately, he had her in the air, flipping her onto her back, his life vest underneath her, protecting her from the rocks. He pushed her knees to her chest, and his tongue swiped heavily through her slit, before he spread her wide. No hesitation, he moved like a man starved, his tongue circled her clit, long and flat, teasing and tasting until he pinpointed exactly where he wanted to be, and her body leaped as he flicked and swirled with an obsession.

Jesus H. Christos. She couldn't pull her eyes from the top of his head as it bobbed frantically between her thighs. His face was fucking buried in her pussy, and she could feel every tiny thrust, every pressure point, every damned stroke. He was the devil. He had to be. There was no other explanation of how his tongue knew exactly where to go, just how much pressure she needed, and when it was too much, he pulled back, only to find a new part of her to tease. She melted into the feeling of satiation that took over her body, bringing her to the brink, and just as she thought she couldn't take anymore, he pulled back, and she gasped in need. But when his mouth was replaced by his dick, slipping and sliding through her slit, against her clit, she felt such a rush of need, she began to beg.

"Please, Ajax. It's too much. I need you inside me. I can't wait any longer. Please, please, please." Her whimpers filled the air when he paused, slowing his pace, finding just the right angle, and she wanted to scream for more, for him to go faster. But she didn't. She only clutched at his arms, running her nails across his shoulders, her attention moving from his wet, perfect lips to the dark abyss of his eyes as he loomed over her.

When he settled between her legs, leaning down on his elbows, his face nestled in her neck, she could feel him inching forward, slowly stretching her, the fullness filling her until she thought she would split open. Her knees had pulled toward her chest, and she wrapped her ankle around his back.

"That's my girl. Take it. Take all of it. All of me. Every part of me…I'm yours, Marti. All yours…fuck, you feel so good."

When she had relaxed, her body rising to keep him seated deep inside of her, he finally pulled back, then thrust again carefully. She could feel his breath against her skin, barely registering his tongue as he lapped at her neck.

Her eyes flew open when he sped up, and a growl ripped from his throat. It reverberated through her body, and she shivered at the heat of him. Letting her feet down onto the rocks, she used the leverage to increase the speed, to fuck him with a violence she didn't know she was capable of. Her nails raked along his back, then up over his shoulders, encouraging everything she so desperately needed.

"Harder, damnit. Faster. Fuck me. Don't hold back."

But he didn't acknowledge her, didn't move from where he'd buried his face. No, she wanted to see him, to remember this moment, his expression, and his eyes when he came. So, she grabbed him by his hair, pulling his face from her neck, and she froze. Was it the darkness of the cave, the dullness of her brain washed in pleasure? His eyes were completely black, even more than before, and she swore he had fangs, but when he looked into her face, and she stared at him in confusion, he blinked rapidly, then pulled back and completely out of her.

She whimpered at the loss of him, before he literally tossed her around, turning her to her stomach and pushing her face into the life vest, leaving her ass in the air. He waited only a second before he pushed inside her again, the angle bringing a cry from her lips. Forgetting everything she thought she saw, her pleasure skyrocketed once again, and he did exactly as she asked.

"This what you want, little one? You want to be railed, fucked so hard you can't walk for a week?"

She couldn't answer, couldn't formulate words, couldn't even tell him how explosive he made her feel. But the slap on her ass stung, and she gasped, partially in surprise, and partially at the way her body reacted. Oh, my God. She'd never had her ass spanked before, and his giant hand had sent shockwaves through her body, her pussy clenching, setting off her body into whole new heights.

"Again." It was the only thing she could stutter, and when the next slap hit, she screamed softly.

"Answer me. Tell me what you want. You want me to slow down?" The hard and fast fucking she was getting slowed to a stop, and she clenched around him, rocking backwards, trying to force him to speed up.

"Use your words, or I do whatever I want." He slowed to a complete stop, and when he pulled back, she could feel him spread her cheeks apart roughly. He slipped his hand down, his bare knuckle spreading her wetness up and over her cheek. He kneaded the now wet thickness of her thigh, skimming his hand across her ass, then slowly began fucking her again. It wasn't enough. This was torture. She needed to come again so badly.

"More, I need more." The sound of her own voice surprised her. It was hoarse and raspy, but she pushed against him, trying to find any leverage against the rocks.

"More what? More of this?" His hand slipped lazily from her hip down across her stomach, and his two fingers massaged her clit slowly, matching the rhythm of his thrusts. She bucked against him, a wildness ripping through her at this new sensation.

"Yes. Harder. Fuck me harder, faster. I don't want to be able to walk."

Without breaking rhythm with his fingers, he used his other hand to steady them both, and as he picked up the pace, slamming into her, she focused on each sensation, suddenly wanting to remember every moment with him. She closed her eyes and concentrated on this exhilaration she'd never felt before—it was overwhelming, but not, all at the same time. The way his hand steadied her ass, and how his other arm felt wrapped around her hip, his finger a steady, deep pressure against her clit, and even the slapping of his balls against her pussy. How infinitely full and stuffed she felt with every thrust. Even his possessiveness and words made her feel wanted. And with a gasp, she couldn't take any more, the high tearing through her body as she came again—an explosion of seemingly infinite spasms that had her drooling and shaking against the rock.

"Such a good girl. My girl. Mine."

She was floating in the aftershock of her climax, flying on cloud nine, when he pushed into her one last time, his low groan hot all by itself as his cum filled her completely. Slow and careful, she barely noticed him pull away, not until he dropped to the rocks on his back, pulling her on top of him, still trying to protect her from the jagged cave floor.

Never before had she felt even a small percentage of this. Nothing compared. Why had she been fighting this? What insanity had made her resist? Now she only had six more days to savor him. And she floated there, in an almost dream-like state, thinking of all the ways she would enjoy the next few days.

It was a long time before he spoke, reality puncturing a hole in her bliss-filled euphoric state. His voice was low and raspy, like he was debating on what he should say.

"We need to talk."

Chapter 14

Ajax

Saturday, September 28
La Jolla, California

"Look, there's no need for declarations of love or promises of a future. I'm okay with just this. It's what I want. I don't know why I fought it this whole time because, fuck, that was amazing. So amazing. Holy smokes." She'd barely moved, the words tumbling out of her, and what she meant didn't register at first, didn't really hit him. "But I realized you'd be gone in a week, so why not make the most of it? Right? And that was definitely making the most of it. That means we have six days left. So, no need to ruin it by trying to make it seem real. I don't need that lovey-dovey stuff. I like simple."

She'd rolled up then, not making eye contact, but stretching to grab her clothes. She was moving on. Going on with her day, not knowing the effect of her casually tossed thoughts. Blissfully unaware that every word she uttered knocked the breath out of him, and he couldn't even look at her while she rambled.

His mind raced from her words to the struggle within him, a choking desperation filling his chest as everything hit him all at once. He had just gone through a hell of a battle with his wolf. He had lost control. Fuck. He'd almost marked her.

He wouldn't do that until she was fully informed, no matter what she said. But his wolf hadn't cared…she'd said she wanted him and was ready. Somewhere in his mind, he knew that her interpretation of those words was not the same as his, yet it hadn't clicked, or he wouldn't have fucked her.

Already, his beast howled within him, frustrated at the lack of connection, angry that he hadn't followed through with a full mating. And now she was telling him that this was nothing. That six more days was all he got from her.

Ajax had thought they'd grown close, that she felt something, that she was falling for him. He sensed her affection, and it was overwhelming in a good way. So much so, that he thought their bond could possibly be strong enough to eclipse his wolf's need for a pack link. Everything had felt so right. Like it was meant to be.

So, what was this? What had he done wrong?

"Marti, that's not what this was. That's not what I wanted. I…I thought you were ready for a commitment. I wouldn't have fucked you if you weren't sure."

"Seriously?" She looked over at him doubtfully. "You require a commitment from all the girls you fuck?" She laughed like he was telling a joke. "Come on. We both knew what this was. You don't like being rejected. And when I ran from you, you needed to finish what you started. It's infatuation, nothing more. You should be happy. This is a win for both of us. You can leave without looking back and go get the future you want. Hell, go back to Texas and make up with your family."

She stood, pulling on her swimsuit and tying all the strings, then the wet coverup followed before tugging on her lifejacket. He did the same in silence, not answering any of the ridiculous words she threw at him. His own breath felt ragged and loud, like he couldn't catch air. And truly, he couldn't. With only her words, she'd ripped every hope away from him in those moments. What she said was logical to her, to humans, but it didn't make it hurt any less.

And it hurt. Fuck, it hurt.

How did he mess up his fated mate so badly that she could fuck him, then throw it all away? Like he was nothing. That wasn't like her, so what had he done? What about him inspired her to want nothing to do with him? Was he really that bad?

That thought echoed within him, a quiet storm reminding him that nothing he did would be good enough, that he couldn't be who people wanted him to be, no matter how hard he tried. Right then, there was a small part of him that wanted to give up, to give in. But he couldn't. He wouldn't. Just…

Shaking his head, he forced himself to move mechanically, every motion torture. He needed to get away. He needed time to think, and to let his wolf run free. He needed to go up to the mountain before he spilled his guts and really ruined everything.

Silence filled his world in those moments. Even his wolf was disheartened and lonely, curling up at their mate's rejection. She didn't speak anymore, and he didn't have anything to say. Climbing out of the obscure tunnel and into their kayaks, they made their way back to the beach.

As he drove them back to the gym, her hands wrapping around his waist was just another cruel reminder of his loss. What could be. When he pulled up in front of her gate, and she slipped off the bike, handing him his helmet, he reached inside his pocket and returned her glasses.

She settled them on her nose, and he studied her, memorizing every inch of her beautiful face, from the curve of her delicate lips to her giant doe eyes. She stared back softly, her eyes searching his and not moving, sensing his unease and the tension between them. Waiting.

Finally, he spoke softly, but resolutely. "Martina Andrade, I am in love with you, whether you think I'm telling the truth or not. I only want you forever. Without you, I have no future." Her eyes widened, and her mouth dropped, but she was speechless, and he took a big breath and looked away. "I don't know how else to convince you because I'm not good at this. To hear you don't want anything to do with me is…painful.

Painful in a way you won't understand. And I get it. But, right now, I need to think, to get away. I'll be back."

With a heavy heart, he drove away, into the darkness of the newly fallen night, and headed straight for Angeles National Forest. It had been his refuge for months now, and he already had a local pack's permission to roam it. He needed to let his wolf work off some steam, and he needed to figure out how to get Marti to understand this commitment.

Shakily, he considered a life without her. Even a day without her. He couldn't. But right now, the hurt was overwhelming.

He wasn't himself, wasn't who she needed him to be when he was like this. He wanted to curl up in a ball and join his wolf in feeling devastated. But he couldn't. He needed to get out of his head, and there was only one way to do that. His wolf needed to be set free, to find some kind of connection, to ground himself. Yet, Ajax also knew the risk he was taking. The longer he was rogue, the more dangerous it was to let his wolf run free. His beast would resist shifting back and would want to stay in animal form longer. He didn't know how long it would take to shift back this time, if at all. But it was a risk he needed to take.

Thirty-six hours. It took thirty-six hours for his wolf to recover and relax, for him to be willing to shift back. And only because he kept the call of their mate in his mind. *Our mate needs us. And we need her. Let's go.*

Monday morning, when he finally wrestled back control, he made his way to where his bike was hidden and headed straight to Los Angeles. He could breathe again, but his mind was on his mate, and a new determination had replaced the devastation that had plagued him since she'd pushed him away. He needed a grand gesture, something that made her realize he was different than the others who came before him. So, he went on a search.

In the fourth bookstore he entered, he found the perfect item. A rarity. She would love it. The second he had walked into her room lasts Saturday morning, and saw her shelves lined with random books, then a top shelf of only a couple special collector's editions, he knew what he would get her. And now, he was at an embroidery shop, holding the softest towel he could find, hoping they could rush his order.

One look at his face, and the old lady practically yanked the towel from his hands, eager to help. And help, she did. She'd stopped what she was doing to immediately complete his request, her giddy ramblings reminding him of how much humans prized romance. He could be romantic, soft, thoughtful. He could for her.

"I've never had such a request before, but I can see it means something." She looked down at the newly embroidered towel, then back up at him. "I'm assuming you're in love? Or maybe you live at home in your mom's basement and want a fancy towel. What do I know about young people nowadays?"

He laughed and thanked her for her help. It was late, and with Los Angeles traffic, he wouldn't make it back tonight before she went to sleep. But that's okay—he would have it ready for her first thing in the morning.

If she was willing to talk to him.

He had already made himself miserable all day Sunday, thinking that he scared her off, that humans didn't believe in love after five days. That, for her, men weren't trustworthy, and there were no words to explain how he was different. She'd probably call an insane asylum on him if he showed her his wolf. So, he'd put himself in between a rock and a hard place, and he needed to work his way back into her good graces and hope she didn't think he was crazy.

But there was one thing that he couldn't get out of his mind, couldn't let go of. Home. The thought of never showing her his world, never bringing her home, seemed…wrong. Maybe she was right, just like his mom. He was letting his ego get in the way.

Carefully, he packed her present away in his saddle bags, staring out at the chaos of LA traffic. It was five in the afternoon here, so it would be seven back home. There was almost no chance he'd still be in his office.

Every excuse rang in his ear, but Marti's words were stronger. Family didn't abandon family. And so, he took off to the corner payphone, shutting down every ounce of pride he still had, and focused on the task before he changed his mind. He punched the numbers into the phone, waiting for the collect call to transfer him, and held his breath. So, when his brother's gruff voice answered, he couldn't speak while he waited to see if he would accept the charged for the collect call.

"I'll accept."

The soft click as he connected had a finality to it, and the silence between them stretched wide.

"Ax. Didn't think you'd be at the office so late."

"If that was true, you wouldn't have called."

He was right, of course. Maybe he'd called this line on purpose, to say he did it, but not really. He closed his eyes, leaning against the phone booth, not fully sure what he was going to say.

"Mom would be so mad at us right now, wouldn't she?" He didn't know what he expected his brother to say, or what he wanted from him, especially when he didn't answer that question. So, he pressed on, realizing that Marti's rambling seemed to be contagious. "I can hear her now, banging the pots in the kitchen, muttering to herself, threatening all of us. Saying our pride was too big for our head."

There was a shuffling on the other line, like he was being taken off speakerphone, and for a second he thought Axel had hung up on him. But then, he could hear him clear his throat softly, so he continued reminiscing.

"She'd send us out on some shitty errand, a punishment really. Tell us to think about whatever we've done, then we'd come back, and there'd be some extravagant meal made. Dad would be sitting at the table, reading his newspaper, but not talking. We'd all pretend nothing happened, and all would be forgiven." He paused again, knowing what he needed to say, but not how. "I guess that's why this is hard. We've never had to fix anything ourselves. She just fixed it for us because we refused. She'd want us to fix this. I'm sorry, Ax. I want to fix it, but I don't know how."

"This isn't a silly squabble. This can't be swept under the rug. You made a decision, and now you have to live with it. There's nothing left to fix anymore."

He didn't know what he thought would happen when he called home, knew there weren't going to be some magic words, and everything would go back to normal. But the desperation he felt to take Marti home, to give her everything he had, took over, and anger colored his words.

"Damnit, I know I fucked up. I want to make it right. But family isn't supposed to abandon family. Father would have never turned his back on me like this. He—"

"He is dead. Mother is dead. What they think and what they would have felt or done do not matter. The only thing that matters is now. And I will not endanger my family or the pack for your selfish whims. I don't care how sorry you are."

"I—"

"You want to speak on family abandoning family? You've spent your whole life with one foot on the outside, trying to leave us. You always had these big dreams, these ideas that would take you away. Do you know how many times I defended you over the years? How often Dad wanted to rage about your plans? Blamed it on too much time in Rathlin? Every time he gave in, every time he loosened up, it was because he knew I would toe the line when you went astray. Because I did. I had to when you wouldn't. I'd always told him we could depend on you. I was wrong."

The air felt like it was sucked out of him, to hear the venom, the pain in his brother's voice…something Axel had never shared with him. But his twin didn't stop, didn't halt the outpouring of frustration he must have been holding on to for years.

"We allowed more and more of our people to leave, did business with more humans, branched out…and you thought it was an achievement. You and Mom celebrated moving into the future. Yet, where did it get us? They're dead because we let down our guard. We loosened the rules. Made exceptions. Now, you want one more."

"I am not a danger to the pack—"

"Neither was the supposed mate of our aunt, yet he turned out to be a treacherous fae, didn't he?"

Ajax didn't answer. He couldn't. Not when that day ran through him, the blood, the widening of his mother's eyes when his father fell. The scream that filled the air before they all leapt into action.

"Didn't he? Answer me."

"He did."

"Do you think I am unfeeling? That I do not wish things were different? That you are the only one with dreams? The difference is that I cannot afford them. I must sacrifice, so others can live. But, you...you are a danger because you do not adhere to what is necessary as a leader. You do not stand firm with this pack, no matter your feelings. And I will not lose the people I have left because of your selfishness. My mate. My son. My pack. Not yours anymore. If they ever were. They are mine. Always have been. I protect what is mine even if it means I lose in the end. You are what I have to lose."

"I can...I can be better." But his voice cracked. He couldn't. He hadn't even told Axel about Marti. A human. His brother was right. He was a danger because he'd be asking for exception after exception. He couldn't lead and have the freedom he valued.

"You cannot. Because even after they died, you couldn't wait to leave, couldn't wait to ask for more."

"I needed to do something, to get out of there. It was too much."

"I, I, I. It's all about you, isn't it? You promised to stand beside me. To lead with me. But I did it by myself. I picked up the pieces alone. I've had to be the strong one, the one to make the tough decisions, and the one people resent. And you? All our lives, you got to be the loved one, the bleeding heart they could plead their case to. But that's okay. I'll take the heat, the anger, all of it, if it means their safety is ensured. I will run this pack, and I will continue our legacy while you search for Goddess knows what with the humans. You speak about family, but you're the one who left. You're the one who walked away. You're the one who abandoned us. Me."

His chest constricted, and his wolf howled mournfully in his head, whining for the connection, as even the sound of his brother's voice was breaking him. Axel was right. He had done this. He had wanted something that shifters didn't have the luxury of getting, and he had been impatient. He'd chosen this, and even asking was putting Axel in a position of hypocrisy.

"I understand."

The labored sound of Axel's breathing filled the space between them for several moments, but neither of them hung up.

"That's all you have to say? I understand?"

"Yes. I understand your reason why. I'm sorry. I never meant to abandon you or the pack. Not like that. But I don't regret it. I only regret the pain it has caused, and I will spend the rest of my life, however long or short, living with those consequences." No, he didn't regret it. His leaving the pack meant he'd found his mate, had found his Marti. "But, it was meant to be. Fate, as Kathleen would say, and we make our own fate, cursed or otherwise."

"Then we have an understanding."

"We do. Despite what you think of me, I care about everything you've said as well, so I will not ask again. May the Goddess protect you, your family, and Tuisa for the rest of our lives."

"Good."

Softly, he placed the phone receiver back in the cradle. Staring at the dirty metal, standing in the midst of the loud LA downtown area, he felt so removed, so out of place from who he was. And so alone. He'd never felt so alone.

Chapter 15

Marti

Monday, September 30
El Luchador Gym

"I see you've been busy while I was gone."

She was on her tip-toes, reaching for the extra cleaning spray, when his voice startled her. The box tipped over, and several full spray bottles rolled out, bouncing off her head and landing with a thud on the floor of the supply closet.

"Jesus, Ben. You scared me."

She turned to pick up the spray bottles, acutely aware of how small the closet was. He stood in the doorway, crowding her, and he didn't even try to help pick them up. She sighed inwardly. Her week had been so much better without him here.

Rubbing her head and wincing at the bump that was already forming, she noticed he wasn't in workout clothes. His hair was slicked back and styled, the light brown shining through a sheen of hair product, and he wore a fitted suit, clearly expensive, and a watch that screamed 'Look at me!'

"I would say welcome back, but you don't look like you are going to work out today. Headed straight to work?" She kept the conversation light because any indication that she liked his clothes would be considered an invitation and a whole other problem to deal with. She tried to put what the Goulden rep said out of her head, not truly believing that he was associated with such a large and ruthless company, but with the suit on, he looked more like them than the gym jock she was used to seeing.

"Yes, I have a big meeting early this morning with business partners from the East Coast, so I don't have time to stay." She expected him to move, to head out, all while she wondered why he stopped by here in the first place.

"Okay, well, have a great day at work, and I'll see you back up here tomorrow, right?" She smiled, hoping to dispel some of the tension that emanated off of him.

"I come here for you, Marti. Every day. Do you understand that?" He was angry for some reason, and there was something violent underlying the tone of his words. She refused to play into his little game.

"Excuse me, I need to get my cleaning done." She tried to push past him, to ignore his words.

"Explain to me why you've been seeing another man all week."

"Another man? I—you're kidding, right? First, we aren't together, and I can do what I want. Secondly, he's the headliner for the tournament, literally the one Goulden insisted on." She glared at him, making sure he knew that she knew all about his association. "I took him to some touristy things, but that's none of your business. What's gotten into you?"

And then, everything between them shifted. He moved quickly, his body flush against hers as he pressed her against the wall, reminding her just how strong he was. She tried to push him away, panic rising in her throat. It was early, even for him, which meant there was no one else around. Grappling desperately, she was no match for his strength, and he grabbed her forearms, holding them in place between them.

"That's where you're wrong. I've given you plenty of time and space to accept this. I own you, and I own this gym. I, along with Goulden, have too much money invested to let it go now."

She gaped at him. "You donated equipment, and we took a loan out ourselves for the remodel. You don't own anything! We have almost paid it off."

His smirk ran cold, the condescension in his eyes freezing her efforts to fight back. "You sure about that?"

"So that man was telling the truth. You are a part of Goulden Enterprises."

He chuckled, leaning in close to her ear and she turned her head, trying to put space between them. "I'm not a part of them. I own them. I run that company, along with a couple others, and there's nothing you can do about it."

"I'm going to take care of that. When I'm done, we won't owe you shit."

"It's cute that you think that. Because even if you did, you can't walk away from me. Bet you didn't know your dad keeps a second set of books. One that has helped me clean a lot of cash, very quickly. And now, we have enough control that I don't need him anymore. Matter of fact, he's just another loose end at this point."

Terror rose in her chest at the thought of losing her father, and she ripped her arms from his grasp, trying to move around him. But he was strong, and faster than he looked.

Instead, he pulled her by her waist, roughly turning her so that she faced away from him, and he pressed himself up against her from behind. One hand held her up against the shelves, and the other ran along the slope of her ass, squeezing, then moving to her hip and around. Overwhelmed and feeling helpless against his strength, she tried bucking, scratching, anything. But it only seemed to excite him, and panic rose in her throat.

She was trapped.

"But you? You are not a loose end. Different from every other woman I've fucked, and the only one who's ever turned me down. I have a very specific purpose for you. One that is coming due very soon, and I have been patient. You may not like it at first, but I promise, you will have an eternity to thank me once it's all done."

Shoving one hand under her shirt, he pulled the front of her bra down violently, a cry rising in her throat. Trapped, she closed her eyes, trying to still the shaking, fearful of what he would do next. She could only hope he would get tired of this game, or that someone else would walk into the gym. Instead, he rolled her nipple between his fingers aggressively, pinching until she cried out. Tears formed in her eyes, and the more she struggled, the more his arms clamped around her.

"This is mine to touch. No one else's. And this?" His hand slid to her crotch aggressively, his breath creeping along her neck as the tears blocked her vision. "This is mine to fuck. I've given you time, but now time's up. Especially since you want to go around fucking other men."

"Fuck you." Tears flowed down her cheeks, but she was angry. She wished she had her pepper spray with her, and if she could get turned around fast enough, she would knee him in the crotch immediately.

"Later, sweet cheeks, later. I promise I've been waiting for that day. It will be special, and you'll remember it for a long time. But, I have a meeting right now."

Abruptly, he released her, and when she swung her arm around to hit him, he grabbed it and pushed her back. Tripping over the dropped spray bottles, she fell to the ground. Glaring up at him, he smirked before straightening his suit jacket and leaving.

"Fucking asshole!"

Overwhelmed and in slight shock, she slid down the wall of the closet, shame and anger filling her. How had she not seen it? Was she really that blind? The more she focused on everything he said, the angrier she was at herself. No, at her father. Little comments, his weird possessiveness, the way Ben had spoken about their future, she had blown it off over the years, assuming he was just lonely. That he was inconsequential. If she had known the power he had over her father, their business, her…she would have been ready. Right? Maybe she was just fooling herself. Or just a fool. Tears poured from her, and she let the sobs take over, accepting that after the last couple days without Ajax, and now confronted with a new problem, she needed a good cry.

While it didn't solve anything, it gave her time to think. Fuck Ben. He was so full of shit. A bully who had gotten out of control. This wasn't some movie, and all these games he wanted to play had consequences. He wanted to pretend to be a big, bad guy, then he would see what happens when she held him accountable. Rising to her feet, she pushed down the roller coaster of feelings that broiled inside of her, and she got to work.

By the time she had gotten the closet straightened up, and came back out with the cleaning supplies, she'd decided she was going to find a way out of whatever they were doing. First up would be to confront her father. There's no way he was keeping separate books. And for what? Money laundering? It was the only thing that made sense for why they needed all these small businesses in their neighborhood. And why he would need control.

Her thoughts ran in circles, her mind wondering what exactly she would need to do when she heard the front door open again, and Felix calling out her name.

"Marti, you alive?"

She knew he was referring to her Friday night drinking session, but she winced at telling him what had just happened. Both he and Ajax would be proven right, that Ben was dangerous, and she needed a fucking escort to keep him away. Funny how it wasn't Goulden that had become her greatest threat.

No way was she telling him right now.

And Ajax...

She still didn't know what to do about him. He hadn't come back, and her Sunday had been miserable. How had she gotten so attached to one man in a matter of days? She shook her head, and smoothing her hair, she made sure she looked presentable before greeting Felix. He couldn't know just yet. He'd go after him alone, and she didn't want her friend getting hurt.

She kept it short and sweet, telling Felix she had a lot of work to catch up on, then rushed back to the office. She needed to do a better search on Goulden Enterprises, but she didn't know where to go. Everything began at home, and that's where she would start first.

Where would extra money be going? She was the damn accountant—how could she not see it? For an hour, she combed back through bank deposits, bill payments, and transfers. She kept all that paperwork filed away neatly, and now that she knew what to look for, she couldn't believe she'd missed it.

Right there, in black and white. Centuries Old Children's Charity. Supposedly, they held a monthly event with rich philanthropists, and her father acted as one of the foundation's board members. That meant he gathered the money from events he hosted and contributed services, donating his skills to teaching self-defense at one of the hotels downtown. He didn't have to do anything but show up and teach a class. Then, he simply dropped all the proceeds off at their bank, then donated it back to the Centuries Children's Charity.

She had never been to any of the events, and her dad was always dismissive about it. He disappeared one Saturday every month for a noon session, then came back with a bank deposit, and then had her write the check to the Charity. Clean money and a tax write-off.

That had to be it. Every month, the deposit had been getting larger and larger, ridiculously so. And then, when she started looking harder, she found two or three other smaller charities. Nothing monthly like this one, but random contributions that she couldn't find real business listings for.

And when it came to the tournaments, that was a huge payout. And she was forced to give tens of thousands to Goulden as a cut in their profit. This one was predicted to be close to a $100,000 profit for the event. It was why she thought they were almost done paying them off.

When her dad walked in at ten, she was furious. Clutching the papers in her hand, she held them up accusingly. "Do you understand what you've done? What this means?"

He froze, his eyes narrowing on her hands. "Um…I…what are you talking about?"

"Don't…don't play dumb." Tears pricked at her eyes, but when her voice cracked, she shook her head and cleared her throat. "These charities? They're a cover for fraud."

A long silence hung between them as realization sank in. There was no more hiding from her, and his eyes lifted to hers, practically begging for understanding. "You weren't supposed to be involved. That was the deal."

"The deal? Are you serious? You kept me in the dark, and now, I don't know if we can walk away from this."

"They said it would be fine. That I would be covered…that, that…" He took the papers from her gingerly, uncrumpling them as he stared vacantly.

"It wouldn't be them going to jail. It would be you. You."

"I…I…I messed up. But there was no choice. Nothing else I could do. They're…you don't understand."

"There's always a choice. Not only did you lie to me, you continued to lie to me, knowing we were being threatened. What were you thinking, Dad?" Anger flowed from her now, but she couldn't help softening her voice.

"God, Marti-bear. I'm so sorry. I've ignored it for so long. Pretended it wasn't happening." Then he looked down at all the bank statements, devastation clouding his features, his next words practically a whisper. "It's my fault…my fault it got out of hand."

"Dad…" She reached for him, her need to protect him overriding the frustration.

"No, you're right. I should have said no. I should have said something to you. I just didn't want to bother you. Didn't want to drag you into my mess back then. I thought I could fix it for myself for once. Without you." He let out a ragged breath, sinking down, and burying his head in his hands. "But clearly that was stupid of me. They came to me years ago, and I turned them down over and over. Then, the day you lost your scholarship, and you came home devastated, I knew I would do anything to make your dreams come true, to get you more than this little gym. I wanted to help. To be your dad. And if that meant my dreams failed, so yours could, then so be it."

"There is nothing, nothing that matters more to me than you. I would have never let you do this."

"I know. And that's exactly why I didn't tell you. It seemed like easy money, but I didn't really read the fine print, and I didn't know what kind of people they were."

"Bad fucking people." She squeezed her eyes shut, flashing back to the fear that had enveloped her this morning. "And what are you getting out of it?"

"Not much, honestly. I tried to back out, especially after I realized I was getting cut out of all the profits. I couldn't even pay for your school after all that. Then they threatened me with you. Said that essentially, I was paying for protection of the business. They would take care of us, make sure we stayed afloat, and you never got hurt. When I asked them why you would be in danger…" He trailed off, plopped down in the chair and wiped his face with his hands wearily.

"What did they say, Dad? I have a right to know." She felt the tears coming, the sobs threatening to take over.

"That there was always a boogeyman out looking for pretty girls to pay the price for their daddy's mistakes." He paused for a long time, staring at the blank wall behind her. "I had hoped you would get married and move away. I hoped for that every day. Someone else to take you away from the mess I made of our lives. Then I could face the fallout by myself. But with you here, I couldn't take the risk in standing up to them. And it became comfortable. But now, they have control of almost all the small businesses in the area, and they constantly want more. I don't have enough capital to start over anywhere else."

His face looked older than his fifty-six years, suddenly droopy and sad. "I'm supposed to take care of you, and I can't. Your mother would be so disappointed in me."

Moving to stand behind him, she leaned down and hugged his huddled figure, wrapping her arms around his neck. "I love you, Daddy. We will figure this out together. You just can't keep anything else from me. I need to know everything, so I can keep myself and you safe."

He stood, pulling her into his arms, and she could hear him sniffing through tears. "That's it. That's everything. Maybe if we get enough savings together, we can start over somewhere else. Just give them the gym. Because they will find us if we fuck them over. They're ruthless. The things I've seen on those days I've been pretending to do the charities…"

"They're not above the law. No one is. I don't see how everyone in our neighborhood has just given in to them. Especially if we band together. I know I can—"

"No. NO." He pulled back, holding her at arm's length, and panic flashed in his expression. "I watched them torture a man one day. His screams, the begging, it still haunts me. There was nothing I could do. All so they could say I was an accessory. That day, they reminded me that I was tied to them forever. I know you think that you can fix this, but you can't. They're more than just a couple of bad people. It's all of them, and I don't want you anywhere near them."

Her mind raced, and she considered keeping Ben's actions a secret, but if she wanted him to be honest, then she had to be too.

"It's too late for that. I'm just as involved as you, unfortunately. Ben is not just a part of them, Dad. He said he owns the whole company, somehow, and he came to see me early this morning. Attacked me, threatened me, said...said, I was his, and I would never get away."

"Wait? You? You...were never supposed to be a part of this. When did this happen?"

"Years now. Ever since I came back, he's been handsy and gross, but I just dealt with it. I thought he was harmless. But, turns out, he's been having someone watch me, and he warned me to stay away from Ajax. He was really aggressive. He's the one who told me to look for the money. He wanted me to know, to feel trapped, like we have no choice."

"Fuck. My baby. I'm so sorry. I never thought..." He squeezed her harder, until she thought her ribs would crack.

"I just know to be careful now. To watch my back and not be alone places." Pushing him to arm's length, again, she cursed at how right Felix and Ajax were, then shook her head. This wasn't their fight. They didn't need to be dragged into it.

"You'll stay here unless I'm with you?"

"I'll be careful. But I have to find a way out of this. Does your friend, Sergeant Ramirez, still work at the police station?"

"Yes, but I can guarantee they have ways around the law. People on the payroll. Otherwise, they wouldn't be so bold. You can't go to the police station. Marti, you can't."

She paused at that. This was all too much. Life wasn't a mafia movie, there was still law and order, and she'd find a way. "I have to try something. Maybe he'll meet me somewhere, like we're going to lunch. I'm going to go get his advice first, then we can brainstorm. We will figure it out, I promise."

After he left, she stared at the wall for a long time, feeling defeated and fearful. She needed to go to the police station, but clearly, Ben had someone watching her everywhere she went. What a fucking creeper. Deep down, she just couldn't believe Goulden or Ben were untouchable. They had all these people in their neighborhood scared, but she refused. She would get through this tournament, and they would find a loophole. They wouldn't do anything right now anyway, so she had time to figure it out. There was too much money on the line this week.

Still, she hesitated before heading out, like she knew she should just wait for him, but why? What did she think he could do? Shaking herself free of the unexplainable need for him, she walked down the hall to his dressing room and unlocked it. Wandering around, she touched bits and pieces of him that he'd left behind. He was a neat man, or maybe he just didn't have much stuff. She didn't know him, not really.

Yet, somehow, she still felt like she couldn't live without him, couldn't see her life with him gone. This was why she didn't want to get attached. The comb, the small amount of clothes, the shaving kit…all of it was replaceable and impersonal. He could leave, and she would never hear from him again. She'd feel hurt and foolish all over again. But, damn, she wanted to believe him. She'd never had someone look at her the way he did.

Her days and nights had been filled with thoughts of him, but it didn't make sense. No, this couldn't be healthy. Her brain jumped from one extreme to the next, and nothing clicked. She just wanted him to come back. He made her feel safe, and right now, she felt anything but safe.

Resolving to be a big girl, she grabbed her bag and headed straight out the door.

"Sarg?"

"Marti! My girl. How are you doing? And your dad? We haven't had a Loteria night in a while."

"I know. That's what I'm here about. We are in a little bit of trouble, and I wanted your professional and personal opinion on what we should do."

Sergeant Ramirez grew up with her father. They graduated high school together, and he used to come into the gym on his days off. So, when she'd called the station, asking him to meet her for lunch, he'd agreed quickly. And now, concern filled his face. "Tell me."

"What do you know of Goulden Enterprises?"

He stared at her, frustration evident. "Not you, too." He shook his head. "They've taken down most of the small businesses. I thought maybe your dad was too old school for them, and he'd be left alone."

She shook her head. "And Ben Barnett? He's become obsessed with me—who knows why. It's become more than threats about money. He insists that I belong to him, and I don't know how to get him to leave me alone."

"Shit. He runs the whole thing. Or is the face of the company, at least. Real bad dude."

"I didn't realize that until this week. Hell, this morning." She could feel the heat in her cheeks, and he frowned knowingly.

He sighed, leaned back in the booth, then wiped his face. "There's something with them. Something more than a crime organization. It's not just that they have ties in the SDPD, because clearly, they do, but it's more. No one has ever been able to pin anything on them, not even our good guys. No evidence. People and things disappear in the night, and they're crazy fast, as in physically. Even good men who tried everything to set them up, say they're uncatchable."

"There has to be something we can do? My dad wants out. And I just found out this morning the extent of what has been going on. He thinks we can run, but I don't want to. This is my home."

"They'd find you if you ran. I can almost guarantee it. You're not the first business showing up at the station, willing to do their own jail time to get out of their connection with them. They disappear before we can do anything to help."

"So, you don't have any advice? Nothing?"

"Depends on how well you can disappear. How far you go, and even then, I can guarantee they have business dealings across the US. Maybe go south. You and your dad can blend into Mexico or even to South America. He speaks Spanish, probably has family down there still. How good is yours?"

"Passable. Shit. This is not what I wanted to hear from you. But thank you. Can I call you if I have more questions?"

"Mija, even calling me might be a bad idea, but it's better than showing up at the station. How about I just come workout next week, after the tournament. Let me see what I can do for an old friend."

Chapter 16

Marti

Tuesday, October 1
El Luchador Gym

She hadn't slept all night, just tossing and turning, listening for every sound outside her window and suddenly wishing she had a giant, scary guard dog. Or Ajax. But he still wasn't back, and she wasn't sure if he would be. She'd messed that up, maybe forever. She didn't want to think about it, didn't want to rehash the words he said to her, and the devastated look in his eyes. He'd looked broken.

And now it was Tuesday, with no sign of Ajax for almost three days now, and life had to go on. Her father had insisted she wait on him, making her promise that she wouldn't go in until later, and she'd agreed just to calm his nerves. But after deactivating Ben's account and revoking his door access, she reminded herself that she hadn't done anything wrong, and no one in Goulden had any reason to come see her today. She refused to hide or change her life. So, Marti dragged herself into her office before her dad was awake, and pouring some water into her coffee pot, stared sleepily at the drip, willing it to hurry.

A watched pot never boils, though, right? She sighed, then made herself busy turning things on. She was already late, and she was sure Felix would be in there any minute. She'd tried calling him last night to ask him to get here earlier, but he hadn't answered. She just needed things to go back to normal, and despite not wanting Ben to actually come see her today, she thought about what would happen when he inevitably banged on that door. Maybe she could convince him to pull back, maybe see how crazy he was being. Try a different approach with him. She certainly couldn't do that with her father or Felix hovering, so maybe it was a good thing if she was there with him alone.

Ugh. Fat chance.

Pushing the power button on the computer, she stepped outside her door and flipped the lights on for the whole gym. Immediately, the place was flooded, and like always, she flinched at the brightness. But this time, when her eyes adjusted, it was too late.

He was in front of her, hands over her mouth, pushing her into the office and up against the wall. She tried screaming, fighting back, scratching at his arms, but he only tightened his grip. His fingers gripped her jaw, aggressively holding back the sounds she tried to make, and the pain pushed pricks of tears from her eyes.

"Stop fighting, and I'll let you go. You understand? If you scream, I'll gag you. If you keep fighting me, I'll tie you down." His voice pierced her thoughts, clouding the panic that had taken over, and his next words rang ominously in her ear. "Do yourself a favor and make this easier for you because you're not hurting me when you struggle. I'd love to tie you up for our first time."

She nodded, fear coursing through her veins as she struggled to breathe through his hand. When his grip loosened, she took deep, gulping breaths, her eyes never leaving his. His hair had mussed in the struggle, and he brushed it back, looking over his shoulder.

"She's a fighter, isn't she?"

He hadn't released his grip on her body, or backed away from the wall, but her eyes darted to the other man in the room, and that was when pure terror shot through her. Ben was familiar, different, but a devil she knew. This other man looked like pure evil.

His eyes were black and soulless, and he smiled sinisterly, like he enjoyed being a villain of sorts. Any other moment in time, she might have considered him good-looking with a wavy mess of styled blonde hair, and a strong Nordic looking face. But she couldn't get past the cold way he looked at her, like she was a juicy steak.

"There is a certain sweetness about her. Change her ridiculous clothes and give her a brush, and she would be a nice addition to the harem."

"No, not her. She's mine." She stared up at Ben, his body not giving her an inch of breathing room, confused by it all, and trying to keep herself from hyperventilating. "Don't worry, that's why I've waited so long to turn you. You're a breath of fresh air. Something different. I'm surrounded by the same starved looking women every day who throw themselves at me, who wait on me hand and foot. I like your fire and flair, your uniqueness, your natural beauty. You'll be special."

"Fuck you." And with every ounce of anger she had in her, she spit in his face.

He flinched, then froze, the spittle dripping down his cheek, his eyes blazing in barely controlled anger. She expected him to beat her, push her away, but she wasn't prepared for what he did next.

He stepped back, releasing her as she slumped against the wall, and with a smooth quickness that jerked pain through her, he ripped her shirt off her body, and she whimpered in surprise. The coldness in his eyes sent chills down her spine as he lifted her ripped shirt and cleaned the spit from his face before dropping it to the ground.

"When they told me you had met up with a cop, that you were planning on running from me, I knew you hadn't taken me seriously, that you still thought you were in charge of anything. But you're wrong. You want to stay alive? Then you will need to learn how to stay in line as part of my operations."

"I'm not a part of anything. I don't want anything to do with you. And I never will. Leave from here, both of you."

He smiled slowly, softly before turning to the other man. "Where are my manners? I didn't introduce you to my associate here. This is Vann. Vann works for Goulden, as does everyone in the San Diego nest. You see, Vann here is a vampire."

She would have laughed if she wasn't worried he'd hit her. "You've really lost your marbles, Ben. You need to get your head checked."

He chuckled. "Wild, isn't it? There are so many things you don't know about in this world, and that's one of them. But you're about to get a crash course, because Vann here is going to turn you while I fuck you. Then you'll be hooked to me forever, and this beautiful body will be enshrined the way it is now." He reached out, running a single finger down her cleavage and over her stomach, hooking into her neon yellow biker shorts.

She slapped it away. "Don't touch me."

"Don't worry, my little tease. I'm almost ready to join you. I'm going to find someone new to bear my children, then they will turn me too. That was going to be you, but it looks like we need to speed up your loyalty, don't we? We will be vampires together, go through our first year of cravings, then…undeniable devotion."

"God, you're fucking sick. And psychotic. You are living in a fantasy land. Let me out of here, and we will get you the help you need." She scooted against the wall, arms crossed over her chest as she tried to make a break for the door.

"Looks like we go to Plan B, Vann. I think I'm going to enjoy this more than I thought."

Grabbing her wrist, he swung her towards the desk, bending her over and holding her arms to her side. She struggled harder, kicking back until she finally made contact. He flinched, releasing one arm, and she turned hard enough to run before he caught her by her braid and yanked her back.

Reaching out, she grabbed the coffee pot handle, and when he pulled her in, she slammed it into his chest, the glass shattering and the scorching liquid covering his chest.

"Fuck. You fucking bitch. You're going to pay for that." Grabbing her by the throat, he pushed her backwards onto the desk, knocking everything onto the floor in the struggle.

By then, Vann had joined him, pulling her hands above her head and holding them there while Ben pushed her legs apart and down. Wedging himself between her thighs, he took off his suit jacket, then loosened his tie, throwing both coffee stained pieces of clothing in the chair.

"Relax, sweet cheeks. I'm going to fuck you while Vann drinks your blood. They say it's the ultimate high, so you should try to enjoy it. Don't fight too hard, though, or he might have too much fun and drain you dry instead. It's a delicate balance, Marti."

Panic and fear filled her as he began unbelting his pants, and she started screaming. "Get off me, you fucking perv. No, no, no!"

Vann leaned into her face, still holding her arms, and smiled. Sharp fangs protruded from his mouth, and terror took over. What the fuck? Vampires couldn't be real. No, no, no.

"You're going to taste delicious." He skimmed his nose across her cheek, then ran his tongue along her neck before pulling back to laugh and look up at Ben. "Ready when you are, boss."

Tears streamed down her face, but she didn't stop screaming. "Get off me. You won't get away with this. People will find out. Felix! Felix will be here any minute. Help! Please…someone!" She screamed, her chest heaving until she began to sob. "Please, no."

The world spun around her, and it seemed like a dream, as she tried blocking everything out. No one was coming, and all she could see was Ben's smirking face, his penis in his hand, stroking her thighs and pulling down her shorts.

She closed her eyes and continued to scream, not registering the new noises in the room. When the pressure against her arms was released, she instinctively rolled off the desk, stumbling to the ground and curling into a ball. Anything to get away.

When she realized the screaming in the room wasn't coming from her anymore, that the sound had taken on a desperate wail that ended abruptly, she glanced up to the horrifying sounds of an animal. Growling and snarling echoed off the walls, and through her tears, she saw Ajax, or what she thought was Ajax, slamming his fists into Ben's face over and over.

When Vann attacked Ajax from behind, he dropped Ben, grabbed the vampire by his throat, and squeezed. After he fell to the floor, Ajax slashed at him over and over, until his head wasn't attached to his body anymore. The blood squirted everywhere, like a never-ending fountain of horror, soaking him, Ajax and her.

In shock, she couldn't make a sound as he turned his rage back to Ben, who was no longer conscious on the floor. When Ajax tore into his chest with his bare hands…claws, the shark bloody talons flicking streams of blood everywhere, she felt herself hyperventilating, her chest heaving up and down, and she crawled backwards, away from the rivulets of blood flowing across the floor towards her.

Her back against the wall, she lifted her hands to cover her face, only to be confronted with the blood smeared on her fingers. She rubbed her face frantically, trying to wipe the blood away, and instead, tasted it in her mouth, and she gagged. The coppery smell invaded her nose, and she couldn't get away, couldn't escape it.

No. No. No. It was everywhere. And her stomach couldn't take it. Down on all fours, she started vomiting, the waves of uncontrolled heaving shaking her body with every cramp, but she couldn't tear her eyes away from the vision of Ben's heart being ripped from his chest.

Sobbing between retching, she struggled to catch her breath, to face this new horror, so when strong arms wrapped around her shoulders, she jumped back in fear, covering her head with her arms.

"Please, no."

"Shhh, it's Ajax. It's over, baby. You're okay. I got you."

But Ajax wasn't himself. She saw a monster, claws, and black eyes, blood flying from the fangs in his mouth, just like the vampire. She pushed against him, trying to scramble away and escape. This nightmare would never end.

"Don't hurt me, please. I'm sorry, I'm so sorry."

"I won't hurt you, little one. Listen to my voice, concentrate on me. I'm going to take you to your dad. But I need you to listen and follow instructions, then soon this will all be over. Can you do that?"

She couldn't speak, couldn't reconcile the man with the animal in front of her. But she'd stopped screaming, stopped trying to push him away, so he scooped her up, pulling her against his body, his voice the only thing rooting her to the memories she had of him. "Keep your eyes closed. Don't look up, not till I tell you."

She tried to calm herself, keeping her eyes closed like he said, and the more she focused on him, the old him, the calmer she felt. Wrapping her arms around his neck, she buried her face in his chest and felt the sway of him walking when they began to move.

"Remember the zoo? They're going to open the Panda exhibit soon. Just a couple more weeks, and we can go together. I'll even wear matching Panda shirts with you. I'll buy you a personal golf cart for anytime you want to go. Whatever you want." She whimpered, feeling the air hit her face as they stepped outside, crossing the grass towards her house. She didn't want her dad to worry, to see the blood. Oh God, she was going to be sick again.

She gagged, realizing that her face was smushed into his chest, his very bloody chest, so she turned her head away, needing to get the smell out of her nose and mouth. Ajax slowed for just a moment, shifting her in his arms. "That's it. You're doing so good. Deep breaths. We are back on that boat, watching the whale. Enjoying the sounds and sway of the ocean, and the beautiful sunset, so warm on your face. And the dolphins? They followed us for miles. Remember how big the whale was, how fresh the salty air felt on your skin?"

She let the deepness of his voice invade her senses, focusing only on him, and let herself be taken back to that moment, anything to be away from here, away from this reality. Her dad's voice was faint, just a noise in the background, and soon, she was being laid in the cool porcelain of her bathtub.

"You can open your eyes now, Marti. I'm going to turn the water on and rinse you off. Is that okay?"

Weakly, she lifted her eyes in the brightness of the bathroom lights, and Ajax's face was only inches away. He was covered in blood too, but she focused on the light green of his eyes, looking for the flecks of imperfections that should be there, refusing to look anywhere else. But there was something calming about the now deep green, something so pure, no imperfections to be found. She'd never really considered that, never thought to muse about how unique his eyes were. Not until now.

She nodded, then closed her eyes again. She was so sleepy, and in a haze, she felt his hands on her, the warm rush of water and a towel wrapped around her before being engulfed in the comfort of her bed.

Distinctly, she felt Ajax's absence when he left, and she ached at the loss, falling deeper into the escape she'd found in sleep. When she'd surface again, jerking awake, unable to rest, the sound of her father's voice singing and his weight against her back filled the void, just like when she was a child. "Arrorró mi niño, arrorró mi sol, arrorró pedazo de mi corazón."

Chapter 17

Ajax

Wednesday, October 2
Marti's Room

Marti woke in a panic, a soft 'no, no, no' filling the air. She was already wrapped in his arms, but he pulled her closer, comforting her.

"You're safe. You're safe. It's okay, I'm here."

His words didn't help, and her chest heaving in agitation, she grabbed his hand from around her waist, yanking it so she could see. He stretched his fingers out, and he frowned at whatever she was looking for. Throughout the night, she had woken several times, convinced there was blood on her or that someone else was in the room. She swore she could hear them. But he hadn't moved from the bed with her since he'd finished cleaning the mess and disposing of the bodies. Well, one body. He had staked the vamp.

It had taken all day, especially since he and Felix decided the gym needed to stay open and operate normally. They didn't want anyone to get suspicious. Not the police, not the vampire nest. Between Felix and her father, they had all taken turns watching over her. She was in shock, and he knew it would take time for her to process it all.

He knew that from experience. His first time spilling actual enemy blood, and not just sparring in a field, had been a violent introduction to death, one that he hadn't been able to forget, and not something he'd ever wanted Marti to see. She shouldn't have to take those memories and shove them down, shouldn't have to accept that brutality, not with him there to protect her. But he had been too late.

It was a lot to deal with at once, and he'd been up all night, replaying the way he'd reacted in front of her, the way he'd allowed himself to go feral, to go back to his instincts. Back to the beast he'd been on a battlefield, back to the moments in the dark alleys of Houston, by himself, fighting the vampires. It's like he hadn't changed at all, hadn't grown from the vicious savage he'd allowed himself to become in his anger. Violence was a part of him, would always be, whether he liked it or not, but it didn't have to be that way for her.

Domingo had been almost as bad as she was, inconsolable and muttering about how everything was his fault. He'd never seen a grown man cry before, never seen someone so broken as he stood over his daughter, sobbing that he never meant for this to happen. Something had snapped in him at the sight, at the way he didn't try to hide his feelings beneath anger and action. Domingo had been unabashedly open, and it had hit him hard. Almost as hard as seeing his mate screaming for mercy underneath that slimy human.

He cursed himself for not being more vigilant, for leaving her alone at all, but for especially leaving the gym the second she had arrived that morning. He had waited till he heard the alarm turn off and she walked in, then he'd slipped out the back and into her home, placing his gifts on her bed and leaving her a note, hoping to surprise her when she came home after work that day. He'd been so excited to see her reaction, to try and start fresh with her, he hadn't considered how much those few minutes would change everything.

But when he had come back through the gym doors, every part of him had raged at the sounds he'd heard coming from the office. Fury boiled his blood, and he didn't slow down, not until both of her attackers were torn to pieces. But then, he'd surfaced from the brutality, from the distinctive feral need of his wolf. Her huddled figure on the ground, the sobs and vomiting wracking her body, and the way her pleas had shaken with terror, had crushed him.

Feral for Love

When she had flinched away, scared of him too, he knew his wolf had gone too far, that he was a monster to her, but it didn't matter. All that mattered was that she was safe.

By the time she was clean and tucked into bed, Felix was already at the door, desperate to make sure his friend was okay. They'd had to start the clean-up right away, but first they had to inform Domingo that vampires were not only a thing, but the whole basis of the Goulden operations.

He'd stared at them in disbelief at first, but it clicked, the acceptance settling into his reddened and weary face. "It makes sense, honestly."

Crossing himself and muttering some words in Spanish that Ajax didn't bother asking about, he'd gone back to his vigil at Marti's bedside. But the man had barely spoken since, the guilt clearly eating him alive.

Once they'd finished cleaning, he and Felix both decided to tell him about shifters. Then about Marti as his mate. He thought this would freak him out, to hear about this whole other world, to be angry with Ajax for trying to take his daughter from him, but no. It took several minutes of silence before he spoke. "So, you are here for her? Your…customs…say you will be committed to her? Forever?"

"Til the day we die, she is tied to me, and me to her. A deep, unbreakable love that I could not walk away from, even if I wanted to. We are destined."

Domingo had only nodded his head slowly, looking at Ajax like he'd given up. "Good. Then you will keep her safe because I have failed her, and she deserves so much more."

And now, hours later, Ajax held her in bed, making sure no one else came for her, and that the vamps didn't try to get revenge on them in the night. He laid there, unmoving, fear of losing her coursing through him, and his thoughts running rampant, darting from his past to his future, anything to keep him from reverting back to the angry, feral beast he was so close to becoming. He ignored his instinct to find the nest and tear every vampire from Goulden apart, struggled to keep from slipping back into the savagery that had almost made him lose himself during the war. It was a possibility, a real one that had taken over his mind before. But back then, he didn't have someone to come home to, someone to remind him why he fought.

Not like Axel had. Ajax hadn't understood then, but he did now. It made sense how his brother had been able to keep himself sane amidst the constant violence. How fortunate Axel was to have been mated to Nubia since he was nineteen and she was eighteen. She had been his rock, Axel's saving grace, where Ajax had none. At first, as they fought alongside their father on the frontlines, his father had just allowed Axel to take breaks, to go home to Nubia, sating his wolf's need for its mate, and to come back with fresh sets of fighters, until Axel had been sent home more permanently, separating the twins. Keeping one of them safe for the future of the pack. The two of them had followed orders without question, knowing why it had to be that way, knowing the dark reality, knowing it was because one of the sons had to live, just in case, so that the line of Tuisa Alphas would remain strong.

But not Ajax. No mate to build a future with, and no need for a break, Ajax had charged on, spying and slipping in and out of camps, whether it was vampires, wolf, or witch, he'd made sure Tuisa's wrath was felt. He'd become numb to the death and gore, and eventually, he'd combated the nightmares with dreams of another life.

And now, he had her. His Marti. As long as he didn't let the dark times take over, not with Marti clinging to him while she slept, whimpering through her fear, he wouldn't leave her, not even for revenge.

Thankfully, he wasn't alone in keeping her safe. Felix was sleeping on the couch, and he had called a couple of pack members to stay with them in the gym. They had taken precautions, and Felix's whole pack was aware of the situation, and on high alert, dozens of them moving into the city to scout. But now, he worried whether he should tell Marti everything at once. She was already falling apart.

Now, they lay there in silence for a long while, like she was running everything through her mind, until she brushed her hand along his, tracing up and down his fingers and turning them over in her hand. "Ajax?"

She sounded worried, but fully awake for the first time, and she turned in the bed, facing him. Her brows were furrowed as her eyes searched his when she lifted her hand to his cheek, running along the stubble, then dragged her thumb over his lips.

"Open your mouth." Her voice was raspy, but determined, so he parted his lips, and she immediately ran her fingers along his teeth. "Maybe it was a dream. Maybe I imagined it all. I'm sorry, I've lost my mind."

She let her hand fall away, and she looked delicate and defeated as she stared up at the ceiling. He couldn't let her feel this way, even if she hated him for it.

"You're not crazy. What you saw was real. Vampires are real, and yes, most of Goulden consists of a vampire nest. It's one of the reasons we were so worried for your safety when they threatened you. They don't make threats lightly, and they are violent and uncaring. It's my fault for leaving. I shouldn't have done that."

She lay on her back, staring up at the ceiling for a long time as she contemplated what he said. It took several minutes, but she pulled his hand to her chest, wrapping both her hands around his and rubbing anxiously before finally whispering, "Are you a vampire too? I…I saw…there was so much blood."

"No, I'm not." He pulled her close, putting her head to his chest. "Do you hear my heart beat? I'm alive. They are not, technically. You've seen me eat food, go out in the sunlight. Those are things most vampires can't do. The older ones have adapted to the sun in short spurts. But no, I'm not a vampire. Is that what you're worried about?"

"I'm worried about everything. You killed two people, Ajax. Are you going to jail? It wasn't your fault, it was mine. I should have told him off a long time ago."

"First, it wouldn't have mattered. Second, nothing is your fault. Nothing. You didn't attack and obsess over anyone. He did. That was his choice. You can do everything right, and sometimes, even then, bad things will still happen. But I'm here, and I won't leave you again. Not for any reason, and I'm definitely not going to jail. No one will find their bodies, but I doubt anyone will look too hard for either of them. I can guarantee they've already appointed a new leader because that's how it works in a nest. No loyalty, just money, business, power. People, vamps, they're disposable. They have a human front that they use and throw money at. They will find a new one."

"Will they…come here? They have to be pissed, they have to know what happened."

"Yeah. They will come after me eventually, but you're a priority for me. You were their target this time, but I'm not sure if that was unique to that one human, or if the whole nest was focused on you. We are working on a plan. Felix is here, and he brought some of his family to stay while we figure this out."

She was quiet for a long time before she looked up at him. She was still pale, and her eyes looked huge in her face, red-rimmed from the tears, but she was beautiful. His heart ached for her, that he wasn't there when she needed him.

"Thank you for coming back, for…for stopping them. You didn't have to do that. I can't stop seeing…everything that you did."

"I told you I'd be back. I'm not going anywhere. I just wish I hadn't left. Then this wouldn't have happened. Like I said, I won't leave you again." He knew he'd be repeating that the rest of his life, knew that he would do everything in his power to keep his mate, and all the people he loved, safe.

She shook her head. "That's not fair. I'm not your responsibility. I know you…said what you said, but people change their minds. This is a lot. I don't want to stop you from your dreams or bring you into my problems. I'm a mess. This is a mess."

He sighed heavily, letting the rise and fall of his chest calm his wolf. His beast didn't like when she talked about leaving. He needed to tell her; he needed her to know everything. It was more dangerous for her to be out of the loop now, and maybe if she knew, then she could process it.

"I need to tell you something else, but I've held back for many reasons. I don't want you to freak out, and I'm not sure this is even a good time, but you need to understand why I can't leave, why I won't leave. And why the vampires will be coming after me, just as much as you. In all likelihood, they were probably already targeting me when they made you get me as a headliner."

She stiffened, studied his face, and he tried to find the words.

"Vampires are real, but so are other supernatural creatures. Our world is full of them. They look like humans, operate in groups or nests or packs or covens. Most of the time, they are not dangerous, and they keep to themselves. Vampires are the opposite. They love living in the city, feeding off humans, using their businesses to build their finances and power. They are perpetually trying to take advantage of others, mainly humans. The other supernaturals are not quite like that. Matter of fact, the rest of them avoid cities and live and operate on their own, avoiding humans altogether."

She frowned. "Supernaturals? Like what? Ghosts?"

"Wolf shifters, witches, fae, and all offshoots and hybrids in between. I'm sure there are others I don't even know about all over the world."

"I…it's…what?" She paused, her voice barely a whisper. "It's like reality has somehow become fiction. Or fiction a reality. This can't be real."

He chuckled softly. "You'd be surprised at reality when you pay attention to the world around you."

"How do you know? How can we tell?"

"There are small things to look for. For humans, it's almost impossible, but for each supernatural, there are ways they can tell. Witches feel auras and the magic inside each person. Fae are similar, more like a vibe. Wolf shifters smell them. For a shifter, very supernatural and every human has their own unique scent."

"So then, how did you know? About Goulden? About the vampire in my office?" She had gone still, waiting for something he knew she already feared, for the words that would make her forever see him differently, whether good or bad.

"I'm a wolf shifter. I can smell them, up close or far away. And for you specifically, on some level, I can sense your feelings, your fears, your happiness. I know that you're afraid, but I need you to know I would never hurt you, and I will kill anyone who tries to."

"So, the claws...and fangs...I saw them. They're real?" She sat up, scooting back in the bed to look at him in alarm.

"Not fangs. Vampires have fangs. Wolf shifters have canines, like typical wolves or dogs. But they only extend in certain situations. And in general, I can control it, use it as needed. If I shift fully, then I look like a large, black wolf. I can still feel and think, but then my wolf is in charge until I shift back to this form."

"This, this is a lot." Her head shook, like she didn't or couldn't believe him. Her words came out as a whisper. "You're okay with just killing people anytime you feel like it?"

"No. Not as a rule. But death is a part of life. We spend most of our time training to fight, defending and attacking other supernaturals that we think should die, but not usually unprovoked. We are natural pack beasts, and we live in communities. If people threaten the community, the people we love, then we will kill. You are the person I love."

Her breath came fast now, and she looked at him with desperation. "How can you know that? You should be with someone like you, not me. I'm nobody."

"Don't say that. You're my soulmate." He attempted to pull her to him, to help her calm, to help his wolf calm, but she pushed back, and he dropped his arms. "The Moon Goddess gives us fated mates, the other half of our soul, and because of the magic within us, our wolf knows immediately once we've met. For humans, it's like having soulmates, and while you don't have magic to tell you automatically, the feelings are still there. You just have more choice in the matter, more ways to lose your mate because you can't tell, because you let other things hold you back, or you choose someone who wasn't meant for you. For us, there is no mistake. Our mates are our greatest strength as shifters. Your scent, your presence, it calls to us, and until we are mated, there is no peace once we find you. My wolf is aggressive for you, and only you."

She took a shaky breath, swallowing hard without looking at him, so he slowed down, letting it sink in.

"Me? But...I don't...I don't understand. I'm not..."

"It doesn't matter. You were meant for me. For us. Every time you've rejected us in the past few days, my beast goes crazy, but it was too soon for you. I keep him under control, waiting for you to decide what you want, but know that I can never truly leave you. Even if you asked me to go, I will always be here, waiting. It's our instinct."

"This is too much. You can't possibly…no. I'm still dreaming, or I've lost my mind. You've lost your mind."

He sat silently, giving her time for things to sink in.

"Show me."

"That's not a good idea. My wolf wants to mark you, and I won't do that until you're ready. He was already pushed to the brink on Saturday night. I won't let him get close again."

"Mark?"

"We don't generally practice human marriage. We mate and mark, then sometimes a ceremony if desired. Then, we are connected for life. I would mark you on your neck by biting into your skin. My shifter magic enters your body, into your bloodstream, mixing with yours, and we are bound forever. The mark fades over time but will never go away, like an almost imperceivable scar. You will belong to me, and I will belong to you. But this is a life you get a choice in. It's not something you are used to, so I will go as slow as you need."

"Show me your wolf. Just enough for me to understand, I need to see for myself." The desperation to believe was in her eyes, and he considered the consequences. "Please. I just need to know that you're not what I see in my head. That you're not…them."

He swallowed hard, pulling her face into both his hands. "This isn't a good idea, Marti. Not if you've never seen a wolf before. Let me get another shifter to show you, to build up to it."

"If you're my soulmate, then why would another wolf be better for me? Why would that make it easier? I just want you."

"Because my wolf is of Alpha blood, some of the strongest and most vicious. And he's not calm right now. He's angry at the vampires, angry at me for not marking you. He's not a cuddly little dog. He will present in a way that is terrifying for you. And I'm scared it will be too much, and you won't see me the same again."

"If it's true, then I already saw him. I saw him rip two men apart like they were pieces of paper. I saw him glory in violence, and I saw him covered in blood. It's all I can see when I look at you right now, Ajax. And if that's all I can see, then I don't know how it could be any worse."

For a long moment, they stared at each other, both stubborn and needing the other to trust them. But he gave in. He gave in to the howling, to her desperate pleas, to his own desire to have her believe in him.

And when he allowed his wolf to surface just a little, letting his facial features morph, his canines to extend, his claws to grow, he watched in distress as her fears were affirmed. Her eyes widened, and she gasped, pushing back into the wall in horror.

Quickly, he pulled his wolf back, taking deep breaths to control him. It was getting harder and harder, and it took everything he had, so he stepped back, away from the bed, and put space between them, not daring to look up at her before his wolf had calmed.

When he could finally breathe, she was holding her knees to her chest in the corner, silent tears streaming down her face. He waited for what seemed like forever for her to speak.

"You were right. It's…a lot. I need space, or time…or something. I don't know what to think or even say."

"I'm sorry. I am. I never meant to push you or scare you."

Her voice broke. "I know. My brain needs to find a way to be okay with all of this. Please, I need space for now."

She wanted him to leave. She wanted to be away from him.

Rejection washed over him again, but he was cognizant, understanding of why. He didn't blame her.

"I will go like you ask, but I can't leave you by yourself. Felix is here with his family. Two…cousins of sorts. Someone will sit outside the door or go with you where you need until it is safe. I want that person to be me, but I understand that it can't be right now. Okay?"

"Yes." She looked relieved that he was leaving, and he had to admit, that hurt, but he pushed it down and left without another word.

Moving down the hall, into the living room, he stopped at the couch where Felix sat up, waiting.

"You heard all that?"

"Yeah. I'm sorry, man. This shouldn't have been the way. Fuck Ben. I should have killed him for her a long time ago, but he seemed so harmless. It was the damn spandex shorts he wore. Made him seem ridiculous and non-threatening."

"Well. I have a feeling the vamps already know but are biding their time. They may not even care about the two deaths. I'm surprised they hadn't killed Ben themselves. They don't tolerate humans long unless it's making them money. And the vamp that was with him was low-level."

"The man that came to see her last week was not low-level. His name was Pennington, and I did a little homework on him over the weekend. He's at the top. He's old, but hasn't been in this area long. Only in the last couple of years has he built the nest though. Rumor is he had a lot of transplants from Houston." Ajax closed his eyes at that, the implication huge. They'd baited him here for a reason. It's why they'd known his name, his reputation. He'd brought this to her doorstep. Felix continued, but they both knew why Houston mattered. There was a grudge there. "I'm thinking he will take over now. He won't care about her as a person, but will still want the money from the tournament. I guarantee he will push that going forward, maybe use the deaths as leverage against Marti's morals. But there has to be something more than the money."

"Revenge. He wants me. Someone is paying big money to get to me."

"I assumed it had to do with you, especially everything that we've heard about Tuisa since the war ended."

"Is it that obvious?"

"Not at first. We've only ever heard rumors about you, and never a name. But it clicked. You can't hide who you are forever. Especially as word spreads that you left."

"Fuck. This was why I left, why I needed to leave. But I can't escape it, can I?"

"That's shifter life. You know that. We can't escape the destiny that our Goddess creates for us. You may not have been meant to lead with your brother, but you were meant for something. And the vampires...they can feel it. They want a taste of Tuisa. You made a lot of enemies during the war."

"Enemies I can handle." He practically snarled that, the anger at himself growing. And Felix's nonchalant truths not helping.

"Maybe you can. But Marti can't."

He thought about that for a moment, about the destiny that had brought him here to her, about the choices he would have to make very soon. He wouldn't be able to do this alone.

"I know that. And I won't take any chances with her. You know this area, these vamps. Do we go through with the tournament? Or call it off and run?"

"I don't know, man. Calling it off will set off a lot of red flags. But not calling it off may be putting her and Domingo in danger."

Rock and a hard place again. As much as he wanted to run, he knew he couldn't. He had to end this somehow. "Then we let Marti decide. Otherwise, she will be upset we are deciding without her. We have two days before then. Then I will take her and hide her. I don't care where. I'll reach out to the Supernatural Council, covens, take her out of the country, whatever I have to do."

"Shit. You know some witches? Haven't seen or heard of any covens around here since before the war. We could use them right now. Could annihilate that nest easy. They'd never see it coming."

Now that was an idea. He smiled at Felix. The first smile in a long time. "Yeah, I do. They're powerful and a little crazy. You know about the Daughters of Danu, right?"

Chapter 18

Marti

Thursday, October 3
El Luchador Gym

"Marti-bear, there is absolutely no reason to be up this early. You're killing me. I was hoping this extended slumber party meant I could sleep in now."

"You're welcome to go back home, Felix. I have a job to do though."

"I'll admit, the towels have gotten low since you've been gone."

"Oh, no. You poor thing, you have to bring your own towel." She looked over at the bench where Felix lay stretched out in his gym clothes, but not actually doing anything. She stared at his boyish face for a while, then he opened his eyes and wiggled his eyebrows playfully.

"You know, you haven't talked about it with me. It's been twenty-four hours since we became joined at the hip, and you haven't said a word. Can't be healthy."

"There's nothing healthy about what happened here. I don't want to relive it. And I don't even know what you know. I just...I don't want to involve you any more than I have to. And I appreciate you bringing your family here to help keep watch, but I feel guilty. Everything comes back to me and my poor decisions."

"How exactly is that? And my cousins jumped at a chance to get away from their house for a while. Only a select few of us ever leave the family estate and they were curious. You're doing them a favor."

She sighed heavily, knowing he was right, that she needed to hear it out loud. "My dad chose to deal with those people because he wanted to make money to pay for my college. My college where I lost a scholarship because of my choices. Ben was obsessed with me because I can't seem to be mean to people or make my boundaries clear. I should have run him off years ago. Ajax is miserable because I can't be what he wants me to be. It's me. I keep messing everything up."

"All that is a load of crap, and you know it. You can only be responsible for yourself. What is it you think Ajax wants you to be anyway?"

"It doesn't matter. You wouldn't understand."

"Shit, Marti. The world isn't falling apart because someone loves you. That's not how it works. I'd kill to find my fated mate. We all would."

Distracted, she scoffed and turned to another machine, wiping at it angrily with her rag. "It's not that simple, Felix. It…he…you just wouldn't understand."

"Or maybe I understand the most."

She shook her head, and when he walked over and stood in front of her, she tried to ignore him as she moved to the next machine. When he grabbed her wrist gently, stopping her, she was annoyed.

There was a seriousness in his eyes, the boyish jokes gone. "If I could do it the right way, then I would have my sister or cousin in here to show you, but we don't have time for that. Get your head out of your ass, Marti. Get out of your own way."

Then, he pulled off his shirt, and dropped his shorts, standing in only his underwear. Before she could avert her eyes, he began to transform, and she gasped, stepping back. In seconds, her best friend had changed into a giant fucking wolf.

"What the fuck." *What the FUCK.*

A dark sandy brown wolf with a tan chest stared back at her, golden eyes bright, and tail swishing back and forth. When he moved forward, his head bumping into her hip, rubbing his body along her thigh, she reached out to touch him hesitantly.

"You're fucking shitting me right now, Felix. I…" She was speechless. He was there, then he wasn't. How in fucking science did that work? Her brain worked overtime, trying to understand the possibility, but it didn't compute. It was like she was in a Tolkien novel, and fantasy had become reality. Had she been training her whole life for this?

He rubbed his head along her hand, then licked her fingers. Circling her legs, he dropped to the floor and rolled around, showing his belly to her. It was such a simple gesture, a familiar one, and she dropped down to one knee, stroking his chest, letting her fingers tangle in his fur.

Inadvertently, she laughed. "You're too big to be rolling around on the floor like a puppy. Felix, I could kill you for this. All these years. This is wild."

Rolling up to standing, he walked slowly over to the clothes he had taken off earlier and looked at her before shifting back into his human form, fully naked. She turned quickly, still trying to process while he got dressed. "All the times I had to look at your naked drunk ass over the years, you'd think you'd be shameless."

"Oh, I am. Most shifters have to be. But, with your mate around, it's a death wish to even shift near you. Especially since you're unmarked, and he's basically in a mating frenzy. It's why he almost killed me that first day we met. It's also why it isn't smart of him to let his wolf out around you right now. Hell, it's not safe for me, either, but he left to run an errand early this morning, or I wouldn't even have considered it."

"There are so many rules. So much violence."

"I guess to humans, it's violence. To us, it's a way of life. We kill for our family, and a mate is the ultimate family. It doesn't help that Ajax is who he is. That makes it worse."

"What does that even mean? I need everyone to stop talking in riddles. I'm not a child."

"Well, it's just not my place to say, just like Ajax couldn't tell you about me. But maybe it can give you perspective. He is an Alpha, born leader of his pack, even if he is the younger twin, it doesn't matter. Biologically, magically, the biggest, strongest of anyone in the pack. It's passed down from parent to child, almost always with males, but there are a few female Alpha leaders now and then. He chose not to lead and left his pack. It doesn't change who he is. And his pack, of all the North American packs? It's the biggest, the strongest, and the meanest."

Felix plopped onto a weight bench and slowly began to complete some reps while he talked. She could only stand there in a daze, trying to process all this information at once.

"They are ultra private, known for their viciousness, especially with the wars that barely just ended. Geez. To be a fly in that battle. I know people who'd kill to see him and his brother clear out a building together—"

"Felix. Focus." She rolled her eyes, her mind already imagining the bloody fighting, visions of Ajax ripping through Ben mixing with everything Felix described.

"Sorry. Where was I? Oh, yeah. Undefeatable and legendary in our world, blah, blah, blah. Which means his wolf is formidable, protective and unpredictable. No matter what Ajax knows and wants, when it comes to you, his wolf can easily take over and lose reason, especially since he's been rogue from his pack for almost a year. He needs the pack link to be stable. A mate helps with that too. But the fact that he hasn't already shown up at the vampire nest and killed every single one of them by hand, is a miracle. You, and only you, are the only one holding him back at this point. Because it would upset you."

Wearily, she sat on the bench across from him. "Jesus. Is there a book somewhere that can teach me all the rules? I don't think I'll ever understand your world."

"Our world, Marti. It's yours now too."

The weight of his words slammed into her. This couldn't be her new life. She was a human, not capable of anything special. Why the hell would she be paired up with someone so strong? He needed someone to run his pack with. Not someone he had to run around protecting.

"I can't, Felix. He deserves someone other than me."

"That's bullshit, Marti. I won't even address that thought."

He stared at her angrily, and she couldn't help but look away. "I'm going to work in the office. There's a lot to do, and we still have the tournament."

"Marti…we should cancel. It's dangerous."

"No. That would only make this worse…Goulden isn't just going away. And…it's the only normal I have left right now."

She'd made her stand, refusing to hear anything else as she walked away. He only shook his head, then leaned back on the bench, picking up a weight bar. Back in her office, there was almost nothing left. They had thrown away the desk, the chairs, even her wall decorations were gone. In its place, she had a new monitor with the old hard drive attached, sitting on a card table and a chair from the front desk. The room had been scrubbed clean, but almost immediately, she decided she didn't want to be in there. Instead, she went to the front desk and powered on the bigger, older computer there. It occurred to her, the beautiful new computer she'd been gifted when they remodeled? From Ben. She let out a shaky breath. He was gone. He couldn't hurt her anymore.

Checking her email, making a to-do list, and settling into her routine, she was grateful for a small semblance of normal. Once she began calling around, checking in on all her vendors, confirming last minute selections, she had crossed off half her to-do list. That felt good. Her brain needed these simple tasks. Out here, as regulars came and went, she was able to see others living their lives and making casual conversation with her. After a couple hours, she started wondering how many of these people might be under the Goulden arm of 'protection,' how many were worried about money or death? How many knew about this supernatural world of people? How many might actually be supernaturals, living conspicuously every day around her?

The phone rang once again, a con for being at the front desk instead of her office, and she answered it, distractedly thinking of the next item on her to-do list.

"El Luchador Gym, can I help you?"

"I see you have a new work area today. Something wrong with your office?"

His voice sent a chill down her spine, and she sat up straight. "Who is this?"

"I think you know, but I'll humor you. Kevin Pennington, new CEO of Goulden Enterprises. Just wanted to check in on our business venture for this weekend. Everything will be continuing as planned, correct?"

She took a big breath, slowly letting it out to calm her racing heart. "Yes. But I think we may need a different headliner. I'm not sure Ice is the best choice. I sent him away."

"That's where you're wrong, Miss Andrade. He's the reason this tournament will be continuing. He is the star. Otherwise, your value to Goulden Enterprises has run its course. I expect you to have him ready, and I will have the other contender ready. Their fight is a non-negotiable. Is that understood?"

She grit her teeth. She didn't want Ajax in the middle of this anymore. She'd thought it was too dangerous for him, and now, she absolutely knew it was. Something about Pennington made her question everything, especially his insistence on Ajax being the headliner. They were coming for him, somehow. "Perfectly. Is there anything else I can do for you?"

"I wanted to thank you for taking care of my little problem. His usefulness was coming to an end anyway, and now it's done. Didn't expect that from you, but it's convenient, nonetheless. Maybe you will be of use to me beyond your business."

"You're sick."

"No, Miss Andrade, I'm sensible." He chuckled softly before continuing. "Your big banners are ready for delivery. Try not to kill any more of my men. Someone will have to replace them, and you don't want to know my choice."

The line went dead, and she sat there for several minutes, frustrated at her lack of control over anything. She just needed to get away from it all. But she couldn't even sit at the front desk without being watched. Overwhelmed as she spiraled, she quietly made her way through the gym, wiping the tears that sprang from her eyes.

Felix wasn't around right then, but she knew his two 'family' members were sparring in the ring, keeping an eye on her. She wondered if they were even related to Felix, or if they were just a part of his wolf pack. She couldn't tell, and maybe that's what frustrated her the most. How much of the world was she ignorant of? How could she live day to day, not knowing what was going to come tomorrow?

She thought she knew everything she needed to know, that she had her life planned out. She knew that her father needed her. She knew that her family was this whole community. People she loved but didn't let get too close because too close meant that it hurt beyond repair when they left. Knowing, especially knowing these things, took the hurt out of a lifetime of pain.

She pushed through the front door of her home, just as her father was headed out to the gym. "Sunshine, you okay?"

"I'm fine, Dad. I just need a second."

But he followed her as she headed inside the house, past Felix, who was now lying on the couch watching TV. She went straight to her room and closed the door, leaning up against it and sliding to the floor.

"Marti-bear? Tell me what's wrong."

Her father's voice was muffled through the door, and she picked at the fuzz on her shirt, her leg bouncing with anxiety.

"What's not wrong?" She laughed bitterly, leaning her head back against the door, unwilling to let her dad see the tears anymore. "Pennington called. He knows they're dead. Thinks I did it. So, at least Ajax is safe. Wanted to thank me for handling his loose ends. Then he made it clear that the tournament will still go on. Otherwise, he has no use for us anymore. We don't make him enough money, apparently. Not without *Ice*."

There was a pause. "I think there's a silver lining there. We know they know. We know what they want. Those are positives."

"Sure, Dad. Positives."

He moved away from the door hesitantly, and she could hear him exit the house, leaving only Felix in the living room. She didn't care anymore. Not about the danger or the rules. She wanted to sit on the beach, alone. She needed it.

Hopping up quickly, before she lost her nerve, she grabbed her bag, tossing it on her desk. She could sneak out the window and run down to the shore, just for an hour. They would never know. Goulden didn't care what she did, not as long as the tournament went on, and he needed her until then. He told her that. What did it matter what she did now?

It had been years since she tried to open that window. Hell, it might be painted shut at this point, so as she leaned over the desk, trying to pull it up, she realized she needed more leverage. She started to empty the clutter from her desk, so she could hop up on it, but when she threw the towel from her bathroom onto the floor, there was a gift box underneath.

She paused, frowning. *Where did this come from?* Almost garish in its coloring, the large, flat box was wrapped in a bright orange paper and green ribbon with a bright green bow on top. Turning it in her hands, there was no card, so she untied the ribbon and tore open the paper. Lifting the lid of the box, she stared hard, and it took her several moments to realize what was inside. Five leatherbound books were spread out over a soft purple towel, and her jaw dropped immediately.

She'd know those covers anywhere. Special collectors' editions of The Hitchhiker's Guide to the Galaxy. They were beautiful, velvety, with gold lettering and fully illustrated inside with color. As she moved the books, picking them up and setting them down excitedly, the embroidery on the towel caught her eye.

Large, with sci-fi-esque block lettering, it said, 'Don't Panic,' and underneath, there was a 42.

Snatching the envelope up, she flipped it over, stopping at the crudely drawn slice of Swiss cheese with a caption: '*Warning — extreme cheese inside.*'

Frantically, but carefully now, she opened it, unfolding the handwritten note with shaky hands.

"My Marti, it didn't take me 7.5 million years to figure out the meaning to my life. It's you. You are my 42. I hope that one day you will let me join you in this life, this journey around the galaxy with you, and whatever you do, don't forget your towel. Love, Thor and Mjölnir."

"Fuck. That's so cheesy. I love it so much." Tears began streaming down her face, and she sank into her mattress, letting herself ugly cry, unable to hide the happy sobs. How did such a scary, muscle-bound man get to be so perfect for her?

For a long time, she held the towel in her hand, her fingers running over the embroidery, imagining this unknown life, how it could possibly work. And even after hours of musing, she couldn't see it, but it didn't matter. Did she really need to?

By the time she stepped out of her room, it was past lunchtime, and she was starving. After splashing water on her face, trying to make it look like she hadn't been crying, she made her way to the kitchen where Felix stood in front of the microwave, popping some popcorn.

"Hey."

"Hey." She pulled out some of her hummus and toasted some pita bread, while chopping up an onion. She looked over at Felix's two cousins on her couch, chowing down on a pizza. "Anybody want a loaded hummus pita? It's yummy."

One of them made a face, and the other asked if there was meat on it. She sighed and looked at Felix. "You're telling me that it's not just a Felix thing? Do all of you wolf people eat like children?"

He shrugged and grinned. "Maybe you're the problem here."

She snorted, tossing her chopped onion, some olives and a sprinkle of feta onto her hummus covered pita bread. "And somehow, I'm the one with dimples in my ass, while the three of you could be made into bronze statues down in Balboa Park."

He looked up from pouring popcorn butter and half the shaker of salt into his bowl. "Good wolfy genetics does help." He leaned against the counter, dropping oily popcorn in his mouth while she cleaned up her mess.

"You still crying your life away in there?"

"You still being an ass?"

"As long as you continue not listening to reason."

Picking up her plate, she plopped down in the chair by the two new guys. They were mindlessly watching MTV music videos, and she couldn't help wondering where Ajax was right now. She knew she asked for space, but he said he wasn't going anywhere, and she hadn't seen him since yesterday morning.

Quietly, hoping Felix couldn't hear over the TV, she started up a conversation with the guys. "Gabe and Jessie, right? Thanks so much for helping me out. I never thought I'd be in this situation."

The older looking one nodded, sipping on a soda before answering her. "No worries. This is a welcome change from home. We don't get to sit around eating pizza and watching MTV. Our Alpha would shit a brick. This is a breeze."

"Well…good."

She waited a beat, finishing up her pita before asking. She glanced at Felix, seeing that he was digging through the fridge, not paying any attention to them. She didn't want to hear him gloat.

"Have you seen Ajax around? Is he over at the gym?"

"Oh, no. He's gone."

"Gone?" Her heart jumped to her throat, and her stomach clenched. No. He said he wouldn't leave her.

"Gone, gone. Hadn't seen him since we got here yesterday, no…Tuesday night. He packed up his stuff and gave us his room."

She dropped her plate on the table, and panic ran through her veins. The slamming of the refrigerator barely registered before Felix called out.

"He's not gone, gone. Don't listen to those two idiots." A handful of popcorn flew across the living room, raining down on Gabe and Jessie. "He was here yesterday, then slept on the floor outside your room. You were just holed up in bed by yourself. He left early this morning, right before you woke up. You told him to give you space, so that's what he is doing. You. Told. Him."

"How did you even hear that?" She frowned at Felix, but relief filled her, and she took a breath. "Is he coming back? Like tonight?"

"First, wolf hearing is almost as good as wolf smell. And second, that I don't know. He had some errands to do in LA before the fight. He didn't say when he'd be back. Maybe tonight, but probably by tomorrow at the latest."

Still holding the bowl of oily popcorn, he slid down over the arm of the chair where she was sitting, smushing his back against her shoulder. "Shit. How much do you weigh, Felix? You're breaking me." She pushed against him, but he didn't budge. Instead, he laughingly tried to feed her the popcorn.

"Why you asking about Ajax? You miss him? You want to kisssss him?"

She rolled her eyes and moved out of her seat, letting him fall backwards awkwardly. "Why did I ever become friends with you?"

"Don't be that way, Marti-tarty, life of the party. Come back! The guys would love to hear about our college days. Their parents are still trying to convince them to go. We need some more educated peoples in the pack."

"Then they wasted their money on you, didn't they?" She grinned, looking over at Gabe and Jessie. "You should go to college, but not because of any exaggerated stories told by Big Poppa over here."

Felix groaned as she walked out of the room, and she yelled back, "I'm taking a nap. Don't bother me with your shenanigans."

She shut the door amid a chorus of 'Big Poppa' teasings and moved quickly. Pennington needed her for the tournament, so he wouldn't try anything, and if he had already been watching her, then he knew about her spot anyway. She needed to get away and think, now more than ever. Her feelings for Ajax were jumbled, and she couldn't decide what to do, or how to make this better.

Thinking about Felix's fancy hearing abilities, she turned on the radio in her room, putting the smooth jazz on like she was going to sleep, and hoped the sound was enough to mask her window opening. Stepping up on the desk and stabbing the cracks of the windowsill with a metal nail file, she was able to slide it open. She stuffed her new towel in her bag, then dropped the bag out the window.

Last minute, she made her pillows look like she was under the covers, then scribbled a note.

"I'm not kidnapped. Just needed to get away for a minute to think without a babysitter. I'll be back soon."

Dropping it out of sight on her pillow, she crawled through her window and pulled it down as far as she could from the ground. Staying clear of any other open windows, she jogged to her car and headed to Black's Beach.

There was a small adrenaline rush, knowing something could go wrong, but she wasn't worried anymore, and the desire to daydream with her mom overrode any risk. Once she made her way down to her usual spot, she grinned as she used her new towel to sit on the ground. There were a couple of people here today, but not many, and they didn't bother her.

It was bright and sunny, the perfect temperature, and taking out her bookmark, she traced the memories of her mother, wondering what she would do, what she would tell her. What she heard instead was her father's voice.

"We knew, Sunshine. She had known she was sick for a while. But nothing would keep her from being happy, even for a short time. And she wanted you so badly, even for a short time. Me and you, Sunshine? We were her world."

No tears this time, and she spread herself out on the blanket, her cheek against the lettering, wondering where Ajax was at that moment. What he was doing, what he was thinking. Did he wonder how this would work too? Did he have doubts? Without meaning to, she fell asleep, dozing in and out, the sounds of the ocean comforting her until there were no sounds at all, and darkness had fallen.

In the silence, it was the sound of a boot hitting a nearby rock that had her jolting awake just in time to see the shadows play along the cliff near her, but she didn't actually see anyone. Shit.

Standing shakily, she called out, "Who's there?"

Straining to see into the moonlit darkness, the ocean barely visible, she studied every shadow, every movement until she was sure she had dreamed it. Just jitters getting to her. It was nothing.

Her heart had calmed until the moment she felt his arm close around her waist, yanking her backwards against a hard body. She screamed and pushed back, battling hard, but getting nowhere.

Chapter 19

Ajax

Thursday, October 3
Black's Beach

The sand moved softly under his feet, and even in the dark, he could see her laying in the sand, up against the cliff wall, and he sighed in relief. Despite seeing her car parked up on the street, he couldn't calm down until he had laid eyes on her. This was foolish, considering everything that had happened with the vampires, but what did he expect? She couldn't be locked up forever.

He knew she came here to be alone, so he was careful to leave her in peace and stick to the shadows, watching over her while she slept. He could see why she came here. It was hauntingly beautiful, a hidden gem compared to the hustle and bustle of the other San Diego beaches. But he'd almost lost his mind when he thought she was missing.

When he came back to her house, and they told him she was taking a nap in her room, he knew she had been gone awhile. Her scent was weak, and he was pissed they hadn't noticed. The fear and panic ran through him, and he'd practically pushed Felix through a wall when he found her room empty, before searching her room for clues.

As soon as he found the note, he knew.

On the beach, he stayed close enough he could hear her breathing if she called out, but far enough away, hidden in a crevice, that she couldn't see him. Once he was settled in his spot, and his wolf content with hearing her heartbeat, he waited silently, keeping watch until she was ready to be back home. Ideally, she would never know he was there.

Eventually, though, she must have sensed his presence, and in her sleep, he heard her call out his name and take a long shuddering breath. He battled whether to go to her, then took the chance when she stretched out, calling for him again. She had startled awake, confused, and looking around. But when she stood, afraid of the unknown presence, he couldn't help slipping behind her, pulling her close to him. She struggled for a second, screaming into the night.

"Shhh, it's me. It's just me. I'm here."

She gasped, wrapping her arms around him, burying her face in his chest before punching him in the stomach softly. "You scared me!"

He flinched. "Sorry. I was trying to let you be alone, but you tempted me in your sleep, little one."

Ajax thought she would pull away, put distance between them once she had calmed down, but instead she clutched him to her, rocking slightly. "I've missed you."

"Really?" Even he heard the surprise in his own voice.

"Is that so hard to believe?" She chuckled up at him, eyes twinkling, and more than anything, he was grateful to see her smile after everything. That one little gesture gave him hope.

"A little. If I was less confident of a man, I would have taken all your rejections to heart. I thought for sure you had at least five more in you."

"The night is young, sir."

"It is. Do you want me to go? I just wanted to make sure you were safe. I couldn't rest until I found you. That note was crap."

"No. Stay. I didn't mean to be here this long, but I fell asleep. Sit with me?"

"Anything."

"I opened your gift." She smoothed her hand across the embroidery in the towel they sat on, but kept her gaze averted. His heart leapt in his chest. Did she think it was too much? Was she afraid of everything it meant? Was it too soon? A million anxieties ran through his head, and he held his breath. He wasn't used to feeling anything but confident with everything he did. His whole life, he was taught that every decision he made was law, and he should consider it carefully. But Marti had broken down every part of him, and he didn't know how to handle any of it. Hell, everything he had done so far had backfired.

"I see that."

"Thank you. It's beyond amazing."

His eyes closed inadvertently, and he took a breath as relief flooded him.

She picked up his hand, squeezing his in hers, snuggling into his side to stare out at the waves, the crashing surf the only sound between them.

"Ajax? I'm…I think I'm just scared."

"Don't worry. Nothing will happen to you while I'm around."

"That's not what I mean."

She hesitated for a long moment, and he sensed she was working up the nerve for something, and his gut wrenched. Would she reject him again? Was this all too much for her? Bringing a human into their world was tough. But he stayed silent.

"I've been scared my whole life, even more so since I gave a relationship a try, and it crashed and burned. I know it sounds unreasonable, but I've always been afraid that I will end up like my mom, dying early and leaving people behind to hurt. That getting attached to anyone would be a waste, that I'd be a problem, a burden, that I'd just cause someone else pain. I'd convinced myself, if I was going to be in pain, then I would be in pain alone." She paused, pulling her knees to her chest like she needed to protect herself. "But every moment I've spent with you made me want more. More you, more life. And that scares me."

She shook her head, unsure of herself, and he knew not to speak, knew that she was working on her decision, but hoped she could give him…no, give them…a chance.

"I thought I could get you out of my system, keep you at an emotional arm's length and just have fun in the moment. But you make that impossible. You're so perfect for me, and I can't believe I've spent so much of my life without you." She laughed. "And too many days this week fighting against you. I should have known. You're undefeated, right?"

Hope sprung in his chest, and the roar in his head was only matched by the howling of his wolf. "Marti, what are you saying? I need to hear it. Please."

"Ajax…I'm in. I've fallen in love with you, and I want to spend the rest of my life figuring this out. With every fiber of my being, I want this to work. Teach me how."

"There's nothing to teach. Everything about you, every piece of you, is already perfect for me."

She giggled, the sound like music to his ears. "I asked Felix for a handbook on wolves. I have a lot to learn."

"He told you?"

"Yeah, he gave me a hard time, basically reminding me I was being unreasonable, and then showed me his wolf. That was wild."

"Less scary than mine, I assume."

"Yes, but that was my fault. You told me."

He shook his head. "Once my beast calms down, I'll shift fully for you, and you'll love him. Just right now, I've been getting stuck as my wolf for days at a time before he relaxes enough for me to shift back. I didn't want to chance getting stuck right now. And my inner fight with him isn't pretty."

"So, what's next? What do we do?"

"Whatever you want. I'll follow you to the ends of the Earth."

"No, I mean, how do we make this official? I don't want you changing your mind on me and escaping my evil clutches."

Gently, he cupped her chin in his hand, forcing her to look at him. "You're not the villain in our story, Marti. You're my savior, my partner, my everything."

He felt frozen, like he couldn't breathe now that she had finally said yes, and he stared into her eyes, lost in their richness and their warmth. She was the one who finally moved, rising to her knees to kiss him softly, hesitantly, straddling his lap and threading her fingers through his hair.

Running his hands along the back of her thighs, then stopping to cup her ass, he let her take charge for a moment, savoring the feeling of her choosing him. She was kind and gentle, so opposite of his own violent and ruthless past. So, when she broke their kiss to place a soft peck on each of his eyes, then his nose, he momentarily felt worried that he would break her or be too rough with her.

He'd never allowed his experiences with human women to be as wild as with wolves—they were more delicate, breakable. But even as he let her touch him freely, letting her explore and be comfortable with her decision, he felt more at ease with her. Like he didn't need to hold back for Marti. He wouldn't doubt fate. He wouldn't wonder what she could handle; he already knew how tough she was.

"I love every inch of you, Ajax, and every time I think I've picked a sliver to call the best, another part of you calls to me."

She worked her way down his neck, and when she tugged on his shirt, he quickly ripped it off, giving her whatever access she wanted.

"Funny, I thought Mjölnir would hold a special part of your heart."

"There are definitely several parts of me who want to hold him close. My mouth for one."

He groaned, the soft heat of her lips moving down his chest, over the slopes of his stomach, then stopping to tug on the waistband of his jeans. She looked up at him, softly trailing her fingers along the outline of his cock, before unbuttoning and unzipping his jeans confidently.

He lifted his hips, letting her pull his jeans and underwear down and off. Tossed into the darkness of the sand, he could only concentrate on her mouth moving up his thigh, and when he groaned, gripping her hair to direct her, she resisted, stopping to lick, then suck and nip at the sensitive insides of his thighs.

"Fuck, little one. You're killing me. Let me taste you. I want to make you feel good."

"Not yet. I'm in charge right now. You'll get your turn." Her breath whispered along the side of his shaft, and when he felt her tongue graze him, he jerked forward. Then her mouth slid over the head, tongue swirling, and he broke out in a sweat, clenching to keep from coming all over her pretty little mouth.

Gritting his teeth, he tugged on her hair as she worked her mouth and hands up and down his dick. Drool dripped from her lips, and when she moaned her own pleasure, the vibrations did him in. He couldn't wait anymore.

"My turn."

He pulled her away from him, and pressing her backwards onto the towel, he held her hands above her head and covered her body with his. He nestled his face into the crook of her neck, inhaling her scent, sucking on the sensitive skin of her shoulder, before pulling back when she whimpered with need, and his wolf responded eagerly in an attempt to mark her. Not yet. His beast could wait a few more minutes.

"Off. All of it off. I want to see every inch of you." Releasing her hands, he pulled her shirt up, and she could barely get it off before the material of her bra stopped him. Impatiently, he grabbed the front and ripped it apart from the middle, tossing it aside so he could admire his mate's perfection.

Her breasts, big enough to spill over in his large hands, begged for his attention, and he ached to taste every inch of her silky soft skin. With a groan, he stroked the dusky brown nipples, and they hardened under his thumb, coming alive at his touch. Working his way down her throat and chest with his mouth, he slowed as she arched, capturing her nipple in his mouth, sucking gently before nipping hard enough to elicit a soft plea in between her moans.

"Mine."

When he sank back between her legs and yanked her leggings off, she took over where he stopped, bringing her hands to her own chest, massaging and pinching her nipples. But he pulled her knuckles to his mouth, away from her body, then kissed each finger tenderly, locking eyes with her.

"Mine."

Then, he put her hands to his chest, leaning forward to loom over her and brush his lips to hers, lightly tracing the curves with his tongue.

"Mine."

And when he slid his length along the slit of her pussy, and she cried out, bucking upwards, he growled.

"All mine."

She clutched at him, and he rocked, letting the tip of his cock push against her clit over and over before pulling back.

"Say it, little one. Who do you belong to?"

"You." She breathed the word, almost silently, lost in the moment.

"Who?"

"You. Ajax." His name was barely more than a groan on her lips, but it was everything to him, and he smiled. She remembered.

His hand skimmed downward, his fingers sliding along her wetness and sinking into her pussy, while his thumb circled her clit leisurely. Pushing his fingers inside of her, he curled upwards, searching for just the right spot, and the faint scream while she bucked against his hand had him smirking.

Taking his time, he set a slow pace and watched her face, watched as she dug her nails into the sand and writhed against him, watched as she bit her lip and called his name. He didn't move faster, only increased, then decreased the pressure, letting her desperation build, savoring the sounds of her begging and moaning. Her tiny sighs and slight humming fascinated him, and he realized he would have the rest of their lives to hear them, to explore all the noises she would make for him. She deserved more than he could give her, and he would take his time to make sure she remembered who she belonged to.

"Mmmh. That's what I want to hear. And what do you want right now?"

"Please, I want to come. More, more, more…please."

"You're beautiful when you beg, little one."

She pulled her knees to her chest as her stomach contracted, and the trembling in her thighs told him everything he needed to know before she drenched his hand. Her pants of need turned to a wail, and she came long and hard, pulsing slightly against his palm. When she was limp and panting, he pulled his fingers from her pussy, slowly and softly continuing to stroke her oversensitive clit, and moved backward. Sliding down to his stomach and wrapping one arm around her thigh to lay his palm on her lower belly, he applied pressure.

"Not good enough. I want everything you got. I want the people in the houses at the top of the cliffs to hear you scream. I want you to shatter over and over until you can no longer walk, and then I will carry you."

Excruciatingly slow, he laid his cheek against her inner thigh and softly kissed before lazily trailing one finger around that sensitive bundle of nerves. He would take his time, and she could come over and over for him until she begged for a break, and then he would keep going. There was nothing holding him back from worshipping her like she deserved anymore, and that started now.

"Ajax?"

Her soft, tired mewling filled the silence, and he settled in, blowing out cold air softly before letting his hot mouth close over her clit, replacing his finger. Her gasp urged him on, and his tongue played over her, lapping up every inch, and soon she was begging again.

"So much. So, so much. I need you. I need you to fuck me, Ajax, now. Oh. My. God."

Her raspy pleas were accompanied by her fingers raking through his hair, pulling the roots, trying to yank him from between her thighs. Not yet, no, she would know what to expect from him, know what she deserved the rest of her life.

Ignoring her desperate pleading, he slid his fingers inside of her again, joining with the rhythm of his tongue, and lifted his gaze to her face. Her brows were furrowed, and she bit her lip just as she locked eyes with him, and he slowed his pace to extend her pleasure even more. She threw her head back, groaning in frustration as she arched, and he watched her chest rise and fall raggedly when he finally pulled away.

"I can't taste you enough, little one. I want you to come in my mouth so that I'll never forget the taste, and then, when you've begged enough, and when I've decided you've been properly worshipped, I will let you come on my cock. Only then will I mark you, claiming you forever, when every part of your body has been satisfied, and you know there will never be anyone else for you."

Gently, he let the stubble on his face graze her sensitive inner thigh as he spoke, teasing her with the sensation even as he slid one finger in and out of her. Until he decided it was enough. Then, and only then, did he give in to her delicate moans for more. Flattening his tongue against her clit, he let the thickness of it slide gracefully, naturally as she jerked upwards, fucking his mouth in short, hungry bursts. Her growing wetness coated his face, dripping down her thighs, so he buried his face in her pussy, pushing down from her stomach, pumping inward with his fingers, and sucking until she sobbed in pleasure.

Her nails slid up his shoulders, digging into his biceps, as she gripped his arms, the tinge of pain only spurring him on, and he worked his lips and tongue until she had come again, her shaking thighs a sign of more to come. Her screams barely registered, and only when she laid there limp and unresponsive did he let up, allowing the last orgasm to fade.

With this small respite, he raised himself to her body, kissing and capturing her lips while she could barely move, barely open her eyes to look at him.

"You are the fucking devil, Ajax, a wicked, wicked devil."

Languidly brushing the backs of his knuckles down her breast and back up again as she caught her breath, he drank in every aspect of her body, every curve and sensitive inch of her skin. When he traced his thumb along her jawline, then up to her lips, dragging her lower lip down for just a second, before pushing it into her mouth, he couldn't help but picture those lips wrapped around him, the heart-shaped cupid's bow and full bottom lip stretched wide. Reflexively, her lips closed around his thumb, sucking hungrily, and he paused, letting the sensation shoot straight to his dick before he slid his arm underneath her body, flipping her and pulling her ass flush against him.

The aggressive movement surprised her, and he pulled them both to their knees, then to their feet, sliding his hand to her throat, pushing her neck back against his shoulder, and exposing her to his mouth. He held them both still, only his lips moving ever so slightly against her ear, and his hand slowly tightening around her neck before he released his hold gently.

"If I'm the devil, then you'll learn to live in this hell with me. You'll like it, beg for it, need it, and I'll give you things you didn't even know you needed. Now grab the wall."

She whimpered, but he could see her excitement, feel it in the way she pushed her ass against his cock, straining for him even as she reached out to lean against the cliff.

"That's my girl."

He nudged her knees apart, and guiding his cock, let it slide against her clit slowly, glorying in the feel of her against his length until she was panting again, reaching behind her desperately to feel him, but he pulled away.

"Grab the wall until I tell you."

Immediately, she put her hands back on the cliff face, but her nails clawed into the dirt, and she arched for more.

"Ajax...I can't take anymore teasing."

He leaned forward, placing his hands alongside hers so he could whisper in her ear, "You'll be taking much more soon, save your begging for the devil."

He sat back, resting on his haunches to get a good look at her delightful ass. Thick and round, much more than a handful, he reveled in the sight before gripping her thighs, sliding up to cup her asscheeks before squeezing them apart. He knelt to get one more taste, burying his tongue into her pussy from behind, mimicking the thrusts that would come soon enough. She pushed against him, begging for more, so he pulled his hand back and slapped her ass hard enough to leave a mark. Her tiny shriek turned into a moan when he massaged it roughly, then repeated.

Every slap of her ass, he could taste how much wetter she was getting, how much she needed for him to fuck her, and he savored it.

"You want me to stop, little one?" He switched cheeks this time, the slap inciting tiny little clenches in her body.

"No. Yes. Fuck. Oh, God, that feels so good, but I need you. Please—"

Slap.

"I didn't think so." Again, he slipped his fingers inside of her. One, two, three this time to make sure she was ready for him. "Tell me exactly what you want now."

She swallowed noticeably, gathering confidence before rocking back towards him. "For the love of all that is holy, please fuck me. I want Mjölnir deep inside me, hard and fast, and don't stop."

Releasing a deep, pent-up breath, he growled as he maintained control of his beast. He strained to treat her with any small amount of gentleness, the wolf in him wanting to take what was his, roughly, without regret. Pushing into her tight pussy inch by inch, and gripping her hips in his hand, he grit his teeth at the sensation of his mate clenched around his cock.

His thrusts slow, deliberate and torturous for both of them, he worked to build her pleasure yet again. "Like this, little one?"

"More, fuck. Just more everything."

"Your pleasure is the Devil's command."

Her long, dark braid slid down her back when she tossed her head to look back towards him, and he grabbed it, wrapping it around his wrist before he forced her to arch just as he slammed into her. His own breath ragged, he held onto her hip with his other hand, driving inside of her mercilessly. Over and over, he pushed her depth to the max, and he could hear the trembling in her moans.

"Yes, fuck me, fuck, fuck, fuck."

This time, he released her braid, both of them dropping to their knees, and pushing her face into the sand, he yanked her ass up high, the bright red in her tanned cheeks making his heart race. He pushed deeper, one hand reaching around to put pressure on her clit for only a few seconds. She screamed into the sand and tightened around his cock as she came from the small touch, but he didn't pause. No, she had more in her.

Instead, he picked her up, flipping her to face him like a rag doll, and stood while she rode the waves of her orgasm. Her back against the cliff, she wrapped her legs around his waist and arms around his neck, and she murmured wearily against his throat.

"No more…too much."

"No such thing, little one." He kissed her long and hard, and cradling her ass in one hand, he slid back inside of her. She gripped him involuntarily, taking his girth one more time, and he leaned her backwards so he could look at her as he fucked her, so he could see his cock slide in and out of her soaked pussy, and heat surged through him at the sight.

"Still so wet, you've got one more for me, don't give up. Give it to me."

With both her knees hooked over his elbows, he fucked her hard and fast this time, and when he felt himself getting closer, and his canines extended to mark her, he groaned loudly.

"Touch yourself. Let me see that beautiful pussy between your fingers. Don't stop until I say."

Her breathing was rapid, and she was almost sobbing, but with one hand hooked around his neck, she slid the other between them. He watched her fingers play across her clit, circling frantically to the beat of his thrusts, and she cried out with her climax.

"Don't stop. Keep going, make it last. Come with me, Martina Andrade Blackwolf."

One last time, he thrust and emptied into her as his wolf surfaced. Pushing away from the wall, he wrapped his arms around her back, pulling her tight, and sinking his teeth into the crevice of her neck. Everything inside his body exploded, and he sank to his knees still inside of her.

Magic streaked across his body, the molten fire of their blood mixing and spreading throughout them both an experience that was comforting and exhilarating all at once. She was his. He was hers. Entwined together forever.

Everything about the moment was more than he could ever imagine, and judging by the way Marti's head dropped back, her fingers digging into his back, her low, guttural wail filling the air, he knew the sweeping shifter magic was overwhelming her as well.

Gently, his canines retracted, and he licked and healed the bite on her neck before laying her on the sand and collapsing on top of her. Everything in his body felt complete, satiated, and loved. His wolf purred with happiness.

His mate lay under him, eyes closed in exhaustion and little strands of hair plastered to her brow with sweat. He knew he was heavy, and he tried not to lay his full weight on her, but for once, he couldn't move, shouldn't move, like his weight belonged there.

After a few minutes, she whispered in his ear. "I hope no one tries to attack us right now. We would both be useless."

"I'd rally. I think." He licked his lips, taking a deep breath and rolling off of her into the sand. Neither of them ended up on the towel, but they didn't care. It was the middle of the night, and they were lying on a beautiful beach with no one near them.

And she was his. Forever.

"Ajax?"

"Yes, little one?"

"You made me sweat."

He chuckled. "Yes, I did. And it won't be the last time."

She groaned loudly. "I think I'm going to have to add exceptions to my rule."

Chapter 20

Ajax

Friday, October 4
El Luchador Gym

"Close your eyes. Blank everything out, the sounds, the lights, your thoughts…everything."

"You don't know how hard that is. The inside of my head has always been a circus, just a bunch of monkeys and chitter chatter. Then on top of it, I can freaking FEEL you now. I could barely keep my dirty little thoughts under wraps all week just with you around. But now, you're living in my head, and you smell so good, and—"

"Little one."

She cracked her eyes at his playful censure, then grinned. "Sorry. I can't help it. This is so cool and exciting all at once. I'm gonna try harder."

"Do I need to go to the other side of the room?"

"No." Her eyes flew open at that suggestion, and she grabbed his wrist. They lay on their backs, side by side in the main sparring ring, their legs dangling over the sides as they took a break from all the preparations she needed to do. "No more rambling."

He couldn't help smirking as she squeezed her eyes shut, but refused to let go of her hand. "So, blank your mind, no overthinking. And then, quickly, picture me."

"Do you have to be clothed when I picture you?"

His snort was met by her giggles, but then…

"Or maybe just shirtless."

"Whatever works."

She gasped and sat up, squeezing his wrist in excitement. "I did it!"

"Now, do it again."

Marti grinned ear to ear, but closed her eyes again and leaned back, but this time, her eyebrows scrunched in concentration. *"Can we do it in this ring after the gym closes tonight?"*

"I will fuck you anywhere you want, as often as you want."

A grin spread across her face, but her eyes didn't open this time. *"This is so wild. And we can speak like this anytime? Anywhere?"*

"There's no specific mind link range, but the further apart we are, the harder it is. Should work up to like twenty or thirty miles. More because of the strength of my wolf, but less because you don't have one."

"This is re-donk-ulous. Can you speak to Felix like this?"

"Only if we're linked by the same Alpha."

"So, if you were a part of his pack, I could link him?"

"Yes, theoretically. My shifter blood magic runs through you now."

"Theoretically? What does that mean?" Her eyes were open, and she furrowed her brows in confusion.

He sat up, stretching his back and leaning forward onto the rope. "It means that we haven't really had a human mate in my pack before, so my knowledge isn't first-hand."

"Never? Like there's never been a human mate to a wolf?" She slid down to the floor, tightening the straps of her flowy sunflower jumpsuit. Underneath that, the stark white of her tube top contrasted sharply with the deep tan of her skin, and he paused for a second, forgetting what she asked. But she sounded panicked for a moment, so he snapped back to reality.

"Just in my pack. Felix says it's more common than I know."

"Why not yours?"

He ignored her question, realizing they'd strayed away from his goal. He needed her to understand how to mindlink him, how to call for his help, and how to read the emotions that would flow between them freely now that they were marked. "Did you feel that connection when we linked? Like there's a string in your brain that leads to me?"

"Oh, um. Kinda. Felt like gelatin was thickening in one spot, then fading away. Like a throbbing and waning."

"Good. And you said you could feel me. How did it feel?"

"Weird?"

"I mean, could you interpret my emotions?" She looked at him quizzically and hesitated, so he tried to explain it a little better. "Across the board, supernaturals' magic is supposed to be balanced. Every group has something that makes them stronger than the other, but then also weaker. I can't wield magic or control nature, but I have healing abilities, superior physical strength, fighting skills, and an ability to shift into an animal that has even more heightened senses. So, with strangers, I can feel their general emotions, their aura, and sometimes their intentions to an extent. It's intuitive, like an animal. But our greatest strength is in having a connection to others, more specifically, a fated mate. Where humans, witches, even fae, can often be fooled into loving the wrong person, or ruining relationships with a lack of understanding and communications, we are given our fate on a platter. As mates, we can sense each other's emotions and love. We can communicate and be in sync. Our mates are our greatest strength. We love hard."

"So, you're saying you'll know every little thought…"

"As in, I can tell when you're feeling angry, sad, curious…frisky." He winked at her, and she turned a little red. "It has some nice benefits."

"Oh…so, that isn't just me feeling that way."

"Is it coming through that string in your mind?"

"Yes?"

"How about now?" He found the connection between them, where it had been flowing freely, then cut it off. He shut it down and shut her out, making it where she couldn't feel him, couldn't hear him, and would have no access to him.

"I don't like that. Stop it." Panic filled her eyes, and she stepped forward between his legs, her hands sliding up his chest desperately.

"But you feel it now?" He opened the connection again, letting it strengthen and flow.

"Yes. Shit. Okay, so I get it. I had just gotten so used to you being around, I hadn't noticed how you wormed your way into my head." She leaned her head against his shoulder, relaxing into him. "So, why would someone cut it off like that?"

"Protection. Distraction. Anger. Pettiness. Take your pick. Just because we're mates doesn't mean we won't argue. We won't always agree. My father often pissed my mother off with his decisions, and real quick, she'd cut him off." He hopped down from the ring, grabbing her hand and walking across the floor of the gym. They'd taken a break, but he knew they had a shit ton of things to do before tomorrow. "I remember once, he had refused one of the pack members' requests to go to college, saying he didn't need any more lawyers right now. Told him to go work the ranch instead. I was only ten at the time, but when that guy came out of my father's office, he was devastated. As Luna of the pack, my mother's abilities were tied to pack emotions. She felt the whole pack on a deeper level. She marched right into my father's office and told him to fix it. He refused, told her he knew what was best for the pack. By the time she'd made it back downstairs, she'd cut their connection, refused to speak with him, and disappeared into the night on a run somewhere."

"Oh, wow. And then?"

"He tore up the whole pack looking for her. Stormed homes of her friends, busted up a stable in the south pasture, and then ran the pack lands in wolf form until he could sniff her out."

"Why wouldn't he just wait till she'd calmed down?"

"That's not how it works for an Alpha, for any wolf, really. Our mates are our lives. To lose them in any way will make a wolf feral."

"Feral? Huh. Feral for love. It's poetic."

"What I'm saying is, I need you to practice shutting it off. And practice figuring out my emotions. That's how we strengthen our relationship, how we get closer. It's our form of communication."

"Right now?"

"Yes. How about this…I'll hang all these banners for you. You just stand there and look pretty, maybe hand me a hammer or a nail once in a while and focus on reading my emotions and mindlinking me."

"Deal."

They'd already unfolded the big banners that had been delivered, laying them out flat to get the creases out, and now, he hefted one over his shoulder and moved towards the big wall.

"I like watching you lift things."

Her voice rang in his head, and he paused, glancing back at her with one eyebrow lifted. *"Why is that?"*

"Same reason I like walking behind you. The view. And also…your emotion is amusement right now. You think I'm funny."

"Too easy. That's obvious without the connection."

"You didn't answer my question from earlier."

He lifted the corner of the banner over his head, then took the hammer and nail from her, tapping it in easily. "Which one?"

"Why doesn't your pack have human mates?"

Immediately, he missed the way her voice sounded in his head, but this was better. She needed to be able to feel their connection without him making it obvious.

"My father, my grandfather, his before him…they've never allowed humans in the pack. Never really allowed us to go outside our pack at all. Not unless you were given a specific job or education for that job."

"Anger. You're feeling anger suddenly…but in other packs, it's normal?"

"Not quite anger. Annoyance because it reminds me of everything that happened before I left." He let silence fill the space between them, but she was right. He had an unreasonable amount of anger in him towards his father's refusal to let him leave. "Okay, maybe anger. To an extent, yes. Many packs allow their younger generations to run around, go to college, get human jobs, find their mates, then come back home with them before they settle into roles they are given. Like Felix."

"I see." But the hesitation in her voice meant she didn't. The lore of his family, their existence, had grown and morphed into a legendary thing because of their secrets, because of the ruthless alliances they'd made that had shut all others out.

It had become the way of their people, the consequence of survival, and then their success.

"Five generations ago, my ancestor, a female born of alpha blood on one side and traces of witch blood on the other, was freed from slavery by her father, the plantation owner's son. Or, rather...she escaped this southern pack's plantation with his encouragement, his land, and his money. Her name was Rosalie." He paused, the memories flooding back, and he relived the moments when his own grandmother had told him and his brother the tale when they were young.

"So, she was a slave..."

"Yes. He sent her with a handful of paperwork—dozens of land grants for Texas that he had procured, that he'd planned on using when he ran away with her mama. But there was an incident...her father's plans were discovered, and her mother was killed in front of them both by her grandfather, then her father punished by his own father." He couldn't encapsulate the fear, the danger, the risk that his greatest-grandmother had taken six generations ago, not the way it was told to him. But he could try. "She was only seventeen, and with crude instructions from her father, and that coveted stack of paperwork, she gathered a few dozen other shifter slaves, ones who she'd been secretly rallying. Shifter wolves whose family had long been a part of that pack, a part of that farm, or even the city, but had been born of African blood lines. Generations of wolves, born into slavery in that very pack, supernatural people who'd never known freedom. They joined her...and she ran."

"I can't imagine. In the 1800s? I'm no history major, but that was..."

"Dangerous." He wished he could laugh at how his brother considered what he'd done dangerous—how Axel had said his running off for a year could have jeopardized everything they'd worked for. It was nothing in comparison. "It was a risk, but our Moon Goddess was on her side. These grown men and women followed her, their new Alpha, as she traveled through Louisiana, then to South Texas. And she'd almost made it. Just a couple of weeks before reaching her destination, she ran into a battle.

One that was taking place between the Austin Colony settlers and our people."

"Our people? I'm confused. She—"

"Our Native American people. Indigenous people who'd called these lands home for thousands of years."

"They were shifters too? How common is it to be a wolf in this country?"

"Not as much as it used to be. Back then…wolf shifters were originally created as sacred protectors of tribes, treated as part of them, yet a separate hierarchy of supernatural people respected for who they were. Mostly, they belonged to themselves, and yet, found homes with human tribes of Indigenous Peoples. They were an open part of the world before Europeans came. When the European explorers began pushing west, giving Native people no choice, some readily assimilated into the cities, passing for Europeans and even lured by farms, money, power, into new ways of life. Like Rosalie's great-grandparents on her father's side. But then, their existence was forced to become a secret, a hidden weapon, and they became a supernatural set of people that some believed in, and some didn't. Eventually, we were dismissed as just a part of indigenous mythology."

"That's…wow. It makes so much sense. I've always thought about all the mythologies in the world, how myths had to come from somewhere, with some truths." She stared off in silence for a moment, then frowned quizzically. "Wait…so they were battling the settlers? And she came up on them. You're gonna tell me she joined the fight, they won, and she fell madly in love with one of them. It has to be. That's how all good books end." Then she took back the hammer as he lifted the next banner to another wall. "And sadness? Nostalgia? That's what I'm getting when you tell the story. Am I right?"

"Getting better." He chuckled at her excitement, then continued his story. "Rosalie and her little pack shifted into their wolves, fought alongside them, killing the settlers who'd attacked. And in short, yes. Legend is that she saved his life during the battle. Her mate was the Alpha of the wolves, Calian. But they weren't exactly happy about that."

"I thought fated mates saw each other and fell desperately in love every time. I mean…I did." Her grin was endearing, and she pushed her glasses up her nose, a subconscious part of her that he loved.

She held the other end of the banner for him, standing on her tippy toes on top of a stool as he considered her question. "Well…most of the time, yes. But remember that Alpha wolves, especially when they already run their own packs, are territorial, aggressive, and maybe a little bit…"

"Arrogant? I see it."

"Wow. I'm hurt."

"You can't pretend it's not true. You're, for sure, full of yourself. That's the number one emotion I get ninety-nine percent of the time."

"Which is why neither of them could agree on anything, and neither of them wanted to give up their power, especially Rosalie. She'd gone through so much, and she already had a plan in place."

"But they figured it out, and they came together. So, happy ending?"

"Eventually, she convinced both the human part of the tribe, as well as the shifter pack, to follow her to a new life, one that wasn't nomadic and dangerous amongst the constant push by the government to settle and tame the lands. She envisioned land and a private world she could make her own, where no one could enter or take anything away from her. A world where they would not only be safe but thrive and be successful. She was determined. And despite Calian's constant stubbornness to just stay hidden, she knew they'd need to play the game. That meant building businesses and selling to the people in the colonies and to the government. She had an eye for business, like her father."

"So, Calian didn't want to deal with the white people."

"Said it was dangerous." When Marti lifted an eyebrow, he laughed.

"Come on. He may not have been wrong at that time. And now, you're feeling proud…of Rosalie or Calian, I can't tell which. Go on."

"That's when the witches showed up. A couple years into claiming the land, parceling it out among families, trying to file that paperwork and get by unnoticed, then struggling to make business moves in a world that only saw both of them as disposable savages, they were desperate for a solution. They needed a façade that would work for them in the new world, especially since those were the years that the US annexed Texas as a state. There wasn't exactly an acceptance of our people by the government. Now, the alliances between Black and Native Americans, it was natural. We shared traumas and experiences, and our people mixed well. Rosalie and Calian combined packs, ruling equally, as Tuisa— meaning two Black Wolves in our language."

"That's so beautiful. Tuisa Ranch? I've heard of them. Everyone has, especially in the human world. How? And you are a part of that history? That is what you have to live up to?"

"My full name is Ajax Blackwolf. Direct descendant. But I wouldn't be here, and we wouldn't have become who we are without Rosalie's determination, and a little help. The real turn came when the witches showed up. It was fate. Rathlin Coven, long considered the origins and source of all witch magic, had left their stronghold on Rathlin Island in Ireland, at the height of the potato famine, looking for a new home, a new place to protect the Daughters of Danu, their Goddess's line of descendants and peacemakers of all Children of Danu. And they washed up on the shores of Texas."

"Oooooh, and an alliance was born. I love these things. I only read about stories like this, in history or in fiction books…but hearing it passed down from generation to generation, it gives me goosebumps."

"The witches needed a new start, land, a way to survive economically, socially…and they found the shifters. An alliance that would benefit them both. They stood in as their partners, used their magic to influence government officials, other ranchers, and even their customers. Suddenly, Tuisa became a name, and not just a Black woman or a Native man. No longer were the prejudices of the world holding them back. And they flourished. People were begging to do business with their cattle, and then the horses they bred quickly became the best in the business."

"But at a price."

"Yes. My family has never trusted humans since. We move cloaked in our business name, never having to truly leave our lands, staying safe within our borders. A whole city trapped in time."

"Do you have…electricity and stuff?"

"Of course. I don't mean trapped technology wise…just tradition wise. Men and women have their roles, and everyone is born into what they're expected to do their whole life. We mate within our pack, sometimes within Rathlin, maybe from other local Texas packs in the past, but that's it. We don't leave, especially lately."

"But you left."

He'd been focused, making sure the last of the banners were hung in just the right spot, but now his eyes found hers. "I knew I couldn't stay. Something told me to leave. It felt right. If I hadn't left, I'd have never found my mate, never found the person who will continuously remind me when I'm wrong or arrogant. I wouldn't have found the woman who made me want to be better, be different than the Alphas before me. I would have grown bitter and angry, and I wouldn't have lasted long in this world."

"You would have been fine."

"No. This was our destiny, our fate. I believe this is the exact moment you needed me, and I needed you. There are bigger things out there and every choice we make leads us to something we are meant to be and meant to do."

"You believe that. With every bit of your heart. I feel it." She pressed two fingers into her chest, rubbing just above her heart, but a worried expression filled her face. "Something is about to happen, isn't it? Something big?"

He hadn't wanted to tell her everything, hadn't wanted for her to know the extent of the vampire infestation in this city, and he especially hadn't wanted her to know that she was too embroiled in it to walk away. He'd have to kill them, and she wouldn't like that. Turning away, he tried to change the subject. "What else can I do? You need these tables moved?"

"You're hiding something. Ajax. You can't shut me out. You literally just said that."

He dragged a table over, popping it up before turning to her. "Wednesday and yesterday? When I was gone all day? I followed the vamps around. Checked out their nest, watched their movements. There are more than both Felix and I thought there were. And they have something brewing too. Lots of vampires coming in from the airport, and even in the daytime, they had people going in and out."

"Shit. You think they're coming here for the fight? You know they insisted on you being here. Maybe you shouldn't show up."

He shook his head, staring into her concerned face. Slowly, he ran his fingers down her braid, playing with the end before letting it drop back to her chest. "I have a feeling there are some transplants from Houston in there. Some of the higher-ups, the older vamps who must have gotten away during the final battles. So, yeah. They're here for me. Either revenge or leverage against Tuisa. Whatever it is, we are going to be ready. I've called in some back-up, and they will be here tomorrow before the tournament."

"Back-up? For what exactly?"

"I can't let anything happen to you. And to prevent that, we will eliminate the threat."

"Eliminate? Why are you speaking in code? Why do I feel your fear?"

He grit his teeth. "I'm afraid you'll get hurt. I wish more than anything I could send you away. Send you somewhere to keep you safe."

"Like hell—"

"But I won't." He grabbed both her hands, feeling the warmth of them in his. "I won't because I know it would upset you. I'm trying to make this happen without involving you."

"That's stupid. I need to know, and I need to be able to help."

"You're helping by just being you. If you do anything different than you normally would, then they will know something is happening. I have a feeling they will make a move on me either after the tournament, or during my fight. I'm wondering why you know nothing about the contender they're sending."

"You're telling me they will try to kill you?"

"Maybe, maybe not. I'm not going to let them."

She yanked her hands from his grasp and stepped back. "You're serious right now. I'm not letting them kill you."

"I'm not going to let them either."

"But you're using yourself as bait. No. I won't let you."

"Trust me, it will be fine. I've taken care of my fair share of vampires. They're not strong, or very smart. Just fast. And that's why I've arranged back-up. Even Felix's pack is sending dozens of shifters to help. I just don't think they will make a move while all the humans are here. They will hold their cards close because they don't like humans, and they don't like them knowing what they're up to."

"How can you be sure?"

"I spent a lot of time living amongst them, seeing the way they operate, how their ranking systems work. They follow the oldest, the strongest, the most powerful. They crave direction, and the older ones have formed networks across the country, sharing and selling information and opportunity. When one nest leader dies, it goes to the next oldest. But especially, if a leader can't advance the nest's access to power and wealth, they will kill him themself. Despite their shared interests, they have no loyalty. So, whether for revenge or money, I am their target. But it is better for them to target me than you, because I will be ready. We all will be when they make their move. It will be after the fight, or the next day. I can feel it. Something's brewing at their nest."

"All of these things are just guesses. Wildly random guesses. You can't be sure of anything."

"Educated guesses. I've killed more than a thousand vampires in my lifetime. I spent a year spying on nests, watching their movements, learning everything about them. Trust me. We have a plan."

"We? Who is we?"

Fear coursed through her and across the bond, and he desperately wanted to make it all better, but nothing he could say would work. "I've been in contact with Felix's Alpha—he is sending a whole troop of shifters to help. More importantly, witches from Rathlin are coming. They are unbeatable. By themselves, they can handle a room of them easily. And if they don't make a move tomorrow night, we will be getting the whole nest the next day. I have a plan."

Tears filled her eyes, despite her trying to blink them away. "I can't lose you."

He pulled her in close, letting her bury her face in his chest. "You won't."

Chapter 21

Marti

Saturday, October 5
El Luchador Gym

"And now, the fight you've all been waiting for, our headliner and up-and-coming UFC fighter, known for his vicious, cold, and ruthless fighting style, the undefeated and unmatched, Ice!"

Her heart pounded in her chest so hard, she barely noticed the roar of the crowd as Ajax stepped into the fighting ring. She stared at every angle of his face, shadows playing across the bronze of his complexion as he stared down his challenger. The glow of the spotlights played across the muscles in his back, the slight sheen of sweat shining tauntingly across every muscle. Between the set of his jaw and his flashing green eyes, he looked dangerous, formidable, and extremely hot.

"His challenger, a hotheaded youngblood from Colorado, the Bull from the Rockies, Taurus!"

Ajax's opponent was huge, just as tall as him, but looked heavier, thicker, like a wrestler. The man smirked like he was hiding something, and it pissed her off.

All day had been a whirlwind of activity, and the first six fights had been a variety of fighters and styles, but she hadn't watched. She was a bundle of nerves worried about all the possibilities, what the vampires might do, or what Pennington wanted from her. Thankfully, the flurry of vendors, paperwork, customers, and outpouring of community showing up had kept her busy. And now, the only thing keeping her sane was her new ability to speak to Ajax in her mind while it was all going on.

Everything about all this felt like she was in a fantasy novel, but the excitement was short-lived when the reality was chaotic and dangerous.

But now, she'd asked him to shut her out so he could concentrate, so her reactions wouldn't distract him during this fight. He'd been hesitant and unwilling, but she knew how she was, how she'd be unable to stop herself from saying things, and that would become a problem. She just knew they would do something to him right now, that there was something about this challenger that wasn't right. He'd only agreed while he was fighting, and she'd promised to stay close to the ring.

"Miss? Miss Andrade?" The voice of the vendor broke through her thoughts, and she glanced over at the man distractedly. The hot dog guy.

"Yeah?"

They touched gloves, she could see the Taurus guy taunting him, talking shit, laughing in his face. But Ajax's outside demeanor didn't change. He stood perfectly still, waiting for the bell to sound the start of the bout.

She had finally wrapped up most of the business for tonight, and she was surrounded by the shifters from Felix's pack. She just couldn't place any of their faces. She knew at least two were supposed to be following her around, but wasn't sure which ones anymore. They'd mixed easily into the crush of the crowd as she moved, and they'd been told to be conspicuous, so she'd easily forgotten about them in the crazy of the night. Ajax had gone over the safety precautions a million times with her, and even more so, they'd walked through the plan for after the fight. The one where they all headed straight over to the vampire nest to shut down the gathering that was there. But not her. She was to stay here under guard, along with her father. She hadn't liked that part of the plan, but he was right. What would she be able to do?

The only time she looked away from Ajax was to look around for Felix. Her best friend should be back any moment now with the witches.

It was the only thing that had gone wrong. Their plane had been delayed all day due to storms in their state, and they'd only just arrived. He'd left at the beginning of the night to go grab them, but they should have been here by now.

"The outlet on the wall isn't working. I think I blew a breaker. Can you tell me where the box is, and I'll flip it?" Even with the vendor yelling over the crowd, he still had to lean in for her to hear him, and she grit her teeth. The breaker box was in a janitor's closet at the back, and of course, it was locked.

"I'll go." It would be faster. She could cut through the crowd and be back quickly, and besides, there was no way she was giving this guy her keys. Frustrated, she kept her eyes on the ring as she moved through the crowd, wondering what the Taurus guy was saying to Ajax. He was smirking, running his mouth about something as he hopped around, but Ajax didn't seem affected, didn't seem like he cared. But panic gripped her chest. She was sure he had some kind of poison or fancy magic she didn't know about. She should have cancelled the tournament and ran. That's what her dad wanted to do, and that's what she was wishing for now. Then she wouldn't have to worry about every person she bumped into being some blood-sucking vampire on a mission.

But she wasn't the goal anymore, and she had to remember that. Pennington had been clear that she wasn't important, that she was only a means to an end for him. She was disposable. Only Ben had wanted anything to do with her, and he was gone, but that's why the witches were here. They could protect Ajax. They were his friends. If they ever arrived.

Just as the bell signaled the round to start, she ducked down the empty back hall, jingling her keys in the lock. In the dark janitor's closet, she fumbled around for a light, then opened the tiny metal door for the breaker box. Nothing seemed wrong. None of the little switches were flipped, and she couldn't just start flipping them on and off now. Maybe his machine was just broken. Oh well, she'd deal with it later.

Hurriedly, she locked the door back, anxious at every roar from the crowd. Just as she moved back towards the main gym, a smooth voice sounded behind her, inches from her ear, and she jumped, freezing in the doorway to the hall.

"Ms. Andrade, it's been a successful night, hasn't it?"

Pennington. She took her time responding, keeping her eye on Ajax as he slowly circled Taurus. "Seems to be that way. Haven't seen you tonight. This the only fight you're here for?"

"Something like that. Wanted to keep Taurus out of here before unleashing him on your headliner. I am very pleased that you were able to secure him for us. Very convenient for what I needed."

She turned her head sharply. "What does that mean?"

"Simply that he is elusive for a reason, and he is more than he pretends to be, which I suspected before, and have now confirmed."

Marti took a calming breath, trying not to give anything away. "What does it matter to you?"

He chuckled, lit a cigarette, and slowly blew out the first drag. "Not long ago, I would have made some excuse, letting your little human self keep your innocence, to allow you to believe you know everything about the world. But you're not innocent anymore, are you, Ms. Andrade?"

"I don't know what you're talking about." She sliced her eyes to his face, boring into his as her anger grew.

"Ice, or Ajax, is more than everyone sees. Even more than you, I believe. I'm betting he didn't tell you how valuable he is to his family, to his friends. How he is not just well-trained or strong but has power running through his veins."

"Ajax left his family behind. He is alone."

Pennington smirked and finally met her eye. "You can leave your family behind, but it doesn't change who and what you are. His death, or his capture, would matter in many ways. Our world, the world that you have so abruptly been thrown into, is barely outside the ending of a violent and bloody war. One that he was not only a part of, but instrumental in. He's a killer. A heartless murderer. And peace treaties are weak and generally unenforceable. What matters now is power, money, magic. All of which he has."

She glared at him. "Why are you telling me this?"

"Because, my dear, you should remember what I told you about me. I'm sensible. Logical. And things have changed. I thought Taurus up there could take care of Ice for me, get me the leverage I needed to auction him off to my buyers from Houston. But in person, I see I was wrong. Taurus won't win this. But that's okay, I had bigger plans anyway. However, it's you, you who surprised me this week. I couldn't figure out how you managed to kill Benjamin, on top of my vampire. But now, I understand." He paused to let his words whisper across her ear, and she swallowed hard. "You didn't kill them. He did. For you. Now, I know Ajax's weakness."

"I don't know what you think you know, but—"

He leaned in even closer, his hand snaking around her waist, the cigarette hanging from his fingers. His grip was strong, but casual to any stray eye. "I can smell it, Ms. Andrade. I've never witnessed a wolf mate with a human in the two hundred years I've been walking this Earth, but here we are. Your scent has changed, and there's a mark on your neck. You've intermingled with a wolf, specifically, the one beating the shit out of my fighter up there."

She tensed, refusing to look at him, keeping her eyes trained on Ajax as he ruthlessly pounded into the other man's face before Taurus was able to get away and regroup. Then, she thought about the shifters who were supposed to be following her around. Her eyes darted through the crowd, flitting over each face. Where were they?

"If you think the little wolves are coming to save you, then you might want to know there was a…slight disturbance just a few minutes ago. A few dozen of my vampires showed up, so I'm betting they are dealing with that little distraction."

"If you have it all planned out so well, then why do you need me or my father?"

"Like I said, things change. But I'll give you a choice, something I don't usually do, in the spirit of our partnership here. After all, you have made me a lot of money these past few years." He blew his cigarette smoke in her face, but she refused to react. "You can go with me willingly, let me turn you, join our nest, and you and your father swear your allegiance to us. Then, I release you. You are immortal and still own this gym. Life goes on."

"Why would I do that? Why would I do anything willingly? You've admitted you are afraid of Ajax. The whole world is, right?"

He chuckled, and she realized his eyes were trained on her mate, watching his every move in that fight. "Because I have several colleagues who want him alive, who want their revenge. And so, with his connection to his new mate severed, he would be greatly impaired and huntable, but he would be alive…for now. He might even make it out of the Hunt alive if he's desperate enough to find you."

"Hunt?" Her whisper was laced with fear, and she cursed herself for her weakness.

"Yes. A little game I rigged up. So many high bidders, bounties on his head, some would call it. I couldn't decide who to go with, so I went with them all. Promised them a weakened Alpha wolf, and a chance to hunt him like the dog he is."

"You're sick."

His laugh was short, nonchalant. "And you? You being turned will weaken him just enough. But at least he'll have a chance, right? If he's such a good fighter, then he should be fine."

"And if I don't cooperate with your little plan?"

"Hmmm. You see, I had great confidence that my contender would have injured him or weakened him in some way, but I underestimated him. I can't allow him to leave this tournament at full strength. He would do great damage to my nest." Slowly, he unbuttoned his suit jacket, sweeping it back behind him just enough for the glint of silver to catch her eye, and her mouth went dry. A gun. "I'm an excellent shot, even from here. I'm perfectly happy with a dying wolf. So, I expect your full cooperation if you want him to have any chance at all."

"No." Her whisper went unheard, but terror filled her throat, a nausea settling in her stomach.

"Tomorrow, with him crippled from losing his mate, my colleagues will be unleashed on the city. They've paid good money for a free-for-all wolf hunt. Hundreds of vampires against him. Some of them even want him alive for whatever purposes, and some just want to use him. Some want him dead. To the victor goes the spoils of war."

"But he has a chance?"

"He has a chance if you choose wisely. Or he could have no chance at all. Just a silver bullet in his heart. And I sell what's left of him for the highest price right now."

She stared at Ajax, the seconds ticking down on the clock for the first round. Against vampires, he could make it out. He had Felix's pack. He had the witches. He was Ice. He was a murderer who'd killed thousands of vampires in the past few years. He would live.

But if she said no, he had no chance, no way to defend himself against a bullet from behind.

She couldn't even warn him, not with the block up. And she would never be able to make it to him in time. There was too much of a crowd, too many people jostling and moving, screaming and cheering, and she was filled with desperation.

"It won't work. He won't let me go. All you'll do is piss him off, and he'll come for you. He'll come for all of you, and I'll be cheering him on."

"So feisty. But he won't know. Not in time. You see, as we speak, your father has already been taken to my home. He didn't get a choice. Only you do. He gets turned no matter what."

"My father?" She shook her head in disbelief. "You're full of shit. I just saw him."

He smiled softly, condescendingly. "Maybe. But remember what I told you. I could always use more loyal followers, and there is one sure way to accomplish that."

"Your plan isn't fool-proof. It won't matter what I do willingly, he will come for me." Glaring at him, she backed up, feeling for the wall behind her, and she struggled not to think of her father and what they would do to him.

The sharp features of his face tightened, and with barely discernable movement, his hands were on either side of her, trapping her against the wall. His face frighteningly close to hers, he whispered, "Maybe that's what I want. For him to chase you. Or you could convince him you don't want him to come for you. Otherwise, I can guarantee he won't make it out alive. Especially in my nest full of veteran vampires who want him dead. There are hundreds of vampires, high-level ones, waiting in my home as we speak. He would never survive if he came for you. And then, I win all the way around."

Pulling a tiny notebook from his suit pocket, and handing her a pen, his voice dropped lower. "Write him a little note, tell him this was all too much to figure out. You change your mind, blah blah blah. I suggest being convincing enough to make him not look for you. And then he has the night to run."

She stared at the paper in front of her, taking a deep breath, and for a brief second, considered actually doing what he said. She wasn't stupid. Even if she went with him willingly, Ajax would follow. She knew he was tricking her, but there was no solution, no way out. All she could do was buy her mate time.

"Tick tock, Ms. Andrade. Or I lose my patience."

Her eyes stung as tears filled them, and she rapidly penned out a useless note.

I can't do this. It's too much to handle. Find someone who is more like you. Don't look for me. It won't change anything. Martina.

She folded it and put it in his outstretched hand. Within seconds, the female she had seen the night of the whale watching trip emerged from the crowd and nodded at Pennington before smirking at her.

"Anita will make sure he gets it as soon as his fight's over. Don't worry. She'll be gentle when she tells him. Now, let's go. I'm sure your father would love to see a familiar face."

Marti stared daggers at the woman, and Anita gave her a little finger wave before disappearing back into the crowd. Then, Pennington's hand closed around her upper arm, yanking her backwards down the empty hall towards the fire exit. One last look at Ajax, and she saw him slowly circling his struggling opponent, who was bleeding heavily, swaying on his feet and moving in circles. A bell rang, signaling the end of the first round, and she melted backwards as his attention ran across the crowd, looking for her.

Outside, she stumbled behind Pennington on the path around the building, and he pulled her to a waiting black Mercedes. Pushing her into the backseat, he slid in beside her, and before the door even closed, the driver was speeding off.

She waited for a beat, then asked, "Where is my father?"

"Waiting for you. You know, things will be much better for you now. It's the sensible thing to do. You'll become a part of Goulden, and things will be simpler. We will fully incorporate the gym into our enterprises, taking on any debts you have, leaving you with no worries. Just do what we tell you, and you become a part of something bigger than you."

She refused to look at him, staring out the window, reconsidering all her misgivings about watching other people die. This man, no, this vampire, with his subtle threats, his smirk, and his sensible-to-only-him logic, made her blood boil, and she didn't think she would mind watching him die. She didn't like how confident he was in killing and using Ajax for his own gain, and she didn't like how he thought he had everything figured out.

Because he didn't. She knew something he didn't. And it only took five minutes before the connection opened up.

"Baby, where are you? What is this note?"

"I'm with Pennington. He made me write it, so you wouldn't come after me. He already took my father and threatened to kill him."

"I'm coming now. What's your location?"

The words rushed through her mind, so fast she could hardly form them, and a desperate fear took over the calm she'd adopted. *"Wait. You can't. That's what he wants, and he's ready for you. He knows you'll come, and he knows who you are. He has a billion vampires gathered at his house. Said they're all there to hunt you. Said that if I went with you, then you would be given a chance to run. I don't know exactly how, but he knows everything about you. This is your chance to get away."*

"He's lying, little one."

"I know. But there's no solution. If I don't go, he kills my dad and still kills you. If you come for me, he's ready for you. If you do nothing, they're going to hunt you for sport. Everything is a trap. I just wanted to give you time to get away."

"I know all this, baby. I spent Wednesday and Thursday staking them out, remember? And I have reinforcements. People wanting to kill me is not new, especially those blood-suckers."

Just then, they pulled up to a large estate surrounded by a brick wall and an intimidating iron gate. It opened automatically, and on the inside, there were at least six people manning the gated entrance with scary looking guns.

Pennington must have sensed her fear, because he chuckled. "Did you think we would be rolling into a picket fence house? Or did you think there were less of us? It's a whole new world here, endless possibilities if you play your cards right."

"They have guns. Really big ones."

"A bullet won't kill me, another perk of being a shifter. Just keep his dirty fangs out of your pretty little neck long enough for me to get there, and it will all be over. I'm on my way."

Something about the way he spoke, even through their mindlink, was calm and reassuring, like he wasn't worried. But either she wasn't close enough, or he hadn't opened it all the way because she couldn't find a hint of his real emotions.

Inside the estate grounds, they moved down a circular path towards a huge gray brick mansion. In the dark cover of the night, she could barely see past the glow of the lampposts lining the driveway, but she could make out a few smaller, matching buildings near it and a gorgeous wide, sweeping staircase covered in ivy at the main entrance to the house. Before she could look around for long, the door opened on the other side, and she was yanked out of the car by her arm.

Once inside, she was surrounded by two other men who escorted her quickly through a large common area. Beautiful women stared at her from over the drinks in their hands, and even more people sat around smoking and playing cards. At least two hundred people were on this floor alone, and she assumed they were all vampires by the way they looked at her with bored interest.

"You're sick. You all just sit around having parties while you plot people's deaths?"

"This place is ginormous, Ajax. There are like two hundred people here. And now they are taking me somewhere in the back. I still haven't seen my dad. Ajax, fuck." Maybe reality was just setting in, or the shock was wearing off, but she felt panic take over, and she could barely breathe.

"I'm close. Don't panic. I'm not leaving you, and I'm not worried about a few bloodsuckers. They die nice and easy. That's why they need guns. They are fragile and dead on the inside. Just keep talking to me. Stay with me. As long as we can link, you'll know I'm close by."

Abruptly, after walking through a long hallway, and towards the back of the house, they stopped in front of a large steel door. They stood, waiting, and she shifted uncomfortably, trying to see all the different threats around her. It wasn't long before Pennington appeared again, then eyed her thoughtfully for a second before waving over another man.

Black hair slicked back, a sharp nose, perfectly groomed and manicured, the shorter man joined them, his eyes moving up and down her body obscenely. "Turn her around. Show me the back."

Before she could even protest, she was flipped and pushed against the wall. "What the—"

"I'll take her."

"Excellent. Take her downstairs."

"What the hell are—"

The steel door opened, and she was pushed down some stairs, the darkness enveloping her, and she stumbled, their hands wrapped around her arms the only thing keeping her from tumbling to the bottom. Once they were downstairs, then down a long hallway, there were two large sets of open cells facing each other. Her father lay on the floor of one, unconscious.

"Dad?! What did you do to him? Dad!"

She was pushed into the other cell, and the door clanged shut, her guards still ignoring her. Pennington appeared just in time to hear her yelling.

"Ms. Andrade, he was given a sleeping drug. He is unharmed so far. It all depends on you though."

"What is wrong with you? You can't just treat people like this. You won't get away with it. Once we are reported missing, the police will be looking for us. People will know."

"You know, Benjamin swore you were gentle, kind, and a pushover, someone we could mold to be a valuable addition to our businesses. He was very adamant. But I'm doubting his perspective on you. If you want any chance of success, you'll need to be smarter about your choices."

Grabbing the bar and sneering at him, she spit at his feet. "I have no desire to have anything to do with you. You can turn me into one of you, but I will never follow you blindly."

"Which is why I will be pivoting my plans for you once again. You keep surprising me, Ms. Andrade, and now, you really will make our little adventure worth it. You've convinced me that it would not be in my best interest to turn you. Congratulations in that regard."

Taken aback, she almost didn't ask the question. Almost. "What's the catch?"

"So smart, yet you still make so many bad choices. You see, as vampires, we prefer a steady live supply for our…proclivities. And the man upstairs, he was enamored of you the second you walked in the door. One look and he offered me a nice, tidy sum to take you off my hands. And that, my dear, will be a much more fitting role for you. You just have to make yourself useful to him. If not, if you can't fulfill his requirements, then he will kill you off."

She practically snarled at him. She was tired of being treated like a commodity, given no choice, her own future discussed between these monsters like she was a piece of meat. "I can guarantee I won't, no matter what they are. Might as well kill me now."

"Be careful, or you'll get what you ask for. As a blood slave, you would just be a feeding bag, like a zombie, only kept alive to supply fresh blood. It's not a fun life to live. And it will also be your father's future at stake if you and him don't cooperate. For now, you have been purchased for use as a blood pet instead. Anything he desires, you will beg to fulfill because you will not only give him blood, but he will give you his, creating an addiction so strong, you would murder your own father if he asked. Pets are treated as queens as long as they can stay alive. Disappoint or bore him, then he will drain you dry and throw you in the ocean."

"Fucking psychos. I'm not doing any of that."

"You don't get a choice. Once you're addicted, no one else will matter to you, not your father, not your mate. And the best part? I will still be finding your wolf mate. His rank alone brought dozens of notorious vamps to my doorstep, many eager for revenge, others bent on utilizing him against his own pack. I'm drowning in the network of big players, all willing to do business with me. Either way it goes, he will be instrumental in securing my position in Texas, a very lucrative area ripe for financial gain."

"You can only dream. You think you're smart, but Ajax would never get caught by you. There's a reason his pack is well-known—they know what they're doing. You think he's suddenly become reckless? You are the fool here. You touch me, and he will personally stake everyone in this house."

"I hope he tries." His eyes gleamed, and never in her life did she wish someone dead as much as she wanted him to die a gory, bloody death. But right then, the door opened, and the man from earlier strode through. Pennington merely looked at him and cocked his eyebrow.

"Money transfer complete." Then he looked over at her and in a flash, his hand had grabbed her wrist, and he pulled her in close, leaning into the bars that separated them. "She goes to my home tonight when I leave, but I want a taste first. You want an audience, my little lamb chop?"

"You're disgusting, and I will slit my throat before I submit to anything you want from me."

"Ajax? Are you close, please. He just sold me as a pet. I don't understand what is happening! Where are you?" Desperation filled their bond, and she knew he was coming as fast as he could, but she was panicking inside, with no clue how to stop them.

"I'm here, little one. Right outside. Stall them a few more minutes. We are just breached. What's your position inside the house?"

"Back hall, there is a steel door. It takes you downstairs into a cell block of sorts, like an old wine cellar. Please, hurry, and be careful. There are so many here. And he knows you're coming. Promise me you'll stay alive."

"Keep the connection open, baby. Feel me as I get closer. Use me to stay strong and fight."

The man who bought her released her wrist, and she stepped to the back of the cell, pressing herself against the wall. He only chuckled, shaking hands with Pennington and staring at her like she was an animal to be caught.

"No point in fighting, Ms. Andrade. Franco here, he can make your life heaven or hell. She's all yours. Let me know if you need extra men to escort her to your home. I would suggest keeping her here until I have the wolf. There is no doubt that, until I have him in silver, he will come for her."

The cell door clanged open, and fear filled her when his eyes reddened unnaturally, and his fangs lengthened.

"No worries, Kevin. I like them feisty. Makes it fun to break them. We start tonight, just a little taste to begin the addiction, and she'll be begging for me to take her home by the time the party is over. Come here, kitten."

Chapter 22

Ajax

Sunday, October 6
Goulden Vampire Nest

Two long tones and one short. It was repeated twice more only seconds later. That was the signal. The walkie sitting between the seats provided all he needed in order to know that everyone was in place. The four of them exited the car silently, quickly making their way along the dark street. From the other end, another set of wolves mirrored them as they approached the iron gates of the vampire nest.

The loud popping of a blown tire filled the air, and another car skidded to a stop twenty yards from the gate. Flattening their bodies against the brick wall, none of them moved, and he held his breath. From the short distance, he could see the small, red-haired woman exit her vehicle and examine her tire. She popped her trunk, looking for tools, and then walked hesitantly to the gate when she couldn't find anything.

"Excuse me? Anyone there? I need to use your phone to call for a tow." Her voice rang out in the night, barely audible over the rising wind. The storm she'd created was blowing in quickly, and thunder rumbled in the distance.

After a few seconds, the gate opened, and he could no longer hear her, but one of the vampires stepped over to her car, looking at the tire before smiling down at her, reaching for her neck with his hand. Suddenly, several more vampires exited the gate, and Ajax took off running towards them, along with all the other wolves surrounding him.

Even as he took action, the vampires near the woman crumpled to the ground, holding their heads and screaming in pain. The lanky, blonde-haired man stepped out of the car, his nightmare fae magic howling almost invisibly around him, and held out his hand to the red-head to help her step over their writhing bodies. They ran towards the gate together, pausing long enough for him to catch up. Behind him, the dozen wolves from Felix's pack finished killing the vampires lying in the road, using the stakes everyone carried on them. They had been ready to move on this place tonight and had even anticipated an attack on him at the tournament. But Cahaira and Linc's late arrival had put a hiccup in those plans. He'd never thought they'd take her. Not his Marti. She shouldn't have been a part of this. Normally, a mere human would never blip on their radar, not like this. He'd known he was their target all along, but he'd been a fool to think she wasn't going to be caught in the middle. He'd been too torn apart by the thought of the fight, by the idea of stepping back into the old Ajax, the one who'd been merciless and destructive. And now, guilt tore him apart. He should have anticipated this. Shouldn't have left her in the crowd.

But he couldn't do anything about the past, only the future. This would end tonight. In whatever way it needed to. He would do whatever was needed to save his mate, even if it meant stepping too close to the feral fire that raged inside of him.

Cahaira looked up at him, her eyes blazing, and she and Lincoln separated, moving in sync to spread out on either side of him once they were inside the gate. "How much time do we have?"

He swallowed hard, every muscle in his body tensing as he felt Marti's fear and panic, her pleas for him to hurry. He looked away from his best friend's worried face, then raised his voice just enough for all the other wolf shifters to hear. "Not much."

"Call it out. I'll lift the sounds through the air." Wind swirled around them, her magic precise and efficient as they moved forward.

"Hit hard and fast. They're moving on her now. She's underground, back hallway, metal door. Shift if needed, Lincoln and Cahaira will stun them en masse. You take them out when they fall. I'm headed straight for Marti."

They moved quickly and quietly as he called out the update. It would have been easier if they were a pack, and he could communicate via link, but they were trained well enough, and these were vampires. They had weaknesses, and he had a witch and a fae.

He just prayed he'd made it in time.

As they beelined straight for the mansion, more vampires poured from the shadows, all with guns pulled, and before he even had to say a word, the wind picked up around Cahaira, siphoned by her power, and created a shield. She ran towards the front of the house, and as the magical gusts of wind whipped around them all, bullets were lost, and vampires were thrown against the house walls.

He tensed as it all began, and an eerie calm descended on him as the robotic urge to kill silenced everything around him. The steady thrum of his heart beating took over, but he didn't hesitate, even when he was thrust into the screaming violence of his memories.

Windows broke as the vampires' bodies slammed into them, and the noise inside the home increased as yelling and chaos ensued. Some of the wolves shifted, attacking the vampires, and others staked them while he, Cahaira, and Lincoln headed inside just as the front door burst open. It was then that Marti had linked him again, terror in her voice, pleading for him to save her. And a furious dread sank through him before erupting into full-fledged rage.

She had been sold. It took everything in him to remain calm, to make it seem like she had nothing to worry about. Letting her feel his fear wouldn't help.

Without hesitation, he worked his way through waves of vampires, Lincoln bringing them to their knees with internal pain and hallucinations, and Cahaira throwing them across the room, stunning them for the other wolves to finish. He flew through the crowds of hissing and screaming undead, visions of smoke and flying debris distorting his concentration, and blood spurted across his face, soaking his shirt as he made his way through. His body was on autopilot, but his mind...his mind fought through the onslaught of nightmares, ones he thought he'd buried in the past year, surfacing to mock him. The only thing that kept him sane was the connection with his mate—the fight in her voice as she screamed invectives at her attacker, snapping him back to the present.

He was pushing his way to the back of the house when a dull pain flashed across his face, but he didn't flinch. It wasn't his. It was Marti's. He could feel every blow now. That meant he was close.

A variety of sharp and methodical pain littered his body as she fought back and was beaten for it. Rage filled him, and he slammed through a group of vampires blocking the back hallway, and he repeated the only comfort he had in this. He could feel her. He was close…he was close. And he would kill everything breathing in this house.

Lincoln was right behind him, and from the strength of the wind in the hallway, Cahaira had to be at their heels. Hand to hand, he fought with an older vampire, his strength more than the others as he slashed out at him, the knife in the vamp's hand slicing across his chest, but Ajax barely noticed. His claws lengthened and with one swipe, almost fully decapitated the last guard. Just as the body hit the ground, he pulled on the handle, but it wouldn't budge.

The steel door was bolted shut, and nothing he did budged it. Every fiber of his body screamed as he pounded harder and harder, the steel unmoving beneath his hands. When the sharp pain of a bite seared across his neck, panic set in.

"Marti, baby, talk to me. I'm almost there." A different pain seeped through when he realized she had attempted to block him out, to save him from experiencing her pain, but wasn't skilled enough yet. So, when he pushed through their bond, he could hear her sobbing, crying for him, and his heart broke. The demons of his past had won. Every brutal act of violence he'd ever committed had been in vain. She had been bitten, and he felt like he was going to collapse from a lack of air when she linked him one last time.

"Ajax, I love you. I'm sorry…I tried, it's too late."

"No, fuck, no. Don't give up, Marti. Marti, I'm not leaving you."

"Move back, Ajax. Move."

Cahaira had rushed behind him to the bleeding body of the decapitated vampire and pulled a set of keys from his pocket. Fumbling with them, she found the correct key, slid open the deadbolt, and he yanked it open.

He scrambled down the stairs before everyone, and the path in front of him blazed with fire, the line of it chasing in front of him, burning up every vampire in his way, courtesy of Cahaira's magic. He could hear Marti screaming, and the sound burned like the fire that now filled the room. His guttural roar fueled a rush of the vampires guarding the cells to run at him, but he only felt their blood spray across his body when he slashed through them without thought. His eyes went straight to his mate, who was in a cell, on her back, being held down by two vampires, one of which had his fangs deep in her neck.

Her screams had died down, and her eyes were closing as both men pulled away and rose to fight him off. The taller one, the vampire elder, stepped forward to intercept him, surprise, fear, and panic in his eyes.

Pennington.

Ajax threw open the cell door, rushing in, and Pennington lifted one hand from the inside of his jacket pocket and pointed a gun straight at his chest. He didn't slow, even when the bullet ripped through him. Grabbing Pennington's arm with one hand, and his neck with the other, he threw him against the wall. When he slumped to the ground, unconscious, Ajax turned to the man who had been drinking his mate's precious blood.

"It's too late for her, wolf. Stop now, and at least she'll stay alive. Don't take another step."

The desperate little man had picked Marti up under her arms, holding her in front of him like a shield. His back against the wall, he looked nervous despite the knife he held to Marti's chest. Looking dazed, a small rivulet of blood trickled from her neck, and her eyes were only half-open.

He paused in his rampage, not because of the slimy vampire's words, but because his body was betraying him. Instead of healing and expelling the bullet like every time before, the bullet was becoming a fiery pit inside of him, eating him from the inside out, and every ounce of strength seemed to exit his body, leaving him to sink to the floor, his chest heaving.

Silver. A wolf's only weakness.

The warm, red liquid gushed from his chest, and he lifted his hands in front of him in disbelief. This couldn't be how it ended. No. No. No. He couldn't fail her.

Covered in blood, venom ran through his veins as he took in the vampire's demeanor change. Realization dawned in the man's eyes, and he smirked, skirting to the side of Ajax, and around the edge of the cell, pulling Marti with him.

"I'd love to sit around and watch you die, but we need to get out of here." Using the inherent speed of vampires, he flashed to the cell door just as Lincoln hit the bottom of the steps.

With an almost imperceptive movement by Lincoln, the vampire dropped to the ground, screaming in pain, and Marti tumbled forward. Instinctively, she curled into a ball, covering her head, and he pulled all his strength together to crawl over to her, pulling her body into his lap.

Nothing mattered anymore, nothing could take back the pain, and he rocked with her.

"I'm so sorry, my Marti. I'm so fucking sorry."

He blocked out the pain of the silver bullet that was roasting his insides, pushed against the waning strength in his body, and focused all of it on her. Tucking her against his chest, he wrapped himself around her, so that nothing or no one else could hurt his Marti. She whimpered in his arms, murmuring his name, and the numbness set in, the whole world around them fading away.

Hot hands prodded at his body, pushing and pulling at his arms, their words drowned out by the roar in his head and the howl of his wolf. They were trying to steal his Marti from him, and he snarled at them, reaching to swipe until his arm was frozen in the air with magic.

"Ajax, listen to me…"

The words floated in and out, and he tightened his grip on Marti.

"It's the silver. We have to…"

"Let her go, Ajax…"

Then his body was forced backwards, magic bending him against his will until he lay on his back. Cahaira's face floated in front of him, and

Lincoln held one arm down. Somehow, he felt the beating of his heart slowing just as a vacuum swirled in his chest, and within seconds, the silver bullet hung in the air in front of his face before Lincoln released him to retrieve it. Relief flooded his body, and a feeling of comfort spread as Cahaira chanted over him.

He felt his strength returning, and he became acutely aware of the heat from Cahaira's hands when she pushed against the wound in his chest. His own wolf roared to life, and his body began repairing itself as his shifter magic healed him.

"Marti…"

"Take a breather, Ajax. We need you alive for her. Don't move just yet."

A rising awareness of Marti's body, still collapsed between his legs, as she rested her head on his stomach, had him going as still as possible. Carefully, he watched her breathe, thankful she was still alive.

"He bit her…is she?"

Cahaira laid her hands on Marti, gently prodding her neck and cupping her cheek to look into her half-closed eyes, her hands glowing with magic as she scanned her body. "He didn't turn her. Was making her his pet. His serum hasn't spread completely, but she is unconscious. I've never done it before, but I think we can reverse it if he didn't finish. He needs to die to end the connection and—"

"Consider that done." Gathering his strength, he gently lifted Marti into Cahaira's arms, then crawled slowly to where the vampire's body lay on the ground bleeding. The vampire would regenerate soon anyway; he needed to die now. Ajax pulled the already bloody stake from his back pocket and plunged it into the vampire's heart. Immediately, the body was reduced to ashes, and he sat back on his knees, panting at the exertion.

"Ajax? I…I …even with him dead, I'm not sure. I don't have the same healing power as my sister, and even if she was here, I can feel it spreading. I don't know how to stop it. Humans…their sickness…even a vampire induced one…it's out of our control."

He looked up at Cahaira desperately, panic coursing through his body, mimicking the sensation he felt through the bond as the vampire's addictive serum flooded her blood, dosing her to make her pliable and euphoric for them to feed.

"There has to be something you can do. We can't give up." His voice was raspy, foreign sounding to his own ears, and he gathered Marti in his arms, her eyes opening and closing sleepily.

"Cut her open. Quick. Let her bleed it out." Felix knelt down beside him, giving the order as several others made their way down the steps, heaving and panting.

"But what if we can't stop the bleeding? What if she loses too much? I can't bring her back from the dead. I can heal, I can strengthen, but I can't give life when there's none left, especially in a human."

"I'm telling you, it's the only way. We've done it before, and it can work. Vampire attacks were bad here during the wars." Felix sounded confident, and Ajax felt hope rise in his chest. "It was on shifters though. They were able to regenerate blood quickly. So, maybe we just be careful how much she loses."

He couldn't help the growl that ripped from his chest at the thought.

"And maybe after, we should rush her to the human hospital for a blood transfusion, just in case."

Ajax glanced quickly at Felix, and he saw the doubt and the worry there despite his words. Looking back at Cahaira, the words caught in his throat, and he could only nod. She pulled a small dagger from her thigh, its familiar design of the Goddess Danu a small reassurance.

"May the Goddess's blessings on my hand safely guide, and your protection and healing continue to provide, for tonight we tempt all logic and fate, dear Goddess, bring this Earthly child back to her mate."

He held his breath, dipping his forehead to touch Marti's and keeping his eye trained on the blade of the knife. Cahaira sliced quickly across the two puncture wounds of the bite, careful to avoid her major arteries, and to not go too deep. Marti gasped in his hands, and her eyes flew open as the trickle of blood began streaming, pressure increasing slowly. She gripped his neck in fear, struggling to sit up and push away.

When the blood soaked her hair and drenched both of their clothes, she struggled, and he looked up at Cahaira desperately. "Can you feel a difference? Just close it up, we can't risk it. There's too much blood. No more."

Marti struggled harder in his arms, causing the blood to gush out at an alarming rate. Blood covered her face, and panic and fear filled her eyes as she reached for him, and it broke him. Even his wolf was eerily silent, and he laid her flat on her back, holding her arms down, so she would stop struggling.

Blood filled her mouth, and she coughed, staring up at him as she choked, confusion and betrayal evident on her face. "Shhh. Marti, hold still. Cahaira's going to stop the blood. Cahaira?"

But a quick glance to his right was just in time to see Cahaira's limp body hit the floor. No, no, no.

His heart skipped a beat, and he looked up in time to see Pennington swinging Cahaira's knife at Lincoln, the element of surprise, and his vampire speed catching everyone off guard after he'd regenerated. They had all forgotten the vampire elder's presence, and now, he fought back viciously.

Slamming Lincoln around, they grappled with the knife for only a few moments before Felix slashed at his back from behind, twisting and turning him away from Lincoln long enough for the fae's magic to fill the room once again, dropping Pennington to his knees in pain.

Within moments, he was outnumbered, and easily, Felix added his blood to the floor before Lincoln drove the stake into his chest.

It was a momentary scuffle, but it changed everything.

Pennington had knocked Cahaira unconscious, leaving Marti to lose a dangerous amount of blood. Marti's strength had waned as the blood continued to stream from her body over the last few minutes. She was now limp and pale, barely breathing. Ajax desperately tried to stop the flow, clamping his hand over the wound as he knelt over her.

"Please, Marti, hold on. Hold on to me, do you hear me? Don't give up. Don't give up on me."

Agony and desperation took over, and he felt useless, helpless and desperate. As Lincoln checked on Cahaira, Jessie pulled his shirt off, pushing the material under Ajax's hand and against her neck. Ajax stood hastily, carrying her as he rushed towards the steps, heaviness filling his chest even as their mate bond became more and more distant.

"We have to go. She's not going to make it."

Chapter 23

Cahaira

Thursday, October 10
Andrade Home

Cahaira leaned forward on her elbow wearily, the corded phone digging into her ear. She sighed. "You're not here, Mom. You can't see it. It's heartbreaking. If we can't fix her, we are going to lose both of them."

"We have to believe that fate will work in the right way, Cahaira. You can't rush in and fix everything with your magic. Let it work itself out."

"Quit with the bullshit circle talk, Mom. I'm not sitting by and letting my best friend suffer if I can do something."

There was silence on the other end of the line, and she realized that despite her mom's inane words about fate that always pissed her off, it wasn't her fault.

"I'm sorry. I didn't mean that, but this is torture. Have you seen anything in the runes?"

"Nothing definitive. The paths are open in too many directions, and it's creating chaos."

Staring at the wall, her mind blank with the seriousness weighing on her, she whispered, "What do we do? What can be done? She's basically catatonic, like the vampire serum is still in her, but I can't feel any. It's been three days since we left the hospital, and I've healed everything on her. There has to be something we can do."

"Can Ajax feel her through the bond?"

"I don't honestly know. He won't leave her side, he won't talk to us, he won't do anything but sleep and stare at her. But I have a hunch he can't feel her, and it's driving his wolf mad."

"I was afraid of that. Can you put him on the phone for me to talk to him?"

"That won't happen. Just this morning, he partially shifted and snapped at me when I got too close to her. He's barely hanging on. Between turning feral from being rogue for so long, and death slowly overtaking Marti, he's going full-wolf. He needs a pack connection."

"Him going feral is a huge possibility at this point. It's been a year. He needs to find a pack to join soon."

"We asked the local pack, but the Alpha is hesitant." Cahaira squeezed her eyes closed, rubbing her temple as she wracked her brain for a solution.

"No one wants a stray alpha wolf joining their pack. It's an invitation for problems, a takeover, tyranny…the possibilities are endless."

"And Marti? I thought for sure we could save her from the vampire serum. Felix was sure. They had done it for wolves during the wars."

"Wolves regenerate. Wolves have their packs to pull their strength from to fight the magic invading their blood. Shifter blood overwhelms the vampire serum because it's superior. Her human blood can't do that. Maybe once she regenerates her own blood completely, like four to six weeks. Maybe once it's her own and not donated blood, she can kick the pull away from the serum."

"We don't have that long. Ajax will snap, and it will be big and soon."

She heard her mother hum, and she could picture her rocking in her chair on the deck of her home. Kathleen would be looking out into the Gulf of Mexico, letting the wind surround her as she thought. It was her power-up, and it helped her think before she spoke. "But she's his mate. When he marked her, he could feel her, correct? Like a normal wolf mating?"

"I assume so. We didn't exactly discuss it."

"Then, in a human way, her blood would have taken on the shifter magic, or some form of it."

"But she lost most of her blood, almost half before I could stop it and before the hospital gave her the transfusions of—"

"—human blood. So, she doesn't have enough shifter blood left in her."

"Do we get her a transfusion of shifter blood?"

"Or Ajax just marks her again, starting over and hope that another marking will jumpstart her body."

"That might work, Mom. You're a genius."

Cahaira heard her mother's throaty chuckle. "Don't celebrate just yet. Talk to him. Make sure he keeps her in places where she feels at home, where she's comfortable, familiar, and safe. Somewhere her mind will want to come back to."

"You think that will work? Have you seen anyone come back from vampire bites?"

It was a long moment before her mother answered. "Not humans."

"And Ajax?"

"Ajax knows what he needs, but he won't do it. Those are his choices. One day, these alphas will learn how to swallow their pride, to work together. It wasn't going to be their father, not that pig-headed fool, but I thought…I thought it would be the twins. They spent so much time here, I thought for sure they would be more balanced, and of the two, Ajax would be the voice of reason. They should have been able to lead a balanced pack together, but even the runes aren't showing me that path anymore."

"They still could, runes be damned. I'm not going to give up trying. Axel will hear me out—he won't let his brother go feral. He can't be that heartless."

"That's between them, dear. We can talk to them till we are blue in the face, but it's still their decision, their path to choose."

"I hate when you do this."

"It's a hard lesson to learn, but all I've had is time to think since your father was taken from us."

"Mom…"

"Cahaira, you have a role, a big one, to play in our world. Your future is certain and has never changed. Not since you were a child. Our fate, the world's fate, depends on you, and it definitely includes those two somehow. You are doing everything you can. It's in your blood. Even now, Ajax needs you. But you can't beat yourself up when they don't listen. Just remember that."

"I won't let their stubbornness tear us all apart. They're our best friends."

Softly, her mother lowered her voice, and the serious gentleness told her more about the future that her mother had seen in the runes than her words ever would. "Everything you do, every decision you make, is important, Cahaira. We've always known, since you were born, the amount of good you would do, but something bigger is coming with the next generation. With Cassandra's birth, and then Makaii's, I could feel a rumble in the timeline. We must put our faith in the future. It's already here."

Long after she hung up with her mother, she sat at the kitchen table in Marti's home. Lincoln and Marti's father had gone with Felix to the gym to run some classes, and she was left to keep watch over Ajax and Marti.

She sighed.

There was nothing to keep watch over. They hadn't left the bedroom in days and barely moved from the bed. She had convinced him to sit her up in the recliner they had moved in there, and he would hold Marti in his lap, reading to her, refusing to leave her side, refusing to do anything that would take him away from her. But that was it.

Marti would eat mechanically, and only then would Ajax eat or drink even. When she was awake, she stared off into the distance, catatonic, unresponsive, emotionless. Physically, her body was healed, but mentally, she was checked out…maybe permanently.

There hadn't been much they could do for Marti, except to just give her time. But it was Ajax who broke her heart. A rock for the fiercest pack in North America, he was huge, brutal, unrelenting, and scary as fuck during the wars. She had fought beside him on several occasions, and the man killed as easily as he breathed, only slowing to wipe blood from his eyes.

But now, he was like a lost lamb, hopeless, yet out of control. And control was something Tuisa prided themselves on—control over themselves, the pack, and their territory.

The few times she had tried to move Ajax physically, to push him to take a shower, eat food, or get him to leave her side for a second, he had snarled at her, his face morphing and transforming involuntarily into his wolf's. Then, he would settle back down and refuse to budge. He didn't even know when he did it anymore, and that was scary. That meant he'd been rogue too long, and he was going feral. If…no, when…he finally lost control, he would be stuck in wolf form, unable to control his shifts, his emotions, his choices. They would lose him forever.

She couldn't let that happen.

Still, she sat and debated her next move. The local Alpha had been willing to lend some pack members at Felix's behest, especially to fight the vampire nest, but despite Felix's status as the Beta's son, the Alpha had only said he would consider adding him to their pack as an external member. It was more than she expected. No pack in its right mind would take on Ajax as a normal member. He was a natural leader, a born alpha, and trained beyond anyone in their pack. It would be considered an invitation to take over and a sign of a weak alpha. Anyone else would have just killed Ajax for being a rogue. It was enough that Felix's Alpha had already allowed Ajax to be so close by and hadn't taken steps to kill him in his weakness right now.

Axel was his only hope. The more she thought about it, the angrier she became. That was his twin. They were identical, had shared a womb, a childhood, a lifetime of family and training to lead their pack together. Axel had turned his back on Ajax after their parents' deaths, and it pissed Cahaira off. She just wanted to shake him or maybe electrocute him with a lightning bolt. Just a small one.

Before she could change her mind, Cahaira picked up the phone and dialed. When Nubia answered, she was grateful. Axel's mate was also close to them growing up, and Nubia was Axel's balance. Sweet, kind, and opposite of Axel, she had a calming effect on everyone, including Cahaira. And she needed that.

Cahaira's temper had never clashed well with Axel's, her wild pride as stubborn as his. She knew her yelling and arguing wouldn't work now, especially since it never had before. So, she would have to do what she'd never allowed herself to do in the past.

For Ajax, she would beg.

"Nubia, how's my little baby nephew doing today? Looking any more like you?" They both chuckled because that 17-month-old baby was huge already, and Axel's look-a-like in every way.

"Makaii's started talking, and you know how mobile he is. Can't keep him contained, especially now that they are building a new packhouse. He's so curious, and he gets so mad, frowning at me like he can just order me around already."

"He's his father's son, isn't he?"

"That he is. You guys want to play some cards this weekend? He'd love to see his aunties."

Cahaira hesitated before pushing forward. She hadn't told them Ajax called her for help when he scouted out the vampires last week. "I'm not exactly in town. I'm in California. Is Axel around? I want you both to hear, and I'm going to need your help with him more than ever."

By the time Nubia found Axel in his office, and put her on speakerphone, she had practiced her speech in her head over and over.

"Axel. I'm not asking for anything new. But you need to hear me now more than ever. I'm begging you. You, me, all of us are going to lose him. It's bad. He's so far gone, he can't make decisions on his own, and he would hate me for even calling and telling you his business, but I don't care anymore. He needs to put his pride aside, and so do you. I won't even be able to bring him to you—you'll have to come here and do it against his will. But you have to. Even if you have to lock him in a prison and make him hate you even more, at least he'll be alive. He's on the edge of being lost forever."

There was a long silence, so she forged ahead. She told him about Marti, the San Diego vampire nest, the many faces of the Houston based vampires they had thought were dead, and how they had integrated with Pennington, how they had plotted together to kidnap Ajax and bring down Tuisa. He heard how Ajax wouldn't let anyone near him, how close he was to shifting permanently.

She told him everything.

And when she finally took a bated breath, waiting for Axel to agree to save his brother, his twin, she could hear Makaii babbling in the background, his whine soft and repetitive, "Dada, Dada, Dada."

"One stubborn, self-destructive wolf will not endanger the lives of thousands in our pack. I will not allow it. If he is attracting attention, putting us in more danger, and doesn't have enough regard for his own life or even his mate's, then why should I? Why should I value his selfish choices over my son's future? My mate's safety? My pack's livelihood?"

"He's family, Axel. He needs help."

"He made those choices that put him there. If he had cared for his mate, he would have protected her, taken her from there, not gambled with her life. We all make choices, Cahaira, and he has to live with his. I didn't leave him, he left us. I can't chase him across the country and fix his mistakes, especially when he still doesn't want it."

"Please, Axel. I can't watch this happen. We've lost so many in the war, we can't lose another during times of peace."

"There's no such thing as times of peace. There will always be someone fighting for our death. This time, he allowed this to happen. He could have prevented it, so take that up with him. As for you, I suggest coming home. It doesn't concern you."

The weight on her chest intensified, and she expected the anger to flood her body, but when she heard Nubia sniff and her tearily say Axel's name, all the emotions she had been holding back the last few days overwhelmed her at once. She felt the tears sliding down her face, and she knew then that her mother was right. This generation was unhelpable. They were only twenty-three years old, and they were already incapable of change. Both of them.

"If I could, I'd put you on the phone to tell him goodbye one last time, but he's already past that. I have to use magic to keep him from attacking me when I go in. Just know, until he's dead, I won't stop. I won't leave him. Even if you won't fight for him, I will. Know that I would do anything for him, just as he would do anything for me. That's what family does. The next call you get from me will be when he's gone. Don't expect anything more. You don't turn your back on family, and he is my family. Hold yours tight, Axel, because one day, you'll lose them too with this outlook on life. If every member of your pack doesn't think you'd fight for them, then why would they keep fighting for you? People are more than numbers, Alpha."

Quickly, she ended the call before lying down with her head in her arms to sob. The heartlessness of running a pack would never make sense to her. Despite her grandfather being an Alpha wolf, their witch genes, not the wolf ones, had run strong through the females, which meant she would never give up hope, could never fathom sacrificing people for numbers. Maybe things wouldn't change with Axel or Ajax, but the sweet babbling of Makaii left her thinking about her mother's words. The next generation would change the future.

There was still hope.

She felt them enter the kitchen, and when Lincoln's arms wrapped around her, she couldn't stop her tears. Leaning into him, she allowed them to run their course, then stood, drying her eyes with a new resolution. Clenching her jaw and looking around the room at the two men's worried expressions, she put her hands on her hips and lifted her chin. She refused to let Ajax go.

"We need to get him to mark her again. My mom thinks it will jumpstart her body, give her the shifter magic she needs to fight through what's left of her mind."

Felix shook his head, sympathy in his voice. "Even the small release for his canines to mark her will allow his wolf more control. If he shifts enough for his canines to come out, I don't know if he can stop his wolf from completely taking over."

"It's a chance we have to take. Anything else I can do to convince your Alpha to allow him in?"

"I'll try again. What if this ensured an alliance between us and Tuisa? Is that something I can put on the table?"

"No. Tuisa wants nothing to do with him. He made that clear again just now." But she sighed heavily, placing a calming hand on Felix's forearm, infusing magic with her words. "Tell him that Ajax will never be a part of the internal pack, that he will only be on the road unless called in to fight. He can even make a pact that he can't ever challenge the Alpha. Whatever it takes."

"I will try again, but if you're going to have him mark Marti again, I don't want to leave you alone just yet."

"You think having another male wolf, from another pack, around his mate is a good idea while he marks her? Even if he likes you, his wolf will be unpredictable. With our magic, we can keep him safe, and we won't be a threat."

"You're right." Felix sighed, looking toward Marti's bedroom door before looking defeated and morose. "She's my best friend. Take care of her."

"And he's mine." He turned to leave, and she looked up at Lincoln. Easy-going, quiet, and thoughtful, she looked to him for logic when she could only think with action. They were alone, and it was the only time she let her guard down and allowed herself to be vulnerable and unsure.

"What do you think?"

"I think love is more powerful than anything, and we need to get out of its way."

Anyone else might not know what that meant, but she did, and she sighed in relief. If the smartest, most logical person she knew thought this would work, then it was the only option.

Inside the dark bedroom, the sun had set, and she could only see their huddled forms on the mattress. Squeezing Lincoln's hand in hers, she approached the bed, settling her weight into the corner by their feet.

"Ajax?"

He didn't move, didn't answer her, but she knew he was awake. She could feel the tension from his wolf. She was too close to Marti. "I'm going to push a calming spell into you. Deidre sent it to me, and she thinks it will help soothe your beast. Is that okay?"

He didn't say anything, so she took that as a good sign. Moving to the top of the bed, she placed both her hands on his chest, and she felt the rumble of the wolf inside. Shifting so that she wasn't touching Marti, she hummed a soft lullaby, concentrating on the feelings and the words she needed.

Once she was done, there was an easing of tension, but it was slight. Better than nothing for what she had to say.

"Mom thinks she needs shifter magic to help fight. She's not sure a human can pull through." Cahaira let that thought sink in, letting Ajax's muddied brain understand that first. "When you marked her, she took on some, right? You could link, you could feel each other. I'm assuming that feeling is almost gone, and it's killing you. I think the magic was too new, not strong enough, and when she bled out, she lost it. She lost a part of you, a part of her."

"She's in there. I still feel her. She's fading though." His voice was hoarse, miserable, and in the dark, she could see him wrapped around her, one arm across her chest stroking her cheek.

"We think if you mark her again, that she can be shocked back to life. Give her a boost of your shifter magic, give her a piece of you to hold on to."

His voice cracked. "I can do that."

"But…"

"I know the risk, Cahaira. I'm not completely gone. But if I lose myself saving her, then it will be worth it."

"I won't give up. Felix is heading back to his pack now to ask his Alpha again."

"And you called *him*."

She didn't question which 'him' Ajax referred to, and she didn't deny it. He hadn't asked a question, and she had a feeling he could hear her phone conversation from here.

"You shouldn't have tried. You don't understand him, but I do. He wasn't going to give in."

"You know I don't put stock in either of your stubbornness. I won't lose either of you."

There was a long silence, and he breathed heavily, purposefully taking several deep breaths. "We need to go somewhere my wolf won't do damage. I can already tell you the shift will come immediately after."

"For her, she needs to be somewhere she feels safe and comfortable. She needs to remember her life and push away from the nothingness."

"She has a place."

Chapter 24

Marti

Friday, October 11
Black's Beach

The first thing that felt real was the lift of the wind, and the tickle of her hair as it danced across her cheek. She hadn't even opened her eyes, but she could hear and feel the ocean, the surf breaking, the birds squawking. Not in a hurry, she focused on the heat surrounding her, and the heaviness of the body lying across her stomach.

It was comfort, like pozole on a cold day, and she didn't want to move, to lose the feeling that she had been chasing for what seemed like a lifetime. When she finally cracked her eyes, the dark blue of the sky was just lighting with the orange-yellow of the sunrise. Focusing on the horizon, the glass blue water was foggy with clouds, and she watched as a few puffy shapes skated across the sky, dissipating in the coming sun. Her world had felt like endless shapes, sounds and fog that she couldn't escape, but this…this was different, and her soul sang.

Her mom was here, she was sure of it.

When her hair tickled her cheek once again, she reached up to sweep it behind her ear, only to figure out that it wasn't her hair, and she wasn't alone. Blinking quickly, she turned her head, involuntarily burying her face in the soft, black hairs of an animal's neck. Startled slightly, but not as much as she should be, she wasn't scared. This was the source of heat and comfort pinning her body to the sand.

His head was laid across the back of her neck, an arm crossing her body to hold her down, her legs tangled in his. Shit, this was a giant…dog? Wolf? Slowly, she tried to sit up without disturbing the animal, but immediately, it moved, and by the time she pulled into a sitting position, he was standing over her on all fours, nuzzling and licking her neck and face.

She giggled, and he pushed her backwards, his tail wagging and excitedly dancing around yipping. In that moment, reality came crashing back, and she realized this had to be Ajax. He was much bigger than Felix's wolf, and pitch black, with beautiful green eyes. She pulled to her knees, hugging his neck, and running her hands along his sides, slightly obsessed with the way his fur felt.

He wasn't scary at all. Why would he have thought she would be scared of his wolf?

"Ajax? You're so beautiful. Did we sleep out here?"

He sat back, then laid down on his front haunches and cocked his head.

His voice filled her head, deep and smooth, but distant. *"I've been waiting for you to wake up for days, little one. You can't imagine how happy I am to hear your voice. I thought I'd lost you forever."*

"Days?" She paused, confused as she tried to think of the last thing she remembered. "I was at the tournament, and…oh." She looked up at him, suddenly panicked. "The vampires…they have my father, and I went with them. I tried to fight them off, but they held me down. Are they…?"

"They're gone. Forever. We made sure of it."

"My dad?"

"He's safe, at home, probably still asleep."

"Thank God."

She stared at him, the weight of all her worries lifted off her shoulders. "I love your wolf, but can you change back? I miss you."

The wolf in front of her whined softly, stretched, and rose to his feet. Slowly, he walked in a circle, softly growling and dancing around, until he eventually plopped down on the ground and stared at her pitifully.

"I can't right now, little one."

She frowned. She could barely hear him now. Yet, she could feel him—it was like he lived inside of her—but he felt far away at the same time. "I'm confused."

"It's hard to explain."

She could feel his pain, his struggle, but she didn't understand it. Instead, she sat next to him, leaning her body into his, nonchalantly rubbing the scruff of his neck. He settled into the sand, huffing into the air, his frustration evident.

"I have all the time in the world."

She felt his struggle every time he tried to speak with her, his voice weak and fighting for control with his wolf. So, when a couple walked up cautiously, she was immediately defensive. Not many people came along this stretch of beach, and when they did, it was usually to walk along the coastline, not the cliff area. But Ajax jumped up and headed straight to them, his large body rising almost to the small woman's chest. But she didn't look afraid. Instead, she reached out and hugged his neck, petting his back, and the man held out his hand, and Ajax licked it excitedly.

"A much more relaxed beast when your mate is out of the danger zone, I see."

Ajax turned back, moving to stand by her before the redhead spoke. "Marti? I know we haven't met officially, but I'm Cahaira, and this is my mate, Lincoln. I grew up with Ajax, so we've been best friends since we could walk."

The woman was stunning. Beautiful red curls, delicate features, pale skin and a curvy figure—she couldn't help but feel a pang of jealousy even as she couldn't control her mouth. "Oh wow. You're gorgeous." She instantly felt awkward and blushed when Cahaira laughed. "Sorry. So, you're the witches we were waiting on?"

"Yes, hell of a time at the airport and unfortunate timing. I'm part wolf, but I don't present with shifter magic, so, yes, I'm a witch. And

Lincoln is a hybrid witch and fae with fae-presenting magic. We live in the neighboring coven, and my family has always run the coven, and his family runs the pack, so he is stuck with me."

She frowned in confusion, absent-mindedly running her hands through Ajax's fur. "So, what's going on? Why am I here? Sorry, I'm just a little lost, and it's hard to talk to him right now. He said he can't shift back."

"Yeah, let me help you get caught up. We are part of the reason he wasn't worried about the vampires at first. We've been killing them for years with him, and Felix's pack came along to help. He just didn't expect them to come for you because he knew he was the target. You should have told her the full plans beforehand." She glanced at Ajax when he made a whining sound. "But he didn't. He didn't want you to worry, but a large number of vampires in that nest were transplants from a Houston nest that we thought was eliminated a couple years ago. As you know, they were gunning for him. He wasn't sure how the vampires would attack, but he thought it would be at the tournament, so we were ready with plans to take them out. You…you were supposed to be under guard at the gym while we handled it. Didn't think they knew you two had a connection."

This was so much information to take in at once, especially connecting everything Pennington had told her with what Cahaira said, and her head spun.

"This is a lot." She glanced down at Ajax, who had laid down, like he was getting disciplined. "Did he get hurt? Is that why he is stuck in wolf form?"

"Well, the story of that night is something I will let him tell you. He's stuck in wolf form because he's a stubborn ass who won't go home."

Ajax's yip, and subsequent restless growling only seemed to prove her point. "He said his brother won't take him back."

"That's true to a degree. They don't agree on many things, and both of them are to blame. But without a pack, a shifter will slowly begin to go wild—feral—until the man no longer has control. The beast will take over and do what it wants. It's very protective of you, and it's feeling relaxed now that you're awake. If Ajax lets his beast have its way, then his demeanor relaxes too. But the more Ajax fights him, the more aggressive he will become. Without a pack, he has no more shifter magic to draw on. He can't shift back."

"How did this happen so fast? He was fine, wasn't he?" She felt a rising panic in her chest. Did this mean he was stuck forever?

"Sort of. He was struggling but maintaining, and probably could have gone for a few more months, especially after connecting with you." Cahaira looked up at Lincoln, who stood like a silent rock in it all. "But you've been out of it for almost six days now, and the thought of losing you drove him over the edge. And then, we decided the only thing that would bring you back was more shifter magic. He would need to mark you again. But doing that would allow his beast to wrestle complete control from him. And now…here we are."

"Holy cow. How do we fix it? We can fix it, right?"

"That's the problem. Most of the time, once a shifter goes rogue, they are killed by local packs because they are uncontrolled, unpredictable, and usually dangerous."

"Wait. Killed? You can't be serious. He didn't do anything."

Cahaira had moved closer, and now she reached around her shoulders, pulling her close. "I know. It's just the way of life for wolf shifters. Kill or be killed. But we are working on it. He would need to be accepted into a pack, but that's not easy because of who he is, how much of a threat to the local Alpha he is, and what they believe about his intentions. If we can convince them he is not a threat, then he can submit to a pack, be accepted, and gain control of his beast again."

"Then we do that, right? Felix can put in a good word." Desperation clung to her, and the happiness she was feeling only minutes before was yanked away. He had sacrificed for her, and now he was losing himself.

"That's where Felix went last night. To try again. He had already asked, but his Alpha was hesitant. Hopefully, we will hear back soon, and there will be good news. Until then, we need to keep his wolf away from others, especially humans. He can only fight for control for so long until his wolf becomes aggressive."

"So, do we stay here?"

"Now that you're awake, I think the mountains are a better place for him. Less people, more room to run free and let his wolf get his fill of the free life. Maybe he will relax, and Ajax can gain control. Now that you're doing better, he can concentrate on that instead of you. Come on. I think we should get out of here. It's getting a little crowded on the beach."

She looked around, realizing she hadn't even noticed the half dozen or so people wandering the beach after sunrise, then studied Ajax. He hadn't said a word to her across the link the whole time, and now the wolf was staring hard at the people wandering too close.

"Linc, you grab Ajax. Up to the car we go."

Within seconds, she watched Lincoln place his hand on Ajax's back, then Cahaira grabbed Linc's arm, then hers. "I'm going to transport us up to the car. Don't panic. Just a little magic, and you'll get used to it."

In the blink of an eye, wind picked up around her, and suddenly, she was standing in front of an SUV. Ajax was stuffed into folded down seats of the trunk, and she climbed in next to him when he got all growly. She wrapped her hands around his neck, pulling him close.

"Is life with you always going to be this interesting? Will I ever have time to read a book and watch the sunset again?" She laughed softly, and snuggled into him, loving his soft fur, but wishing for his warm skin and hot lips. "I kinda have plans for your human body, so I need you to get it together for me."

He rumbled, then snorted, before settling down for the ride. Back at her home, they were careful to get Ajax inside without drawing attention, and he curled up in her bed while she took a good, long shower. While she dried off and got dressed, she could hear the murmur of voices outside, so she hurried out of the bathroom door. Inside her room, Ajax stood at the door, the hair on his back standing straight up, a low growl filling the room.

"Ajax?"

He didn't move, only stared intently at the door, the rumble of his growl getting louder as she came closer. The voices outside her door stopped, then she heard Cahaira call out.

"Ajax. You're not giving me a choice here. Stand down or else."

Instead of following her orders, he backed up, closer to Marti, like he was protecting her, then lunged at the door, his large body cracking it.

"Jesus. Ajax! Stop!"

The room had gone eerily quiet, and then she felt an unearthly tension before he whimpered softly and dropped to the floor at her feet. "Oh, shit."

Quickly, she knelt down, checking him for signs of pain, and Cahaira opened the door slowly. "You okay?"

"What happened to him?" Tearfully, her hands searched his body.

"Nothing, I just used a sleeping spell. He's getting antsy, and his wolf has an instinct to protect you, even if it's unnecessary. There are other wolves in the house that pose a threat in his beast's eyes. No one wants a shifter fight right now. I don't think it would end well." Cahaira stepped aside, and her father stumbled around Ajax's limp wolf, practically tackling her in his classic bear hug.

"Thank God. Thank God." His arms were like a vise, a good one, and she closed her eyes tight, sinking into her father's arms. Things had changed so much in the past couple of weeks, she didn't realize just how much she needed this.

"I thought they'd killed you. I was so scared." Shakily, she tried to push the vision of her father lying on the floor of that cell to the side, but it was hard. It had been seared into her memory.

"It would take a lot to kill an old dog like me. I'll be around for a long, long time." His words were small puffs against her hair, and she welcomed he familiarity of it all.

When they finally pulled apart, she stared up into her father's face, the deep creases and dark undereyes more pronounced now than they'd ever been. He looked like hell. "I've messed things up."

"Hush that talk now, Sunshine. You couldn't do that if you tried. Just gotta get it all back on track. And you got plenty of friends for that." He pulled away, and for a good reason. Felix stood in the doorway, looking like a lost puppy, eager for her attention. And when he pushed into the room, not even acknowledging Ajax's body when he stepped over it, her father moved aside.

"Marti. I thought we lost you for good." His arms wrapped around her in a tight hug, and she sank into his familiar warmth. No, Ajax's beast would have lost his shit. She could tell that now. Tears sprang to her eyes, and she realized this whole world was overwhelming, and not as fun and fantastical as a fantasy book would make it seem. Bloody death was around every corner, with real tragedies, and real war, and things couldn't be solved by just talking.

"What are we going to do, Felix? It's so much."

"I know. We think we have a solution, but you're not going to like it, and we think you should stay here."

She pushed back, looking up at his worried face. "Like hell. If something is happening with Ajax, then I want to be there."

"I agree. It's not a good idea, Marti." Cahaira chewed her lip as she considered the situation. "It's hard to explain."

Felix shook his head and sighed. "You don't understand wolf ways, Marti. What has to happen is perfectly normal for us, but you will find it brutal and scary. With you there, it would make Ajax's beast's instincts kick in even more. We want to bring Ajax back into control, but his beast will fight to protect you. It's a distraction."

Her resolve wavered at that thought. If her presence would make it harder on him, she didn't want that. "If I am to live this life with him, then I need to see how it all works firsthand. He can't keep me from it forever, right? It's now or never. I have to be able to hang."

"She's not wrong." Lincoln was the voice of reason and seemed to be the only person on her side. "If you think separating them will make Ajax calmer, then you're thinking too logically. His beast doesn't make sense when it comes to her. Remember that. If you want him calmer, then he will need her there, by his side, where he can see her."

Felix studied her for a second, then looked at Lincoln, his gaze finally settling on Cahaira. "Is he always this logical?"

"Yes. And he's never wrong, damnit."

Hope rose within her. "So?"

"Get changed. Something comfortable, but long-sleeved. Hiking boots too. We are headed into the mountains."

Within an hour, they were on the road, Ajax loaded in the back, folded down seats of the SUV, still unconscious, her father in the passenger seat, Felix driving, and Cahaira in the back with her. Lincoln and others drove the other SUV, the one everyone else would transfer into when they reached their destination.

She listened with trepidation as Felix tried to explain the dynamics of pack Alphas, alpha-borns, and the need for a pack connection. What scared her the most was what needed to be done for Ajax to be accepted into his pack. It sounded insane, and most importantly, people could die, probably Ajax.

"But that's where we come in. Felix's pack explained our magic to their Alpha, and he was willing to help if we kept Ajax under control. Otherwise, it's too dangerous for all of them." Cahaira's words were a slight comfort, but not much, especially when she considered the risk.

"So, saving him wouldn't be worth it to them." She said this flatly, trying to understand how supernaturals disregarded each other's lives so casually. Even Felix treated the situation like it was inevitable.

"It's the shifter way, Marti. It's how we stay alive in this world. We do what's good for the pack, not the individual."

"Seems like a terrible way to live and think."

"Exactly why Ajax left." Cahaira's comment was strained, and she could see the tension in her face. She had been quiet most of this trip, listening and brooding in the front seat while Felix drove, explaining all the semantics, and then how it would go when they got there. Or how it would *hopefully* go.

Since Marti had insisted on going, and Lincoln had pointed out the obvious, their plan changed a little, and now she would be integral to the timeline. First, they would stop when they were almost there, letting everyone else get out, leaving her alone. She would be the one to drive

Ajax far enough away, and Cahaira would release the sleeping spell. She would park at a Trailhead in the Cleveland National Park, close to the Morena Valley Pack territory. From there, her job was to keep him calm, and to talk him through what would happen next.

She could do this. She would. For him.

Once they reached the transfer point, Felix pulled over, and everyone piled out. She slid into the driver's seat, and quickly realized her dad hadn't moved.

"I'm going with you. You're not doing this alone."

She'd never seen her father as a stubborn man, but now, his jaw was set, and there was a distinct resolution in his voice. Felix tried talking him out of the car for a minute, but it was no use.

"Son, if Ajax doesn't like this old man around his daughter, then we will deal with it. Go on."

Taking a deep breath, she reached over, squeezing her dad's arm. "Thanks, Dad. I'd love to have you come." So, it was decided.

They'd only been driving for a couple of minutes when she felt Ajax stirring behind her. Taking several deep breaths, she tried to relax, not wanting him to feel her nervousness.

When his nose nuzzled her neck from behind, and he whined a little, licking her ear, she smiled. "Hey."

She could see he was trying to climb into the front seat with her, and he grumbled around, nudging her father's arm, but no sign of aggression, so she sighed with relief.

"Hey now, Ice. I know she's yours now, but she'll always be my baby. I get a few more minutes with her, and you're way too big to sit in my lap. Settle down, and we'll be there in a minute." She almost laughed when her father patted Ajax on his head, before summarily dismissing him.

Ajax snorted, clearly offended, but accepting the decision. Probably more because he was too big to even sit on the center console. Instead, he settled for stretching from the backseat to the front, resting his snout on her right arm as she drove.

"Ajax? We are going into the mountains. You need some space to run and be free. I'll stay with you the whole time, okay?"

A heavy sigh, then a slight whine was his only response, and she glanced at her father. "This could be weirder, right?"

Domingo laughed, the hearty rumble a welcome comfort. "Certainly interesting. Almost like those books you were reading prepared us for this."

"Almost." She couldn't help the smile that tugged at her lips, careful to keep her eyes on the barely visible markers along the dirt road.

"I just want you to know how proud I am of you. And your mama too. She'd be tickled pink at everything you've done."

"You mean she'd be proud at how good I was as vampire fodder?"

"As in, your whole life. I don't say it enough anymore, but she would absolutely be happy with you. You're both so much alike. It's like she's still here sometimes."

"Yeah?"

"Yeah. You live the way you want, and don't let anyone or anything sway you from your path. You're loyal and brave. So much more than I could ever be."

"I don't feel very brave right now."

"Things don't feel brave when they're happening. It's always after when you realize how hard you worked through it. But I know you got this."

"I hope so."

"One day, you're going to look back at this and think about how many things you've survived in your life. It's those moments, those hard decisions that make it all worth it."

She nodded, the lump in her throat keeping her from speaking. She couldn't cry right now. Ajax needed her. He needed her to be brave.

It didn't take long to make it the few miles down Los Pinos Rd, then past the Corte Madera Rd, and just like instructed, she pulled off and parked. Ajax seemed instantly alert, but excited to get out. Giving her father one last hug, Domingo stayed back at the SUV, ready to take them home, all of them, hopefully, when it was over.

"I'll be here waiting for you. Both of you." Ignoring her father's words at first, Ajax practically tumbled from the SUV, overcome with energy, but managed to pause when Domingo called his name. "Ajax. Don't forget what you promised me, son. You said forever, and forever is far from over. Do what you need to do."

She swallowed hard, not sure what they'd spoken of before, but Ajax's wolf stood still for only a moment before looking at her, waiting for her to join him. There was still a piece of him in there. Of that, she was sure.

Together she and Ajax walked, more like jogged, since he was itching to break out into a run, toward the Corte Madera Peak. He would rush off, then come back and circle her, until finally, she leaned down, pulling him close as she panted.

"Ajax, remember I told you my one rule? No sweating. And I'm breaking it already, so go ahead and run to your heart's content. I'll meet you at the top. Just remember the things I do for you!"

Before she even finished her sentence, he had taken off running, and within ten minutes, he had run the whole area, scouted it out, and was back by her side just as she reached their destination. Pulling herself up on a big rock, still far enough away from the edge, she caught her breath as she took in the beauty of the landscape. As far as she could see, there were rolling hills and mountains, foggy cliffs, outcroppings, and wide open space. The silence of it all lent a somberness to their lives that felt too heavy to bear.

Ajax's wolf, finally getting his fill of running, sidled up next to her, alert as always, but he panted with a carefree happiness only an animal in the wild could have, and she was suddenly scared that all of this would go badly.

"Ajax? You still in there?"

There was a long beat before she heard his voice in her head. He still sounded distant and strained, but it was comforting. *"I'm still fighting, little one, but you're alive. That's all I needed."*

"It's not all I need though. I need you. I need every part of you. I don't think I will be able to survive without you. I can't lose another person I love, and you promised me a future. Existing is not enough. That's what I've been doing, and now I want more. You showed me there is more to life than making it through, more than duty, more

than just being alive for the sake of it. You gave me hope. So, I won't accept just existing. I need to really live. And I can't live without you."

"I'm sorry, little one."

"No, I don't accept. You can't show me a glimpse of a life with you and expect me to let it go. I'm going to fight for you. Even if you don't like it. I would tell you that I am sorry for what is about to happen, but I'm not. It's our best chance, and I know your wolf is convincing you that he is in charge, but he's not. You are. Fight him."

A tear slid down her cheek at how different Ajax sounded, how his feral beast convinced him this was the best way to protect her. Her Ajax wouldn't give up. He would want to be next to her, to spend his life with her.

He'd gone feral for her, for love.

And for him, she'd do everything she could to bring him back.

But he didn't answer, and when he stiffened, she knew he sensed the company that approached from all sides. He started forward, then circled with a low growl, moving to block her body from the wolves slowly encroaching upon their location.

"What did you do? He's dangerous. I can't control him anymore, Marti. You don't understand." Ajax's distinct presence in her mind faded as the beast's instincts filled her with his anger.

"These wolves are here to help, Ajax. The Alpha is willing to let you join his pack, but you must submit. I know that goes against everything you are, but it's the only way. I want to spend my life with you. This will give us that freedom. Ajax?" Her words came out in a tumble, a rushed whisper as he began snarling at the seemingly endless wolves.

None of them were in human form, and there were so many. She didn't see Felix, Cahaira, or Lincoln anywhere. She swallowed, suddenly worried about this. They seemed vicious and wild, and she didn't see how they could have Ajax's best interests in mind. They were snarling, growling, and a few snapped at them when they circled close enough for Ajax to lash out.

His wolf dwarfed all of theirs, but to her, it didn't matter when he was outnumbered thirty to one. They had paused in their movement, almost in a formation when the largest of them moved forward up the middle. He was dark grey with amber eyes glowing with a fire that seemed anything but friendly. He didn't growl or appear aggressive. Instead, he held his head high, almost regally, and waited about ten yards away.

Ajax turned all his attention to him, facing him head on, and she could see why Ajax would be seen as a threat. If this was their Alpha, Ajax was still much larger than him, and her sweet, cuddly black wolf had turned into a deadly fighter, his hair sleek in the sun, ears laid back, and now, instead of growling, he crouched low, stealthily moving forward on the Alpha. But the other wolf didn't move.

From nowhere, Cahaira and Lincoln appeared next to the other Alpha, facing Ajax. Felix stood next to the red-haired witch, in human form, lifting his chin, but not aggressively. Ajax froze, recognizing his friends in some way, but his manner didn't soften, not even when Cahaira stepped forward, slightly in front of the Alpha, and spoke.

"Ajax. This is Alpha Montez, from the Morena Valley Pack. He wants you to join his pack with conditions. You will be free to travel as you want, but you must come back every month to keep your connection strong. You can't stay rogue. You will also agree to be banned from challenging the Alpha for his role. You have to submit to him today, or you will not be allowed to roam free anymore as a rogue. Submit or be killed."

Chapter 25

Ajax

Friday, October 11
Corte Madura Mountain

The urge to rip the Alpha's throat out in front of his pack was overwhelming. He itched to feel his blood drip down his throat and show him who should be submitting to who. But her voice held him back.

"Ajax, please. For us."

He had barely acknowledged Cahaira's words, their weight not registering until he felt Marti at his side, and even his wolf paused. He didn't turn towards her, his beast refusing to let the Alpha out of his sight, but she moved away from him, putting a gap between them to stand next to Cahaira, and he was conflicted.

His beast's thoughts had become his own, and he had ceased to understand the difference between the man's desires and the wolf's. The longer he stayed in this form, the more at one with his beast he became. That had always been true, but now, more than ever.

Protect her.

He snarled. Did his beast think he couldn't? Did he doubt himself?

"Fight for me, Ajax. I know what you would want. Trust me and submit to him."

Every instinct he had urged him to fight this Alpha, to show him who was in charge. And seeing his mate stand so close to the man enraged him, and he wanted to tear the Alpha apart. But something stopped him.

His internal struggle played out physically, and his body grumbled, then shook. He looked between his mate and the Alpha, and an angry howl ripped from his body. Almost immediately, the pack tightened their formation, closing in on him, and he calculated the weakest spots, looking for the smaller wolves, those with hesitation, and any crevices along the mountain that could create a trap, ensuring his success.

As he shifted stealthily, eyeing the flaws in their plan to trick him into submission, he still focused on Marti. *Protect her.*

He needed to get Marti out of the way first—they were tricking her; he just knew it. His mind flew out of control, his beast's doubt merging with his own, and he rose in a challenge, moving straight toward the Alpha first. Take him out swiftly, use the right side as his next attack, making sure Marti could get behind him on the cliff.

With a snarl, he pivoted to lunge forward when Marti stepped between them, blocking the Alpha from Ajax's attack, and he froze. He dropped his gaze to the Alpha, who moved subtly around her, and he continued in his path, determined to keep her safe. But when he looked into her eyes, and her voice filled his head, he realized she was afraid, and not of these wolves.

She was afraid of him.

"Please. Stop, Ajax. You're scaring me."

He was supposed to be protecting her, keeping her safe. It was his one job as her mate, and here he was, letting her get hurt again, not taking control of the situation. This time, she was afraid of *his* beast.

But he could do something about that.

He backed up slowly, not breaking eye contact with her, and when his back haunches touched the large boulder behind him, the other Alpha moved around Marti, protecting her *from him.*

The Alpha still hadn't issued a challenge or tried fighting him. In fact, somewhere in the back of his mind, he realized the other wolves had backed off, laying down in positions of submission. The Alpha had given an Alpha Command, and it had passed through his own alpha wolf without notice. His beast had no inherent need to be led by another, was naturally the leader himself. He could run free, since he didn't need anyone.

But the man did. The man needed someone.

The Alpha issued his Command once again, closing the distance between them, and now he heard it in his bones.

Submit.

His beast lifted his head high, refusing to submit, but the man wrestled him for what he truly needed to be happy.

Submit.

One last growl ripped out of him, but her voice, her tears, filled his head. Her sobs and pleas registering finally. *"I need Ajax. The man. Please submit."*

Submit.

And this time, he did. Ajax overpowered his beast, finding the control he'd always prided himself on, and forced his beast down to his haunches, and then finally, averted his head to the ground at the Alpha's feet…in submission.

The silence of the mountains felt overwhelming as the Alpha forced his beast into submission, and the shifter magic of the new pack flooded him. Almost instantly, his beast's fierce presence in his mind shrank. His own consciousness loomed over him, and everything became clear. The irrational notion that this pack was out to kill him disappeared, and the weight of his wolf's savage need to fight dwindled as he focused on thinking rationally.

"Shift."

His new Alpha's voice rang through his mind, and his beast obeyed, succumbing to his new leader. He stood tall, naked and free, and he could finally breathe. The call and animalistic need to connect with a pack had lifted from his mind, and he belonged once again.

His new Alpha shifted in front of him and stood silently, assessing him before he put his hand out. Ajax reached out as well, shaking his hand heartily.

"Thank you for giving me my life back."

"Felix better not be wrong about you. He put his position in this pack on the line as well."

"I won't disappoint. You will have an ally for eternity."

Alpha Montez nodded, then turned back, shifting as he walked and took off in a run with the rest of the pack. As they disappeared, four people were left standing in front of him, and he swallowed hard. Marti was frozen in place, and he was ashamed of himself. He should have fought harder for her. He'd been weak. What did she think of him now?

Without a word, Cahaira reached out and grabbed her mate and Felix by the arm, transporting them away in a blink. He barely noticed.

"Marti? I'm so sorry."

She raised her hand to her mouth and tears streamed from her eyes. Then she ran straight for him and leaped into his arms, wrapping her legs around his waist and clinging to him.

"Oh my God, I was so scared I lost you. Please never do that again. Never leave me. I can't handle it." Her hysterical sobs were muffled as she buried her face in his neck, and relief flooded him. He didn't think she'd still want him after what he put her through. He squeezed her tight, not wanting to let her go either.

"Never. From now on, I do whatever you want, all the time."

She laughed through her tears. "You're full of shit, but I'm going to hold you to it." She took a deep breath, inhaling his scent. "I couldn't breathe without you."

She pulled back to look into his face, and her beautiful, brown eyes had him mesmerized. He balanced her on one arm, and he used his thumb to wipe the tears from under her eyes. "I love you, Marti. You're stuck with me forever now. I marked you twice."

"Ha. Jokes on you. You're the one stuck with me. You've made me sweat twice, and I'm going to punish you forever for that."

A deep contented growl rumbled through his chest, and he pulled her lips to his, their softness melting away all his worries. When she whimpered softly into his mouth, he threaded his hand through the back of her hair, pulling her head back and biting her lip playfully.

Then, he trailed his mouth along her neck, sucking and licking until he nuzzled the shell of her ear, letting his breath tickle her.

"Little one, I'll be spending a lifetime making you sweat, so please, punish me accordingly."

Epilogue

Ajax

Almost four years later…

"I'm done."

Marti looked up absent-mindedly from her notebook where she was brainstorming places to hold Alex's birthday party next month.

"Hmmmm. What if we take him to a dinosaur park? There's a State Park in Texas with real dino tracks, and even a drive-thru safari nearby." She flipped the pages, looking at the notes she made. "Glen Rose has the Brazos River too. We could go tubing, rent a big cabin, invite the girls from Rathlin, see if Nubia would want to bring Makaii and Keoni, make a whole weekend of it? We haven't seen them in months."

Alex hung around his neck, jumping on the mattress behind him, then used him as a jungle gym before leaping back onto the bed. He watched his son bounce around happily, before turning his attention back to Marti.

"Marti. I'm done. As in, I want out of the UFC. Four years is enough. I want to settle down."

She stared at him over the rim of her glasses, blinking rapidly as she focused on what he was saying. He reached out, pushing them up her nose for her, then grabbed her hand and squeezed. She was beautiful, especially when he had her speechless. That almost never happened.

"Done? With fighting? Everything? What will you do? Why?"

He shook his head and smiled softly. He had been making plans to get out for a couple of months, but until he was sure, he hadn't said anything. He knew she would be annoyed with that.

"That fight with the young wolf a couple of months ago? It had me thinking. I'm getting too old for this."

"You're twenty-seven, not forty-seven. He was nowhere close to beating you. It was just weird fighting a shifter for once."

"I know. It's not that. I want to fight more wolves—it made me feel alive. That's always been my goal, to bring wolf packs together, a UFC type fighting tournament, but across shifter packs, for fun. We spend so much time fighting each other over bullshit. I always thought if we had ways to get our aggression out, then peace would be easier."

"Yeah, that's not new. You've talked about that for years. What's changed now?" She cut right to the chase, always seeing through his tendency to drag things out.

"I don't want Alex to grow up on the road, and you deserve a normal life, not driving fight to fight, living in an RV."

She frowned at him. "I like doing this with you. I've slept in some beautiful places because of this RV."

"I know, and we still can. But we are missing other things that matter. Cahaira just gave birth, and we missed that. How many other birthdays, holidays, and Friday night poker games will we give up because of this life? I'm too old to keep this path. It's time to go to the next level."

"And how do we do that? You know your brother won't let us live in Tuisa, no matter how many vacations we spend outside the pack with you two silently pretending you're both invisible."

He ignored her slight jab at the precarious relationship he and Axel had agreed on so that their families could still spend time together. He wanted Alex to grow up with Makaii, Keoni, and now Aífe. He couldn't wait to meet Cahaira's child, and it felt like time. He was missing too many things that mattered, and he'd found a way to make it all work. He just had to push his pride down even more.

"Not Tuisa, but Alex needs a pack. A real one, not the once a month visits we make to Morena Valley. So, I've been working on a solution.

And before you get mad, I didn't tell you because I wanted the details to be final before I surprised you."

"And?"

"Remember me telling you about the Aisling Pack? The warded pack adjacent to Tuisa's lands?"

"The one with the Alpha who killed Kathleen's brother and took over the pack her parents formed? The one Rathlin and Tuisa both hate with a passion?"

He flashed a huge smile. "That's the one. It's less than a thirty-minute drive from Tuisa, and a five minute boat ride from Rathlin, and they have warded boundaries to keep you and Alex safe. And I worked out a deal with the Alpha."

"You sound like a realtor trying to get me to buy a fixer-upper." She sat back and crossed her arms.

"He said I could build a gym within the wards, train wolves from all around the country, and I would be in charge of all his wolves' training for the pack. I can probably convince him to let me hold wolf tournaments too."

"That's…a lot to think about. Your own gym? Training wolves, holding tournaments? Can you come and go like you do with Morena Valley?"

"Yeah, that's the beauty of Aisling. Because of the wards, rules are relaxed as long as you're part of the pack. Go in and out as you please, and it's full of all kinds of wolves from all over. Diverse, open, and full of opportunity. The Alpha is an ass, but what Alpha isn't, right?" He smiled wide, knowing her weakness.

"Clearly, Alphas are all real pains. I guess you have thought this through." She tapped the pen against the paper thoughtfully. "Will we get a house? Or do we build one?"

"I already have land that's been deeded to me by Kathleen. They still own the deeds to big parts of the land, and the Alpha doesn't know it. We build a house right on the water, and we build the gym right across from it. Just like your dads. We can go to Rathlin or Tuisa every weekend, come back and forth to visit your dad, even go on vacations with Felix still."

"God knows my dad will never leave his gym or San Diego. I mean…it all sounds great." She thought for a second, reaching for Alex as he leaped into her arms.

"Mama! I'm a velociraptor! Cacaw!"

"Did you tell your brother?"

He hesitated, not wanting to think about the call he'd made, the one where he'd spoken, and Axel had sat in silence before hanging up. "He knows. Nothing's changed."

She cocked an eyebrow, knowing exactly what that meant without him saying a word. "Let's do this."

Thank you for reading Feral for Love!
Hope you enjoyed Ajax and Marti's story.

This was only the beginning. A prequel.
Check out *Cursed by Fate* and fast forward twenty years into the future.
Meet Aífe and Makaii, and see just what impact Ajax had on them all.
Immerse yourself into a world filled with broken trust, warring supernaturals,
and ruthless alliances. You won't regret it.

Next up:
Cursed by Fate

Follow VJ on her socials and sign up for her newsletter by navigating to
https://subscribepage.io/Fs2dAO

Or

Website: violetjeanwrites.com

*I know, I know. I hate all those subscriptions too.
I promise, minimal emails. Only updates on new releases.*

About the Author

VJ Silvey writes paranormal romances with a hint of fantasy, always with headstrong and sassy heroines, and realistic-is themes. A lifelong Texan, teacher, and avid reader, she loves to travel with her family, and to imagine alternate, secretive worlds just below the surface of every destination.

Check out VJ's socials and sign up for her newsletter!
Or you can navigate to her website listed below.

Contact info:
Violetjeanwrites.com
vjsilvey@violetjeanwrites.com

Newsletter: https://subscribepage.io/Fs2dAO
IG: @violetjeanwrites
Twitter: @vjsilvey
TikTok: @violetjeanwrites
Facebook: Violet Silvey

Ruthless Alliances Collection

Between Ruin and Salvation

Cursed by Fate

Unravelled by Darkness

Avenged by Fire

Destroyed by Redemption

Between Fear and Obsession

Wild in Spirit

Wild at Heart

Wild for Love

Standalones

Wrecked by Chance

Feral for Love